DITCHED

JOSIE GORDON

Lambda Literary award-winning author

Bella BOOKS

2011

Bella Books, Inc.
P.O. Box 10543
Tallahassee, FL 32302

Printed in the United States of America on acid-free paper
First published 2011

This book is a work of fiction. Names, characters, places and events are either used fictitiously or entirely imagined. Any resemblances to actual events or places or persons living or dead are coincidental.

Editor: Katherine V. Forrest
Cover Designer: Kiaro Creative Ltd.

ISBN 13:978-1-59493-226-7

Other Bella books by Josie Gordon

Whacked
Toasted

For Casper
everyone's therapy dog

Acknowledgments

Thank heavens no one will grade my depiction of Michigan geography. I'd fail. But that's why I write fiction. While quirky places with unique histories and vivacious lives do dot Michigan's Great Lakes coasts, and while almost every place that Lonnie visits on her trip in this book actually exists—or did when I took my research trip a few years ago—I made some stuff up. Middelburg doesn't really exist. Nor does the county I placed it in. I stretched the whole coastline to make room for that little town and its people. Still, I recommend to everyone a visit to the northern lower peninsula and the upper peninsula. Country of astonishing beauty, and great pasties!

Many thanks to my tribe of big-hearted people who, thankfully, really do exist: Rhoda, Carla, Pat (and her dining room table), MMC, Jared the car guy, everyone in my family, Casper and Desmond who snore while I type and then demand to play ball, Hattie who naps on my desk, Tim who makes sure I get my exercise picking up paperclips, Nikolaas (the only truly Dutch one of all of us) and most of all, Jen. I couldn't do it without them. Special thanks to my editor, Katherine V. Forrest, whom it is an honor to know. Any errors in this text are mine, not theirs.

Special thanks to all of Lonnie's fans. I confess that I'm a lousy blogger, but you can find me at www.josiegordon.com and on Facebook. I'd love to talk to you.

About the Author

Josie Gordon's first mystery novel *Whacked* (2008) won the Lambda Literary Award for the Best Lesbian Mystery of 2008. The second in the series, *Toasted*, was a finalist for the same award in 2009.

This was a happy ending to a rather scary episode: once upon a time, Josie actually found a dead body in the woods. And though every amateur sleuth she has ever encountered in books or on TV would have seized the chance to march right up and investigate, Josie ran like the dickens in the other direction! Later, while waiting for the police, she resolved to write a book in which the sleuth would be as freaked out by finding a dead guy as she was.

Recently Josie has decided to learn to draw and has begun to practice art journaling and making comics. She lives with her partner in the woods and walks every day in places where there are more trees (and turkeys and woodpeckers and on a good day, even deer) than people.

Ditched is the third Lonnie Squires mystery.

You can learn more at www.josiegordon.com.

CHAPTER ONE

I leaned back in my office chair and tossed down the report from my Committee on Liturgy. The line one caller ID announced my best friend Marion's work number. Her latest drama would do nicely for a break in this long morning of reports and meetings, so I grabbed the receiver. "Good morning!"

"Grab your loved ones, Lonnie, and hold 'em tight!" said Marion. "'Cause if I were a religious woman—and you know I'm not—I'd declare it a sign of the impending Rapture."

I smiled. "If you get Raptured, can I have your car?"

"You need it, that piece of crap you drive." She was probably shaking her head in pity. "But I'm the Eclectic Believer here. I'm the one supposedly getting left behind."

"Plenty of folks would tell you Episcopal priests will be hanging around too." I stretched the morning's tension from my shoulders, wondering what had gotten Marion into this state.

"Well, you haven't got a thing I want. Except that lovely dog. And if anyone on this planet is going to heaven—"

"It's Linus." I reached out with my foot and rubbed the eight-month-old black German shepherd's ribs as he slept beneath my desk—his usual spot despite the bed in the corner of my office. "Agreed. And you're so sure the Rapture is upon us because?"

"Bad energy everywhere today."

"Did the soccer game get canceled?" I spun to look out the window and check the weather. The red-golden leaves of the silver maple in the parish house's backyard snapped in the October sunlight. It hadn't rained all summer or fall, so of course we'd all dreaded that it would start today, the day of the very first Women's League soccer game in Middelburg. The first game my over-thirty team, the Hot Flashes, would ever play. But it looked sunny.

"Star Hannes is here, in The Grind," Marion whispered. "Eating a piece of boeterkoek and liking it. With her crew filming the whole thing!"

"Whoa." It *was* a sign of the end times. Star hadn't been in Marion's restaurant in months, even before trying to get her shut down last August for supposedly poisoning people.

"She's yuckin' it up with my regulars, talking about how The Grind is a bastion of local heritage."

"Well, it *is* a bastion of local heritage," I said. "Much as I hate to agree with the woman. It's The Windmill Grind Kaffe Klatsch and All Dutch All the Time Café, for God's sake." Middelburg was founded by Dutch people. Their descendents still populated this place.

"But here's the thing." Marion whispered now. "My chi has been out of whack all week. The first not-good sign. And then in she comes. Another very-not-good sign. Everything is wonky."

I glanced down at *The Middelburg Review* on my desk. Ballooning ARM mortgages driving foreclosures in the town and the county to an all-time high. The local high school's basketball team, The Middelburg Warships, losing to Holland Christian in overtime. Bow hunting season starting tomorrow. Star Hannes' standing in the congressional election polls dropping as election day approached.

"It isn't all bad," I said, eyeing Star's numbers.

"Are you going to tell me I'm being too dramatic?" Marion asked. "Because I can hang up now."

"No, no." I leaned forward as if she were in the office with me. "I'm just saying that if Star's sudden appreciation of your food has you foreseeing karmic cataclysm, maybe you should reconsider joining the Episcopal church. We're a bit more stoic about such things." Linus sighed, scootching himself around so my foot would hit more of his belly.

"Yeah, well." I heard a metallic slap and splash in the background. Marion must be calling from the restaurant's kitchen. "I haven't told you about the stranger yet."

Outsiders didn't show up in Middelburg much, except for the rich folks from Chicago who owned mansions along Lake Michigan's beaches. And over the course of the summer, we got to know them. So the locals have a big case of *stranger danger.* As a stranger here myself—I'd moved here from Chicago's South Side only six months ago—I knew.

"And what? You think he's bringing the Rapture?"

"No. He's an attorney from Chicago. Never seen this guy before. Little guy. Goatee. Bow tie. Trussed up tight like if he popped a button he'd fall to pieces." She paused, then dropped the bomb. "And he's got questions. *About you.*"

A tiger clawed upward from my insides. I checked my watch. It was something I always did when trouble struck—something I'd picked up from years of watching old cop dramas on television with my dad. 11:53. The beginning of the end times. At least, for me in Middelburg.

If that sounds too dire, let me explain. My ex-girlfriend Jamie dumped me last spring and set up with a new chick, an attorney. Jamie kept most everything from our years of cohabitation, which was okay with me. But she'd cleaned out our joint bank accounts for a "safer" bank, which was not okay. I asked her for half the balances and she stalled all summer. Last week I called and threatened to come after it. She'd argued that New Chick said I had no right to it since I'd left her, moved out of our Chicago home to take on a new life in Michigan. I pointed out that I wasn't the one who left her bleeding on the ground after a nearly fatal attack by a shovel-wielding murderer.

"I called nine-one-one!" Jamie whined and I wondered how I'd ever loved anyone who could sound like that. "Besides you don't remember what happened. You had a skull fracture."

"I know you said bye-bye before the ambulance got there. I know you didn't even follow me to the hospital. I've got witnesses to that, head injury be damned."

"You shouldn't swear. You're a priest."

"Give me half the money," I said and she hung up on me.

I knew it wasn't over but I hadn't expected an attorney to show up. Maybe New Chick had put her foot down about the money and sent a colleague to threaten me.

"Get him out of there," I said, "before Star—"

Marion gasped. "Crap! Star just got up from her booth and is bearing down on him with the Middelburg How-Dee-Do Third Degree. Kaylee!" Marion shrieked at her restaurant's assistant manager as pots and pans clattered crazily. "Stop her!"

Star Hannes, town councilwoman and congresswoman wannabe hated my guts on a good day, ever since I uncovered her plot to defraud pretty much the whole town last May. With less than a month until the election and her standing in the polls slipping, she'd do anything for attention, including exposing the local woman priest as gay. Given my bishop's aversion to bad publicity, if Star got wind of Jamie, of the truth about me, I was through.

"Bring him out your kitchen door. I'll meet you in the park," I said. "I'll answer his questions and get him out of town."

"Everyone will see."

Middelburg's Central Park sprawled right across the street from Woman at the Well Episcopal Church and parish house, in full view of many downtown homes and businesses.

"They'll all know within the hour anyhow," I said. "Might as well act as if I have nothing to hide."

"Do you?" Marion asked.

I hung up.

She, of course, didn't know the truth about me. No one did. Ultraconservative Middelburg was too dangerous a place for me to be out, even to trusted friends like Marion. One innocent slip and I'd lose my job for sure—something I couldn't afford. No telling what other harassment I'd have to endure.

My stomach soured. If this attorney was here to talk about Jamie and our money, I guess Marion was about to find out. Just one more thing to deal with today.

As I stood, Linus leapt up from beneath the desk, knocking his head on the bottom of the drawer. He'd grown so fast, he still didn't fully understand the dimensions of his gangly body.

"Help, help, help," I prayed as I rushed through a clean-up, wishing I'd worn my clergy clothes instead of jeans, a white turtleneck and a crimson fleece. The priestly costume put the fear of God into most people. Because I want people to feel welcome at church, not afraid, I usually didn't wear it. But now I didn't have an ounce of intimidation factor going for me. My short hair lurched out funny on the right, I had black dog hair stuck all over the fleece, and I looked like I needed more coffee.

Linus and I hopped down the stairs in the old Victorian house the church used for parish offices and meeting rooms, landing in what had once been a front parlor and was now a homey reception room. Ashleigh Moore, the extravagantly beautiful twenty-something who'd joined us this summer, sat at her desk chatting with Bova Poster, a middle-aged parishioner, chair of my Committee on Liturgy and one of my very own Hot Flashes. Sitting on the nubbly couch behind Bova, Isabella Koontz tapped the screen of her cell phone, dark hair hanging in her face.

"Gotta run out quick!" I high-fived Bova's raised hand.

"But! We! Have! A Meeting!" Bova folded her arms across her chest causing the embroidered chipmunks on the front of her orange sweatshirt to kiss.

"Back in ten." I sidestepped toward the door. "Ashleigh will get you tea. And there's chips." I grabbed Linus' collar. "Have chips."

"We're fine," said Isabella, barely raising her head.

That stopped me. Isabella was always the first to offer a broad smile. That was, unless—

"How are you today, Isabella?" I asked.

Bova and Ashleigh looked at her.

Isabella nodded, still tapping away on her phone. "Oh,

great! The kids are doing great in school. I got them matching Christmas dresses at the resale store in Holland yesterday that are going to make my mother just die they are so cute." All this without ever looking up.

"And Ivor?"

Still she tapped. Very unusual. She did wave her phone though. "Just checking in with him. He wanted to have a quick lunch. But I'm here." She roughened her voice. "'You're always at that church when I want to spend time with you.'" She shrugged.

I tried to catch her eyes, to see her face behind her hair. In the last few months, she'd managed to sprout a variety of bruises, some on her face, some on her arms. Once she wound up on crutches with a sprained ankle. She claimed she was a klutz. Almost everyone took her at her word or—even if they didn't believe her—didn't push it because, well, it wasn't nice. When I'd tried to find out if she was safe at home, she'd shut me down. So mostly, I just kept careful watch.

"Go! Go!" Bova shooed me. "We'll compare! Wafer! Suppliers! While! You're gone!"

I dashed out the door and down the porch steps, holding Linus' collar. His leash lived in the car for when we walked downtown, but most days we just ran in the church yard or the park. The fall air chilled my denim, which moved cold and heavy against my thighs. Once we crossed the street Linus dashed ahead, chasing the park's black squirrels up ancient maples glowing in the slanted sunshine. Leaves shushed and ticked as they blew by, curled from weeks of no rain.

Marion and a suited man with dark hair and goatee rounded the corner from Middelburg's two-block-long downtown. She gesticulated wildly, sunny yellow swing coat flapping behind her arms.

Suddenly, I thought I might throw up.

CHAPTER TWO

I called Linus and as he sat in front of me—the results of our daily obedience training during my lunch breaks—I grabbed his collar. We walked to a leaf-covered picnic table and I pointed to the ground. "Down."

Slowly, eyes rolling with dissatisfaction, he lowered his body like a creaky drawbridge until his chest touched the ground.

"Good dog."

He flopped on his side and twisted, belly up, big paws waving, hoping for a belly rub. I felt my nausea recede a bit.

As Marion and the attorney approached I brushed the leaves off the table and stood, one eye on Linus, one eye on them. My best friend's color scheme for the week was, evidently, yellow. She wore a bright turban over her auburn hair, yellow coat and dark green spandex pants that made her look like an out-of-season daffodil. As always she balanced her round frame on skimpy sandals with spiked heels—also sunny yellow. Her fingernails and toenails flashed yellow with, I thought, flaming suns handpainted on the big toes. Marion had her nails done every Tuesday over at Colleen's Cuttery and the color change pretty much indicated the dominant scheme of wardrobe for the coming week.

On those heels, Marion towered over the attorney and at six foot even, I did too. He had a pink bald spot on the top of his head, which flashed as his head bobbed in greeting. "Maurice Brand." He offered a business card with the hand that wasn't gripping the worn leather satchel. The card proclaimed his name in sensible type and unfolded to detail the pedigree of the law firm in which he was a partner.

Looked like Jamie and New Chick were going all out to shut me down. I considered caving right there, telling him that Jamie could keep my damn money. But I couldn't bear being bullied. Screw her. I'd fight.

"Before business, we eat!" Marion pulled a silver thermos, three insulated mugs and a huge foil package from her tote. "Broodjes are perfect for a picnic."

I just wanted to get this over with. Plus I had a meeting to get to. But Marion's look told me to obey, so I sat down.

She set plates and two broodjes before each of us. Rye rolls, split in half, each topped with sprouts, Havarti and tomato and cucumber, and finally a sliced hard-boiled egg.

I thought it looked suspiciously like health food and not at all like a perfect picnic.

A few minutes later, Brand patted the napkin to his goatee. "Simply fantastic! I had no idea Dutch food could be so tasty. One tends to lump it with British food for some reason. You know, rainy and dark."

"Oh, no!" Marion's horror was not pretend. "Dutch food is some of the most tasteful and creative in Europe. I know everyone makes a big deal of French or Italian cuisine, but the Dutch is so underrated. It was Dutch food that built this nation, you know. After all, it was the Dutch who settled much of the New World!"

Brand nodded as he took another bite of the miraculous broodje. "I'm truly grateful to have learned this."

Marion leaned back from the table and looked at me in triumph. She had softened him up for me, made my job easier. Just like she did during a soccer game, finishing on a perfect cross. Marion Freeley, superbestfriend to the rescue once again.

"I'm sorry," I said, "but I need to get back to the office. I have an appointment waiting."

"Indeed." Brand dabbed his mouth again and shifted his cuffs. "I'm glad this sunny angel directed me here, because your mother was unwilling to provide me with your exact address, the name of your church or your cell phone number."

My mother? How had she gotten involved? Jamie knew where I lived.

"Your church has no Internet presence—hard to believe in this day and age." Brand shook his head.

"It's coming," I said. It was on the docket for our Committee on Communication. "Facebook too."

Brand smiled politely. "Well, since time is of the essence. I decided to simply come find you. The will cannot wait."

"What will?" asked Marion.

Brand looked at her then back at me.

"You can say anything in front of her," I said. Might as well.

"The will of your aunt."

"What?" I must have sounded shocked because Linus popped up beside me and eyed Brand. "She's been dead nearly a decade. We read her will then."

"Not all of it," he said.

"Yes, all of it." I well remembered my sister Cassie's outrage when I'd received far more of Aunt Kate's money than she, earmarked to pay my seminary tuition. My sister had begged me not to go, to give her half the money instead. But the money couldn't be used for anything else. Kate was a proud Episcopalian, even if she'd been a controlling bitch who'd treated me as her personal slave while I was a kid. "The money she left us is long gone."

"Not so." Brand pulled his satchel onto the table and dug inside.

A cool wind scattered leaves across the grass. A squirrel catcalled from halfway up the trunk of the nearest maple. Linus' ears turned toward the sound.

"Oh, fabulous!" Marion laughed. "Has she actually been living in Tahiti all this time? I wouldn't put it past her!"

"Shut up," I said, "or I'll kick you out of here."

"She died nine years, one month, and twenty-six days ago," Brand said. "My condolences."

Linus nosed my plate. I gave him a bite of broodje. "And the will?"

"The will contained directions to us, her executors, that were to be kept in confidence until two weeks before your thirty-fifth birthday, which I believe is coming up. Next Friday? October tenth?"

Marion cocked an eyebrow at me. The squirrel on the tree chattered, flipping his tail.

I didn't like the sound of this. "Yes. But I don't get it."

Brand snuffed, studied the stack of papers. "It is rather strange. But I've brought all the details."

Terrific. My crazy great-aunt, with whom I'd spent my teenaged summers while my parents went through their ugly, unnecessary divorce—the woman who had hounded me, then haunted me ever since I'd moved back to this burg—now she was rising from the grave to screw up my life again. *Just terrific.*

"What does she want from me now?" It had always been like that with Aunt Kate. Pretending to give but really demanding something. I had no hope that her being long dead would change anything.

He shrugged, pulled tiny reading classes from his vest pocket and flipped pages. "She has given you the potential to inherit $467,863 and some change."

Marion whooped and shot her arms up so fast she nearly knocked over her coffee and Brand's. "Half a million dollars!" She whooped again.

"Potential?" I asked. "You said potential." I could smell Aunt Kate's shenanigans over the broodjes. "What does that mean, exactly?"

"Half a million dollars!" Marion clapped her hands.

"Fabulous exotic vacation here I come."

Brand hadn't looked up from the papers. "That is in addition, of course, to the value of the race car."

Marion froze, hands mid-clap. "Race car?"

I ran my hands through my hair. My great-aunt had worked as part of a medical team on a local racetrack way back in the Fifties or something. Before she'd made a bundle by investing in cable T.V. But I'd never heard of a car. "Aunt Kate had no race car."

Brand kept reading. "A nineteen sixty-six Ford Fairlane 500 two-door hardtop racer. One of only fifty-seven built. Named 'The Pearly Gates.'"

Marion's grin spread slowly. "God, I love your aunt!"

Brand peered through his glasses. "I have a lot of technical details here. Certificates of documentation from Ford. It has fewer than seven hundred miles on it and all original parts. At last appraisal it was worth almost eighty-two thousand dollars."

Marion's jaw dropped. I think mine did too. Neither of us spoke.

"Your great-aunt provided that it be kept in running condition until you picked it up on your thirty-fifth birthday."

"Picked it up from where?" I asked.

"Conveniently, right here in town." Brand pulled his glasses off. "Carson's Car Care."

"Red has your car?" Marion clearly couldn't believe it.

Neither could I. Red Carson was a county sheriff's deputy I'd met when I'd stumbled upon a body last spring. Since then she and I had become pretty good friends. Well, at least, we hiked together most Sunday afternoons. And she was undeniably cute. Her father had run a garage on the south end of town for decades and her brother had taken it over after their dad's death. Red helped out occasionally, but since her brother had shipped out to Afghanistan last winter, they hadn't done any work.

"Why has no one told me this before?" I asked.

"Terms of the will. No mention of any of it allowed until this week."

Of course. Typical Aunt Kate. Secrets. Plots. Manipulations.

"Regarding the car," Brand said, "I'd advise you to get it

appraised again if ownership is transferred. After the trip." A quick breeze tousled his hair and he spread his hand to flatten it again.

"*If* ownership is transferred?" *Here it comes.* The scheme. The demands.

"Trip?" Marion asked. "I knew it! Some place with umbrella drinks, I hope! 'Cause I'm going too!"

Brand sighed. "The terms of the wills are these: Katherine Squires has left you a vintage race car, The Pearly Gates, in running order. However, you only inherit it on the condition that you pick it up on your thirty-fifth birthday, a Friday, and use it to take the trip laid out by your aunt, here." He offered me a thick folder of papers but Marion snatched them. "The trip will take until Sunday night. It has a prescribed itinerary which you must follow exactly, taking pictures of yourself and the car at various points along the way."

"This trip is around Lake Michigan!" Marion said, flipping papers from the folder.

Linus nudged me and I handed him my last bite of broodje. "Pure Aunt Kate," I said. "Everything comes with conditions."

"You have to take a friend with you," Brand said and Marion kicked me under the table. "To take photos of you and the car."

The squirrel chattered again and Linus woofed, scaring it back into the thick red leaves above.

"First stop: the Singing Fountain in Grand Haven," said Marion. "Can you believe I've never been there?"

"At the end of the trip," Brand continued, "on Sunday evening, I'll meet you here and receive the evidence of your compliance. If all conditions are met, you inherit the car and the entirety of the estate."

Marion kicked me again. "Half a million bucks!"

A knot twisted in the center of my chest—a knot I hadn't felt in over nine years. "What if I miss a photo? Or want to go alone?"

"Hey!" said Marion.

"Or if I'm busy this weekend? I'm a priest, Mr. Brand. I work on Sundays." My aunt would have guessed this a good possibility. After all, she'd left me the money for seminary. And she'd have calculated what day of the week my thirty-fifth birthday would fall on. She knew this little game of hers would get me into professional hot water. I began to boil.

"There's a submarine in here." Marion flipped pages in the folder. "And a waterfall. And the world's largest crucifix!"

"If you don't go, don't take a friend, you get nothing," said Brand. "The entire estate goes to the secondary beneficiary. If you attempt the trip but fail to complete it for some reason—any reason—you may keep the car, but everything else goes to the secondary beneficiary."

I dug a finger into the grain of the wooden picnic table. "Who is that? Someone in my family?"

Brand fingered the edges of his leather bag. "I'm not at liberty to say."

"Of course you aren't." I wiped my hands on a napkin. Only Aunt Kate could hijack my birthday from the grave. Or try to. I stood and Linus leapt to his feet. "Thanks, Mr. Brand, but no thanks."

Brand looked like he might cry. "Please, Reverend, I know it's a shock. I urge you not to make a hasty decision."

"God forbid my aunt do anything truly generous. She just expects me to drop everything or else no money. No love unless you submit utterly."

"It's only three days," Brand said. "And quite a bit of money."

"My life doesn't stop for my Aunt Kate's money," I said. "I can't miss a Sunday on such short notice." Tears bit at my eyes. Just like Aunt Kate to try to yank my chain like this, screw up my life, make my birthday all about her. Well, I wasn't going to let her get the best of me like she had when I was just a kid. No way. "I'm sorry she wasted your time."

"Lonnie!" Marion held up the folder. "You need to think about this. Seriously."

"No, I don't." I patted my leg to call Linus to follow me back to the church. I forced myself to smile. "Thanks for your efforts, Mr. Brand. And you." I pointed at Marion and felt a genuine smile growing. "See you tonight at the game."

CHAPTER THREE

"Trouble?" asked Isabella as Linus and I climbed the steps to the parish house porch.

She and Bova sat in the peeling wicker rockers amidst curled papery leaves. I'd have to have those chairs brought in soon. Yet another item on the priest's To Do list.

"No." I studied Isabella's face. No purple shadows or fading yellow patches. Just bright open eyes above a long crooked nose. Not for the first time I wondered if Ivor, her husband, had broken it.

I sat on the steps and we had our meeting on the porch, in the crisp breeze and sunny air. I'm amazed over and over again at the crazy things parishioners want to haggle over. Today it was the size of the type in the worship bulletins relative to the amount of paper needed to print them. Were our efforts to be a green organization more important than considering the eyesight of the older members of the parish? The font discussion took half an hour. And that was just the start of a long agenda.

Linus' jagged snore punctuated the entire meeting, reminding me that my life had more to it than crazy great-aunts and church.

After two I reentered the parish house. Ashleigh cuddled Linus and gave me the best news of the day: "No messages."

Linus and I climbed the creaking stairs to my garret office in the back room of the second floor. I loved it here. The top of my head just brushed the ceiling in the center of the sloped room, but on each side I was usually seated or bent, at my desk or perusing my shelves. I'd covered the black wooden floor with a colorful wool rug I'd found at the Goodwill in Holland—another Dutch town south of here but considerably more cosmopolitan. I'd also tucked a bed for Linus in the corner in front of a second door I never used, that led to a kind of creepy landing and narrow stairs down to the back porch.

This had been a storeroom made into a temporary office for me when I'd first arrived to consult with the former rector. I'd been held at gunpoint here. I'd helped my dad win a huge trivia contest from here. I'd counseled kids and adults, shared in celebrations and condolences, hoped for my future. When I became interim rector on a two-year contract, the parish leaders had tried to get me to move to the big airy office in the turret room downstairs, but I'd declined. I liked this one best. The turret room was better suited for adult education space anyhow.

I settled in to start Sunday's sermon. The Old Testament reading was the Ten Commandments from Exodus, always a tough one, as people around here loved to grab onto laws, pretend they were clear and start casting stones at others. Especially dangerous to gay people in this day and age. But the other readings offered a little more. A psalm that talked about laws making people wise and joyous. Paul's letter to Philippians about how religious law failed to bring righteousness. I'd barely started brainstorming ideas when the phone rang and I grabbed it without looking.

"The Right Reverend Tappen would like to speak to you,"

announced the woman's voice as if God himself had descended from on high to request an audience. Lydia, my bishop's secretary, worshipped him. She had more job security than any of us.

Fantastic. First Star, then my aunt, and now my bishop. Maybe Marion's intuition about an oncoming cataclysm was right.

"Lorraine!" The bishop boomed. I pulled the phone away from my ear. "How delightful it is to speak to you, my little sister in Christ!"

Thank God he wasn't here in person. Otherwise he'd be standing with arms spread for the mandatory hug. That heavy pewter pectoral cross he always wore would cut into my breast as he squeezed. Plus, he wore too much cologne.

"How can I help you, sir?" I wanted to get back to my sermon. My nice, quiet, reliable, logical sermon.

"Lorraine, how sweet of you to offer to help!" The phone vibrated in my hand with each syllable. "There is a little something I need you to do for me. I'm sure you won't mind and it won't add a minute to your already busy schedule."

Well, *that* sounded too good to be true.

"Happy to help," I lied.

"You know that all-clergy meeting at Frontline Church of Christ? I want you to represent not only your own church, but the entire diocese as well. I simply can't make it, and I'm sure you'll do a dynamite job."

I had no idea what he was talking about.

"Afterward send me a thorough report and if I need to, I'll follow up with Pastor Wesselynk."

"Okay." I stalled. Had I forgotten some huge meeting, something so big that my bishop had been invited to it?

"Of course, I could have selected a more senior priest to represent me, but this seemed such an excellent opportunity for you to show your stuff. Theologically, of course." He guffawed at the marvelousness of his sense of humor.

Truth was he didn't want to go. He was just sending me in to do his dirty work. I knew it. But I said nothing while I checked my calendar online and my e-mail inbox. I skimmed my trash and spam. Nothing from Brady Wesselynk.

"And of course," he continued, "I look forward to you giving the community a good impression of our church. When you see Pastor Wesselynk," he continued, "be sure to thank him on my behalf for the letter of invitation."

A letter! I started shuffling through the stack of untouched mail on my side table. Linus watched my flurry with interest. I barely listened as the bishop droned on about broad minds and tradition. "It sounds like an interesting thing, this Faithful Heritage Initiative. Perhaps a model for something similar in our own diocese."

I tossed the mail back on the table. Nothing. A burning suspicion snuck its way up my neck. What if I hadn't been invited to this *all-clergy* meeting? What if I were the one minister of the twenty in town—one for every congregation of Christ the Lord's Own Sainted Elect Reformed Church, the Methodist and me—left out? Set up to look like a fool?

Brady Wesselynk wouldn't do that. We weren't exactly friends, but he respected me, especially after I'd helped clear suspicion from his church when a man died there. He wouldn't snub me, but he wouldn't stop anyone else who wanted to. Like Star Hannes. Brady was one of her biggest butt-kissers.

"If you could get that report to me within forty-eight hours," the bishop said, "I'd be grateful. It'll be off your plate by Thursday evening, and you can focus on your sermon for Sunday. Ah, the clarity of the Ten Commandments. If only all of the Bible were that easy to preach about."

"Wait!" I thought hard. He wanted the report by Thursday evening? Forty-eight hours? That meant—that panicked urge to vomit burbled in my gut again. Tonight? This stupid meeting was *tonight*?

At the same time as *my soccer team's very first game ever?*

I wanted to slam my head onto my desk. Or cry. Or kick Star Hannes. Or all of the above.

"Yes, Lorraine?"

I couldn't ask what time the meeting started. He'd know I hadn't been invited. That would just create more trouble and I was in enough as it was. "What time Thursday evening sir? Forty-eight hours from the start of the meeting? Or the end? What would you prefer?"

"Turn it in by five thirty. Forty-seven hours. Show me you're on the ball." He chuckled again.

That meant the meeting tonight started at six thirty at Frontline. Something about a Faithful Heritage Initiative. Something that Star Hannes didn't want me at so badly that she'd not only left me off the invite list but she'd also scheduled it—I just bet—to occur opposite the Hot Flashes' first league game.

Like Marion had said, a sure sign of the end times.

CHAPTER FOUR

When I stepped out of my '88 Honda Civic wagon at Frontline Church of Christ, thunder rumbled in the west. Only about twenty cars, lonely spectators, sat in the middle of the acres of parking lots. A hundred percent of the clergy of this town. Twenty little cars. I had to laugh.

Keep it in perspective, Lon. The world is a much bigger place than this.

I checked my watch. 6:23. My goal was to find out as much as I needed to know and get the heck over to the rec center to change as close to seven thirty as possible. That's when the game started. My blood surged at the thought: *Soccer!*

If I were lucky this would be dull and I could slip out early. It killed me to miss the pre-game with the Flashes, but I couldn't just blow this off, what with my vow of obedience to my bishop. Marion would act as team captain until I got there.

Thunder grumbled again. The blue sky faded behind stacked mountains of thick black clouds, tinted red and purple by the sunset.

Just hold off until after my game.

I closed the car door and checked myself out. No dust or dog hair on the clergy duds—black heeled shoes, black slacks, black shirt with white plastic collar. The fiery red jacket embroidered with gold thread sat squarely on my shoulders. A quick glance at the window's reflection showed my gelled hair had stayed in place.

Good to go.

I passed through the sliding doors into Frontline with my game face on. Just like walking onto the field at the start of a soccer game. Show no weakness. I half expected someone to ask me for my invitation, to kick me out when I couldn't produce one. I wanted someone to try.

No one did, of course. In fact, no one said anything to me at all. Two hunched men with peppery balding heads, tweed suitcoats, and quick steps glanced at me in the lobby then hurried into Frontline's sanctuary.

I wondered if I should bring it down a notch, enter less stoked for battle and more in a spirit of community. I was halfway through a change of heart when the sliders sucked open behind me and Star Hannes walked in, full entourage in tow, and lust for domination swept every other impulse away.

Trim and tall, with the high shining cheekbones and luminous eyes of so many of the Dutch-descended, Star had a sophisticated style that turned everyone's heads. Tonight she strode forward in a kiwi-colored wool suit and silk blouse with a plunging front that took no prisoners. A simple gold cross hung there. She turned to laugh at something said by the young man on her right and her tri-foiled hair tossed and flashed in the lobby's artificial lights. Everyone in the group laughed with her.

Tonight that group included Star's number one toadie, Mimi Manser, who walked as usual on Star's left and slightly behind. Mimi played for the Hot Flashes only because in high school she'd played on our original church team, The Well's Belles. Since then, she'd gone to the dark side, but when I'd been one person short of a full team last summer, we'd taken her on our team. None of us trusted her anymore, but she could still play left wing with the best of them.

The young man on Star's right was Frederick something—a young guy just out of college in Chicago, whom Star had hired last month as her publicist. Two lithe brunettes trailed, one lugging a television camera, the other a bulky backpack of additional technical equipment. Lauren and Annie, Marion had told me. Trailing them came the reporter, Artesia Collins, the twenty-something platinum blonde who'd signed on to be chronicler of Star's rise to fame. Marion, who knew everything since The Grind was the hub of town gossip, said that Artesia yearned to be a reporter but found narrating Star's propaganda less than satisfying.

And last, and perhaps least, Star's string bean of a husband, Gil, brought up the rear, all limp hair and spidery mustache, wearing a starched white shirt, ironed jeans and penny loafers with no socks.

Star rested her eye on me for barely a second, then scooted it away, not wanting to acknowledge my presence.

I followed them into the sanctuary. The worship space at Frontline was more modern Broadway than traditional religious. Plush theatre seats for hundreds, double aisles, a raised stage wide and deep enough to hold a performance of *Wicked* (not that that show would ever get booked in this town). I'd spent a good deal of time here in August working security for Cousin Donna Hancock's Loaves and Fishes Evangelical Cooking School Road Show. I'd seen the sophisticated lighting, the computerized sound systems. What I had never seen was the place so empty for an event.

The twenty-some of us flowed into a puddle in the center of the front three rows of the immense auditorium at the dark foot of the brightly lit stage. They chattered with each other, occasionally looking up at the podium festooned with vases of splayed tropical flowers: birds of paradise, bougainvillea and greenery. That explained Star's kiwi suit—she'd dressed to match the stage setting.

I spotted Brady Wesselynk hovering in the aisle, wringing

his hands. As always, he wore creased khakis and a Ralph Lauren shirt—tonight a pale blue. As I sidled up to him I noticed wrinkles in his normally sharp pants. "Hey."

He blinked his surprise. "Lorraine! So—glad—to see you." He grinned his big-toothed grin and slapped me on the back.

I played it cool. "Sorry to crash, Brady, but my bishop sent me."

Pink flowered in his cheeks.

"So," I said, "what are you and Star up to?"

His eyes widened, round and white, like a frightened horse's. Actually, Brady looked a lot like a horse, with a long rectangular face, blond forelock, big square teeth and a hee-haw sort of laugh. But he wasn't laughing now. "We are up to nothing," he said. He ran his palms down the front of his shirt, smoothing out imaginary creases.

I nodded slowly. "Because you know that allowing a candidate to campaign on church property would risk your nonprofit status. Hate to see you lose your tax breaks on this place."

His enormous Adam's apple bobbed with his swallow. A sudden explosion of thunder rocketed through the room. Everyone paused, then began speaking all at once.

I raised an eyebrow. "Is that a sign of divine disdain, Brady?" I enjoyed his squirming.

"Star is not campaigning," he said. "She is acting in her elected capacity as member of the town council, making a special announcement to the clergy of the town."

"Mmm." I scanned the audience. "Not a single other member of the council here, though."

"Lorraine. All is right with whatever goes on in this church. 'For in it the righteousness of God is revealed through faith.'" He winked. "That's St. Paul to the Romans."

Before I could snap at him for pulling Biblical words out of context, he hurried over to Star's group, now circled up at the corner of the stage.

I slid into the third row, settling one seat over from a heavy-set man with great black eyebrows and a balding gray head. He busied himself searching his pockets, then pretended to be too busy examining the crumpled paper he'd pulled from his jacket to greet me.

No surprise. The clergymen of this town didn't really know what to do with me on two counts: I wasn't a member of the CLOSER church and I was a woman. Brady and I had the first in common, so I guess that's why he talked to me. He was about the only one who did.

Everyone hushed as Star, moving like a well-oiled machine, glided to the podium. "Thank you for coming." The lights slowly faded until we sat in dimness and she glowed in the single golden spot. From the aisle behind me, her crew's video equipment showed its red eyes. Recording.

Star gazed out at us with fake maternal love. I wondered if anyone in the room bought it.

"As one of your town council representatives—"

Ah, so she was smart enough to dodge the rule against campaigning in a church.

"—I've come to share with you an exciting new initiative." She glanced down. "One I developed myself, researched myself, and am passionately dedicated to."

Campaign ahoy. Thunder crashed again, then a crazy thrumming. Rain. Hard rain. Still, we could play in rain. But the lightning had to stop, or we'd get canceled.

"I'm thrilled to introduce to you Middelburg's Faithful Heritage Initiative. As the church leaders of this town, I know you'll support this initiative one thousand percent." She paused for applause and the men obliged.

"Middelburg was founded nearly one hundred years ago because the Christian Reformed Church had become too secularized. Our forefathers bought this entire town and re-dedicated it to the new church they founded, Christ the Lord's Own Sainted Elect Reformed. You are the representatives of that church here on earth."

True. CLOSER churches existed nowhere else.

"Middelburg's founding was too unique, too risky to have come from man alone. The Holy Spirit, gentlemen, guided the founders. They, in their infinite humility, simply acted as mouthpieces for the wisdom of our Lord."

She looked down at Brady who lurched forward to start the applause. Everyone else joined in.

I'd learned months ago that the separation of church and state didn't exist in Middelburg, Michigan, but it still made me squirrelly. My foot jiggled. I hoped I wasn't missing a Hot Flashes game just to sit here and listen to her stir up local patriotism.

"We have, of late, lost that connection to our divine destiny!" Star gripped the podium and leaned so hard that the flowers trembled. "We need to return to that wisdom! Only it bears the authority of tradition *and* the authority of divine inspiration."

Brady-induced applause again, followed by another enormous clap of thunder.

"And the path, gentlemen, is simple. We need to return to living in the light of revelation as preserved forever in Middelburg's founding document, The Town Charter."

Murmurs of appreciation.

Star paused and surveyed each and every person in the room—skipping me, of course—her golden/auburn/chestnut tri-foiled hair glinting in the light. She sipped from the glittering Waterford glass then pulled a dusty tome bound in dark brown leather out from beneath the podium and set it next to the glass.

"Few realize—in fact, gentlemen, I'd be willing to bet none of you even realize, if betting weren't illegal in Middelburg—how many of the laws in this charter are no longer observed!"

A lot of eyes darted back and forth, but no one said anything.

Star smiled, held a hand up. "No shame in that. For neither did I. Not until I began to wonder why we suffered two murders in the last six months after decades of crime-free existence."

The air around me turned to ice. I'd been involved in those murders—finding the bodies, solving the crimes. Star loved pointing out that the crime rate exploded at the same time I'd moved to town.

She caressed the book. "There is wisdom here, friends. Revelation. It is a good book."

I almost laughed out loud. I checked out the rest of my clergy colleagues to see if anyone was getting her crap. *Good book. Please!*

As if she were Moses descending with the tablets. But everyone else listened seriously.

"There are laws in this book that no one has observed for a very long time. And this failure has led to the moral cracking of Middelburg's foundation."

"Yes!" cried a man from the front row. Others murmured assent.

"This failure to follow the law threatens the survival of our families!" Star rocked the heavy wooden podium with her fervor. "And our spirits!"

"Yes, yes." Voices from all around me.

"We must once again observe the laws written by our founders." Star paused to sip while enthusiastic conversation broke out all around me.

I wanted to stand up and shout. *Can't you see what she's doing? Fear-mongering, blame-casting and fantasizing about an impossible future. You're smarter than that!*

But instead I checked my watch. 7:03. If Star wound this up quickly, I could make the start of the game.

"The town council has adopted my Faithful Heritage Initiative for a trial period. It is a return to the many laws tragically unobserved and unenforced for so long. In order to ease the transition back into lawful living, I have chosen seven passages from the Charter which we will begin observing immediately."

Seven passages? Was she kidding?

She studied us to make sure she had our full attention. "These seven laws have been handpicked by me to have the most immediate positive observable effect on communities and our families."

Uh-oh.

"We will, of course, help people adjust," Star said. "Starting tomorrow, warning tickets will be issued through Sunday. Only then will actual legal action against infractions take place. Very charitable, considering these are not new laws."

More nods.

"This trial period will last for one month. Then the town council will vote on whether or not to officially adopt the initiative, bringing all of the laws of the charter back into full observation." She smiled. "It's time for some tough love, gentlemen. Love the sinner—" She held out her hands, cuing us to speak.

"—hate the sin!" shouted the men around me.

Star pulled a piece of paper out of the book in front of her. "Here are the seven passages I've chosen for us to observe."

I held my breath. What antique craziness would Star have cherry-picked to manipulate these folks into voting for her? Because that had to be what this was all about. Getting votes.

"Number One," Star read. "No cursing in public."

A pain in the ass, but livable.

"Number Two: No dogs allowed in any parks within city limits at any time."

"What?" I turned to the man beside me. "That's crazy! What are parks for then?"

Star didn't pause. "Number Three: No dogs allowed in any public spaces except in the roads and on the sidewalks."

"What?" I shouted this.

"Number Four: Any dog outside of a building must be on a six-foot leash at all times, including on private property unless contained behind a fence. Number Five: No dog may eliminate itself on any property not owned by the dog's owner unless in the property owner's presence. Number Six: No children under the age of twelve may walk a dog off their parents' property without adult supervision."

"Come on!" I yelled. I couldn't even play ball with Linus in the churchyard? Marion's kids couldn't walk him? "These laws don't make sense for our lives today!"

For the first time Star looked at me. "Ah, our Episcopal priest." She leaned forward. "I think that is exactly the point. Today, we do not live in the ways that we should. Number Seven," Star said with a flourish. "No one may speak to a minister serving a congregation within twenty-four hours of that minister's Sunday church duties, thus allowing said minister appropriate time for prayer and reflection while leading the town's people in their worship. Exceptions include the imminent death of family members or farm livestock."

She smiled at us. "That last one, ladies and gentlemen, should make your lives much easier."

Everyone laughed and nodded. "Finally some peace and quiet!" the man next to me told another.

Star looked down again. "All of these bear the same consequence: first offense punishable by a fine equivalent to one week's wages or fifty dollars for the unemployed or indigent. Subsequent offenses: jail time and additional contrition as determined by the seated magistrate for the town. Except, of course, in cases where the violation is brought about by a child under the age of sixteen, in which case the father shall pay the debt. A very charitable, Christian approach."

I sprang upward. "There's nothing Christian about this. It's idolatrous love of the law. It's false righteousness. It's stupid and dangerous!" I looked at my fellow clergy. "Surely you all know this." None of them looked at me.

Star gave me the smallest shrug. "Perhaps what we humble CLOSER people know is different than what you Episcopalians know." She slowly slipped the piece of paper back into her book. "Our founders were guided by divine inspiration, gentlemen. If we question them, we question God. If we ignore them and the laws they wrote, we turn our backs on God. That cavalier attitude has caused the catastrophe we call culture today. We cannot let it happen to Middelburg. So I came to you first, as men of the Lord, so that you could help me and the town council remind all Middelburgers whose people we truly are. I rely on you. All of Middelburg relies on you. The Lord our God relies on you."

As I walked up the aisle, I turned back for one last look. The men had swarmed her. Her cameras rolled. She must've felt my anger sweeping over her, because she looked up, looked straight into my eyes for the first time all evening, and smiled.

I nodded back. And then in my head I heard the words of one of the greatest strategic masterminds of all time, Bugs Bunny: "You realize, of course, that this means war."

CHAPTER FIVE

I hear them gaining on me and there's no place to hide.

My feet slap in puddles, slipping across the grassy muddy mix. The outside of my right knee shrieks with pain. Chilling rain slices across my face, nearly blinding me.

Drops spin from my hair as I look around. Nothing. No options. No help. I want to wipe the streams of sweat and rain from my eyes, but I need my arms to pump, to keep my feet flying.

I can't keep running like this for long. They'll catch me. But what else can I do?

Maybe thirty yards ahead in the rainy October night, a weak light shines. The goal.

I kick my heels up a little higher behind me, ignoring the searing tendon. Maybe I can spray dirty water like an eighteen-wheeler on a slushy road.

Twenty yards.

Over the *woof!* of my own breathing I hear them behind me—one of them, anyhow—cursing in desperate rhythm. Not winded at all.

Mental note: I'm getting too old for this shit. A priest's life is supposed to involve sherry and warm hearths. Grateful octogenarians and cherubic children.

Don't battle.

That inner voice, usually so wise. But what? I should just stop? Then what? They'll just fly on by me like in some cartoon?

I actually snort my laugh. Then tell my legs to go harder.

The air changes around me—pressure or motion, I'm not sure which—but suddenly someone is close enough to touch me. I can hear them cursing with each raspy breath.

I arc my body into a block but my feet slip just enough to throw off my balance. Rivulets of water run down my bare thighs as I double-step to regain my balance. My knee groans. I throw out an elbow because they are close, so close I imagine I can feel the hot breath that forces those curses out.

Ten yards.

Nine.

"Go!" I scream to my feet, my knees, my thighs, my heart, my lungs. I dip my head, dig into the earth, plunge one last time into my last reserve of energy. I can win this.

Five yards to go when a foot crosses mine and everything drops away. I flail as a hip collides with mine tossing me into the air. I fly outstretched like George Reeves' Superman. Well, more like a jet landing with no tires and no brakes in a cold pit of sloppy mud.

My hands hit and slide. Hips, chest, the side of my face.

Bells clang behind my eyes. Freezing water slices into my ear. I leave a wake as I skim the brown water.

I reach out, trying to grab an ankle to stop them. Then their foot finds my ribs and I curl to protect myself.

My heart reaches into my gut and threatens to heave it all up and out. My vision swirls and I can't catch air.

Lost.

Waves of blood pound my head. I shouldn't have run. But I didn't know what else to do.

Another foot in my ribs. A toe nudge, really. I try to look up into darkness and rain.

Marion looks down at me. Her fiery hair flops into her eyes, running into the mascara dripping there. Her cheeks blaze and her mouth forms a nearly perfect O as she heaves to catch her breath.

"You okay, Rev Lon?" Puff, puff, puff.

"I could've saved—" I mumble, but I'm not sure it comes out.

"Lonnie?" She bends closer now. Drops from her hair fall on her face.

A scream from across the field electrifies the air. I try to lift my head, to see.

"Great goddess, Lonnie, you're bleeding!"

I feel my eyes roll back trying to see through the darkness. *Where did they go? What—*

I hear the whistle and moan. They've scored. I slide back and down a deep wet hole.

Shouting. Marion's clammy hand on my forehead. I resurface, pick up snatches of words.

"—now she's passed out too—good goddess—kill yourselves—it's only a soccer game!"

Then cold blackness everywhere.

CHAPTER SIX

"So you got run down by an eighteen-year-old. So what?" Wanda Mueller, left fullback, slapped me on the shoulder. I'd discovered her last summer defending parfaits from would-be food thieves and knew she'd be a heck of a defender on the soccer pitch. "She wound up with an asthma attack."

My teammates and I walked in a huddle from the dark, ditchy field toward the blazing lights of Middelburg's new recreation center. Rain still sliced at us. Around us, onlookers and members of the other team dodged puddles as they ran for their cars.

"You know what they say," cracked Romee Vrooman, our crazy goalie. "It's not a good soccer game until the paramedics have to bust out their gear!"

"Well!" Bova Poster puffed alongside us. "Thank! Heavens! All! She! Needed! Was her own! Inhaler!"

"You did a great job," I said. Bova had played midfield in her first game ever tonight.

Colleen Brink, substitute left winger and Middelburg's hair and nail stylist, gave me a light punch. "Don't feel bad, Lonnie. You barely survived a neurotoxin attack two months ago. You're still recovering."

"Plus she was half your age," added Bets Alderink, left midfielder mom, and my church organist.

"No," I said. "I'm only thirty-four."

"Only until next week!" Romee danced through an ankle-deep pool. "Then someone has a birthday and officially joins the middle-aged. Like the rest of us."

"I just didn't get a proper warm-up." I limped on my aching knee.

Damn Star Hannes. If it hadn't been for her and her Faithful Heritage Initiative I'd have been here. Warming up. Psyching up. Not reinjuring the knee that had ruined my soccer career. Not walking in with us down two, helping us tie in the last minute. Not failing to outrun some eighteen-year-old hotshot for what should have been an easy breakaway goal!

"Reverend! Hey, Reverend!"

I turned toward the voice and my team stopped and turned along with me. A young woman, broad shouldered, thick-legged, with pony-tailed hair almost to her hips, jogged up. She looked like a finalist in a wet T-shirt contest despite the mud.

"No hard feelings, huh?" She flicked her fingertips into my bicep. "You ran hard, you know?"

For an old person, I imagined her thinking but not saying. "Your lungs okay?" I asked, knowing she tripped me on purpose. I didn't blame her—anything for the ball.

"Hey." She shrugged, "I deal with worse shit all the time."

"Tina, let's go!" called a teammate and she bounced off like a lion cub toward a warming car. In the glow of the car's interior light, I spotted Star Hannes standing nearby, holding a giant umbrella in one hand and pointing deputy Don Loomis toward the opposing team's car with the other. An accusing gorgon. The big bear of a man looked a bit sick.

"Are we! Going out! For drinks?" asked Bova.

Don leaned forward, said something to the girls in the car. Tina laughed. The others looked stunned.

I grabbed Marion. "Watch this. Something's up."

Don took out his ticket book. Tina flailed in protest. Then Don ripped off a ticket and handed it to her.

"Bad energy," Marion said as they slammed the car doors. The inner light went out. Don turned back to Star, who nodded.

"Big trouble," I said. "Wait until I fill you in." I'd joined the game the minute I'd arrived—I hadn't told anyone about what I'd heard at the meeting.

"Showers and beers," cried Romee and everyone responded with whoops. "I bet I can drink faster than—"

"Ladies!" Don Loomis' voice boomed out of the darkness. "Middelburg Team! Hold on a moment, please."

We all looked at each other.

"Here it comes," I whispered to Marion.

Don's big wet body creaked with damp leather and heavy uniform as he jogged up to us. "Just a word to the wise, ladies."

I looked past him, saw Star still standing beneath her umbrella, dry as a bone and satisfied.

"There's a law on the books against cursing in public places here in town." He stared at his booted feet, engulfed in a puddle. "Hasn't been enforced much, but will be starting this week. A lot of swearing goes on in these games."

"Soccer players swear," said Romee. "What happens on the field stays on the field."

Don scratched his thick neck at the edge of his blond buzz cut. Rain had beaded among the short stiff hairs. "Yeah, well." He pulled out his ticket book and began ripping off tickets, handing one to each of us.

"You've got to be kidding!" shouted Romee.

"Just warnings, ladies, just warnings." He handed me mine. "But it's serious stuff. Big fines. And someone will be here at every game. Probably practices too."

"Yet another fantastic use of our police force," said Colleen. Her son D.J. had been driven out of his garage-based bike repair business by some silly ordinance last spring.

"Citizens can make these complaints as well," Don said.

"Tickets can be issued later, based on tapes. Video. Doesn't have to be police."

"What?" Romee screamed. "What? That's insane! Are you insane?"

Colleen shushed her.

Don scowled. "Ms. Vrooman, it's the law. Our heritage. Our town founders wrote it."

"This crowd giving you trouble, Don?" Deputy Red Carson, Don's partner, stepped out from between two parked cars. He looked surprised to see her.

In the distance, Star frowned.

Red walked through my teammates like Moses crossing the Red Sea. She didn't have on her sheriff deputy's uniform tonight—just soggy jeans, hiking boots and a dark plum rain jacket. Her curly hair burst out from beneath the edges of a University of Michigan ball hat.

"He's ticketing us for swearing!" Romee waved her ticket in Red's face. "In a soccer game!"

Red looked at Don who looked flustered. "Don't remember being on duty tonight."

"The F-f-faithful Heritage Initiative," he stuttered.

"The town council is reviving a bunch of old blue laws from Middelburg's charter," I said. "It's Star's latest scheme to boost her election numbers."

"Great Holy Mother, help us," murmured Marion.

"Doesn't she know soccer players vote?" asked Romee.

"Not! Enough! Of us!" said Bova, "To count!"

"And most folks in town will eat it up," added Colleen, whose business, like Marion's, gave her a great sense of the pulse of town. "They can out-righteous each other."

Good thing Mimi Manser had never made it to the game to hear and report all this.

Red's eyes narrowed at Don. "I haven't heard about this."

He shrugged his bowling ball shoulders. "The councilwoman told me just a few minutes ago. Demanded I meet her out here because of major law-breaking." He held up his ticket book. "She showed me the council decision. Made me issue warnings."

"Made you." Red glanced at me. "And, Lonnie, you know this how?"

"I was at the meeting earlier tonight. There are seven crazy—"

Red held up a hand. "If it's official—if—I'm sure we'll hear more about it tomorrow." She glanced toward Star who still stood, watching. "Go home and get some sleep, Don." She smiled at him. "Opening day tomorrow."

Hunting season.

Don nodded with clear relief and trotted back to his squad car.

"You ladies head on down to the rec center," Red said. "The staff will want to close up after you've finished in the locker room." The Hot Flashes turned as a group and headed for the rec center.

As I started with them, Marion gave my shoulder a shove. "Thank the officer." Then she jogged off.

"Thank you, officer," I said obediently.

"How's your head?" Red asked.

I rolled my eyes. "I should've outrun her. I had a huge lead." She looked about to speak so I jumped in. "And don't say anything about that kid being half my age or I'll slug you, cop or no cop."

She studied me, eyes steady. "I was going to suggest you get someone to look at that knee."

My ex, Jamie, was a doctor. In the seven years I'd been with her she'd never even asked about my knee.

"So tell me what's going on with Star," she said.

I told her all of it, including how I'd been purposely left out of the loop. "If it wasn't for my bishop being so lazy, I wouldn't have known anything about it. Star has everyone wrapped around her little finger."

Red tipped her head. "Yeah. But maybe they were trying to be nice. Like, they knew you weren't invited and they didn't talk about it because they didn't want to rub your face in it."

"Like a middle school party? Please."

"Could be."

"I'm not sure that makes me feel better." I shook my head as a ripple of rainwater snaked down my neck. "West Michigan

Nice strikes again. It's a source of endless wonder to me how being nice serves as an excuse for all kinds of heinous behavior around here." Marion had tipped me off to the evils of West Michigan Nice when I'd first moved back. Nice to your face, but otherwise, look out.

We walked through the empty lot toward the rec center, me limping through puddles. "I suppose that's why you kept my Aunt Katherine's car all these years and never said a thing to me about it? To be nice?"

I sounded snotty, I knew it. I *felt* snotty.

Red glanced quickly at me. "Nothing nice about that at all. Business. My dad made the deal, promised the car would be cared for and its ownership kept secret. He died. We kept the deal. Good thing too, since right now the fee for taking care of it pays the taxes on the garage until—"

She kept her head down. I knew she meant until her brother came back from the war.

"Can I ask you something?" she said.

Nerves jumped across my skin. "Sure." We were friends, but it was a new friendship. Plus, truth be told, I got a little tingly every time I saw her. I didn't want my Aunt Kate to wreck this. Though if anyone could do it, even after being nine years dead, my great-aunt could.

"I hear you've turned down the inheritance. What's up with that?"

"My aunt and I had a complicated relationship." If Kate had been friends with Red's dad, I didn't want to tell her that I thought my aunt was batshit crazy and had belittled, taunted and teased me throughout my teens. I hadn't told anyone that, actually. I'd just grown up and let it be.

"If you don't mind me saying so," Red said, her eyes on me as we walked, "my dad always said she was a bit of a nut."

"What did you think?"

"I barely knew her." We splashed through a puddle as wide as the road, mud slippery beneath us. "Saw her around town. Big purple hats. Always saying stuff to shock people. Sort of the Crazy Cat Lady without the cats."

We didn't speak for a few seconds, then Red said, "But now

she's dead, Lon. Why not take the money? Maybe she left it as a peace offering?"

"Please," I said. "If there is anything my Aunt Katherine wasn't, it was West Michigan Nice. No, she's back from the dead and up to no good. Like a zombie."

Red laughed.

"Look," I said, stopping as we neared the rec center's back door. "You've got to find out what Star's doing," I said.

"I'm sure we'll get briefed tomorrow. I won't have time for anything else with bow season starting. I work like thirty hours a day, ten days a week for the next eight weeks."

"Like Lent, only longer."

Red smiled. "I wouldn't worry about these tickets Star's threatening. If Don and I ticket anyone, it'll be because I've been searching trucks for poached animals, not listening for athletes using swear words."

I ran my hand through my hair, tossing the rain out of it. "You search vehicles for dead animals?"

"Random checks. You got a dead deer, you'd better be able to show me the tag that says you had the right to kill it."

"People just drive around with poached deer out in the open?"

Red chuckled. "You bet. Odds are they won't get stopped. I ticketed a guy last year who said he'd been shooting deer without a license for thirty-seven years."

I grimaced. "Wait. He told you that?"

She made a can-you-believe-it face. "Yep. As if I was the one screwing everything up. And he wasn't even drunk. The ones who have been drinking can be hilarious."

"Hilarious? They're armed, right?"

She shrugged. "More a danger to themselves than to me."

We stood, both not really looking at each other. Rain dripped into my eyes. "I suppose I should get going."

"Me too. I'll miss our walk Sunday. Extra shifts for a while, with hunting and all."

I nodded.

"Which reminds me." Red's face opened, suddenly serious. "Keep Linus out of the woods this month. Yourself too. Go to the beach. At least until hunting is over. And as for Star—well, until we really know what's going on, keep yourselves out of the woods there too, if you know what I mean."

"But dogs aren't allowed on the beach. It's the law."

"No one pays attention to that during hunting season." Red grinned. "Like I said: all the cops will be in the woods, unless we get called out for something more dire. Not Star's tickets. Don just doesn't have a spine. Trust me, it will be fine."

CHAPTER SEVEN

A few minutes later, my cleats clattered across the tile in the deserted back hall of the rec center. I had a chill, though I felt plenty warm on the inside. Red Carson was a cute little thing, all right.

"I don't care if you *think* you did it right," came a beefy male voice from around a corner, "it keeps switching off!"

"Not possible." Steady but angry. A voice I knew. Jack Putnam, maybe the most laid-back guy in all of Middelburg. He had retired early from his job as a counselor in the local kindergarten through eighth grade public school. Now he ran a small electrician service. "I just finished checking the timers, all the cameras, again. Nothing's wrong. Someone is screwing with the system."

I paused in the hall, not wanting my cleats to interrupt. I had to turn the corner to get to the locker room door but I didn't need to walk into that. Maybe if I waited a second they'd go away.

"Oh, right." The deep voice again. "Why would anyone screw with your system?"

"Perhaps," Jack said, voice smooth, "because they want to be in this rec center undetected, after hours."

The deep voice sputtered laughter. "Nothing's been stolen. Nothing even out of place. Your system's just glitchy."

"It didn't get glitchy until the keys were given out last week."

"Here they are!" The singsong of Star's voice chilled me more than the rain soaking my uniform. "I told Gil I heard male voices. Strange, after a women's soccer game."

"I found him sneaking around back here," said Jack.

"I work for Koontz. We're doing electric for the building." Mr. Deep Voice sounded a little panicky.

"Not at this hour of the evening," Jack said.

"And what on earth were you doing here, Jack?" Star asked.

No love lost between the two of them. They'd had a bad run-in a few months ago, when Ivor Koontz and Star had teamed up to capsize Jack's new business.

"Checking the security system I installed."

"It's glitchy." The deep voice.

"It has shut itself off a time or two in the middle of the night," came Gil Hannes' reedy voice.

"Well," Star purred. "When you contract work out to the lowest bidder and—"

"There is nothing wrong with my systems," Jack said, "that someone else didn't cause."

"And why would someone do that?" I could practically see Star shaking her head with sorrow over this poor man's deranged ideas.

"Maybe you can tell me," Jack said.

"Are you suggesting—" she screeched.

"Star, darling." Gil interrupted. A moment of silence followed. "I appreciate your conscientiousness, Jack."

"Yeah, well, why don't either of you seem to care that he's here?" asked Jack.

"Hey!" Beefy Voice didn't like attention brought back to him.

"Dale?" Gil asked. "Why are you here?"

Long pause. I shivered, clammy and chilled to the bone. I needed a hot shower.

"Well, I left a reciprocating saw, okay? Somewhere." Dale sounded deflated. "It's Koontz's property and you know how he gets. I don't want to have to check in tomorrow short. He'll pull my pay and I need it."

"You are under a lot of pressure," said Gil.

"Times are hard for all of us," Star said. "It's why we all need to vote for change next month."

My teeth chattered during a violent shiver. I couldn't wait any longer for hot water. I took a few clattering steps and rounded the corner.

Star's green eyes flashed annoyance, but it was the only sign of anything but composure. Though she'd been out in the pouring rain like the rest of us, her kiwi-colored heels shone spotless on the tile floor and her satin legs had not a spot of mud on them. Gil, on the other hand, looked a rumpled mess. The only thing about his stringy self not tousled, wrinkled or wrought was the woman's raincoat draped over his arm. "What are you—" He stopped when Star touched him.

"Darling," she said to him without taking her eyes from me. "You'll want to call the custodial staff for an overtime shift to clean up the halls and locker room after Reverend Squires leaves." Her eyes narrowed. "Yet again, she proves a burden to the people of this community."

The corners of his thin mouth turned up beneath his pencil thin mustache. All four pairs of eyes slowly studied me.

Every single inch of me from toe to chest was coated in mud. Knowing how hard my head had hit the ground, I imagined my head was too. I looked behind me. I had indeed left a dirty trail. How in heaven's name had the other Flashes walked through here without leaving a mess? Cleats off, of course. A soccer player never walked into a building in cleats. I'd been thinking about Red—I'd forgotten.

Heat rose past my neck and Star saw the weakness. She

placed an arm up in front of her husband and forced him back, stepping beside him to the opposite side of the wide hall, like I had leprosy or something. "Let's just give her plenty of space. For now."

They stepped aside as I walked past. "Sorry you lost," Jack said. "Heard it was a good game though."

"Yeah." I slunk into the locker room.

The girls stood around in various states of clean-up, chatting, but I strode past them all, past my locker, straight into the shower room, uniform and cleats and shin guards and all. I cranked on the nearest spigot and turned toward it, letting the hot, clear water wash everything away.

CHAPTER EIGHT

"Cursing is protected by the Constitution!" Romee Vrooman waved a square of pepperoni and double onion thin crust pizza at the table. Skinny's Special Number Two. "It's free speech."

"It's an election ploy," Wanda said. She paused to count the pieces left on the pizza she'd split with me—pepperoni, green pepper, onions, mushrooms. "I think that piece there belongs to me."

I shoved it toward her. "It's targeted at me. I mean no cursing, no dogs and no talking to clergy on Sundays? What's left? Outlawing women's sports?"

"Don't say it out loud!" Marion said. "You'll manifest it with negative energy."

Romee lifted her glass. "Manifest me more beer."

Someone slid one of the pitchers down the table. After soccer games and practices, the Hot Flashes hung out at Skinny's B-B-Cue, combination pool hall and dive bar restaurant in downtown Middelburg. It was the one "bad" place in town where folks could walk on the wild side, then go home feeling dangerous and unscathed. After The Grind, it was the most popular restaurant in town.

The air hung gray with carcinogenic haze, but the pitchers cost four dollars and Skinny made the best thin crust pizza in the world. When I was a kid, living here summers with my great-aunt, I'd viewed this place as some mysterious adult mecca. I'd heard people had died here. Aunt Kate told me a baby had been born on the pool table. The summer I turned eighteen my soccer team, the Well's Belles, most of whom were now Hot Flashes, had brought me here for a pizza and a Swisher Sweet cherry cigar. Since the drinking age was twenty-one, no one had even tried to slip me a beer. But they made it clear I was an adult anyhow.

"Lonnie, I seriously doubt Star convinced the town council to support this plan just to annoy you." Colleen looked at me as if I were her eight-year-old son D.J.

"Maybe there only were seven laws," Bets Alderink said.

I traced my finger in the condensation on my glass. "I don't know. It was an awfully big book."

"We could go! Check! It! Out! Ourselves!" Bova declared. The purple and blue embroidered butterflies leapt and danced across her bosom with each heave.

"Why?" asked Gaby. "To bring up more laws for these nuts to enforce?" She slugged her beer. "That'll just make everything worse. Trust me, I got five kids. Let sleeping dogs lie."

Everyone stared into their glasses.

"We should stand up and fight." I looked at each one of them in turn. "Look how upset you all are with these ordinances. What about everybody else? Maybe all we need to do is encourage everyone to stand up for themselves."

"Against the Town! Council?" Bova's eyes rounded at the thought.

"Why not? You stand up to me all the time!" She was a perpetual thorn in my side at church.

"But you're! My! Priest!" As if that should explain it.

"Come on! We fought the council last spring to help D.J." I looked at Colleen. "Remember?"

She dropped her gaze.

"That was the team," Rika VanRenselaar said. "Working for the team."

"For a little kid," Romee added. "This is different."

"How? Now you'd be working for every little kid who wants to walk a dog!" I couldn't believe it. One minute they were bitching up a storm, the next, they wouldn't look me in the eye.

"Because mounting a public campaign against the town council's decision wouldn't be nice," Marion said, not bothering to hide the bite in her voice. "Right, ladies?"

"Hey!" Romee looked insulted. "I don't care about being nice. But I have to live in this town."

"Maybe it would be easier to leave town," I said, none too nicely.

Silence. Marion nudged me.

"My husband's leaving town." Bets crumpled her paper napkin and tossed it onto her plate. "At three a.m. To kill innocent deer with a bow that looks more like something from *Star Wars* than *Robin Hood*."

Everyone began jabbering about hunting season and their men's urges to go out and kill things for food.

"I'd rather have a nice cut of just about anything from the butcher over a gutted dear hanging from the rafters of my garage," Bets said.

"For sure!" Marion shuddered. "That's some bad karma. Get it? Car-ma? Garage?"

"But what can I say?" said Bets. "He loves it as much as I love soccer and you guys."

"Does! Your husband! Bring out! *The! Box!?*" Bova asked.

They all cracked up. "Like it's the Ark of the Covenant!" Lucy Vogel, who played anywhere in our forward line, said.

"Yes!" They all laughed again.

I leaned into Marion. "Denny doesn't hunt, does he?"

She shook her head. "But he loves to decorate for Christmas. So I know what it's like to have a man obsessed in the house pulling out the *box*. His gear for his annual ritual."

"Two arks," Lucy added. "He buys more of it every year!"

"A camouflage suit designed to help him melt into pine thickets," said Bets.

"Another! for hardwood! Forests!" added Bova.

"All of it breathable and waterproof," said Rika.

"Maybe we could use them this Saturday!" Romee said. "For Dainty Ditches day?"

Dainty Ditches Day was another Star-inspired town council community project, a pseudo-environmental publicity stunt designed to get her space in the newspapers, time on television stations and votes in next month's elections. Still, the ditches around town did have a lot of garbage in them, so we'd signed up to do some cleaning north of town by the Zaloumi brothers' blueberry fields.

"No way in hell is Tom letting me use any of his stuff for anything dainty!" Bets laughed. "There's a lot of it, but it's all his."

"And there's even more for gun season!" added Wanda. "The guys in the office talk about it constantly."

"Infrared scopes!" shouted Rika, holding up her hand.

"Night vision goggles," added Lucy.

"Insulated clothes good in Antarctica," said Marion.

"I know," said Wanda. "Let's snitch the gear and start a spy syndicate."

"Can't use Tom's stuff," Bets said. "He doesn't share."

"Jake does, but that's a problem. He's loaned half his stuff out. Including those brand-new goggles." Lucy said. "People are lined up to try those things out." She pointed to Bets. "Including your husband."

Bets rolled her eyes and pulled her hair back behind her ears. "Great. Now he'll want some for Christmas. Night vision goggles on Christmas morning. So much for this year's family pictures."

"Speaking of presents." Colleen grinned. "I got that fabulous something special we talked about, ladies. For you-know-who's birthday!"

They all looked at me and grinned. I did love them.

"Speaking of you-know-who," Marion said. "Look." She pointed to the TV mounted in the corner of the ceiling.

There I stood, in full clergy armor, in the center of Brady's church, shouting at Star.

"Not everyone was happy to hear about the town council's Faithful Heritage Initiative," came the voiceover by Artesia Collins.

Cut to me: "There's nothing Christian about this. It's idolatrous love of the law. It's false righteousness. It's stupid and dangerous!" Freeze-frame of me, arm flailing, teeth bared. Underneath that in big letters: Reverend Lorraine Squires, Episcopal Priest, Middelburg.

Everyone and everything in Skinny's went silent.

Cut to Artesia, milking the camera so energetically it felt like she might burst from the television. "Reverend Squires achieved fame this summer as a sort of Sherlock Holmes with a collar. Or maybe Jessica Fletcher as priest. She solved two murders when local authorities failed. She is Middelburg's Ecclesiastical Super Sleuth."

Cut to another picture of me on a gurney, being carted away from my church this past summer, when I'd nearly been killed by a murderer who wanted me silenced. God, couldn't they find a better picture of me anywhere?

"In a phone interview from the Bahamas, local billionaire businessman Christopher Orion credited Reverend Squires with saving his life during a civic event last spring." The TV screen showed a still of Chris, his wife Elyse and their son Bill standing in front of Woman at the Well. The membership photo from our church directory.

"Too bad Elyse isn't here to keep Star in check," murmured Marion.

"Not everyone's a fan, though," said Artesia as the visual cut to her and Star somewhere in the Frontline lobby.

"Perhaps Reverend Squires doesn't value ages-old orthodox Christian tradition the way we in the CLOSER faith do," said Star, her eyes deep with faked compassion. "From what I've seen of the Episcopal Church in the news in the last few years, I'm not surprised. They seem to be quite at odds with themselves—and with all of Christian history. I feel sorry for them. For her."

I felt a bubble of untouchability form around me as everyone in the bar looked at me.

"Wow," said Romee.

"Yeah!" agreed Bova.

"Feel that knife in your back, Lon?" asked Marion. She picked up a beer glass and toasted me. "That was West Michigan Nice."

CHAPTER NINE

The next morning, as I drove past woods and blueberry fields to get into town, pickup trucks dotted the normally empty roadsides, parked parallel and tipped into ditches full of water. Hunters. I imagined arrows flying through the woods and rubbed Linus' head. "No walks in the woods for us, buddy." The vision of Linus with an arrow between his ribs flashed into my head and I shook it away. Over my dead body. "No way," I said out loud. He flopped his foot over my wrist.

As I pulled into town, an SUV passed, a dead buck roped across the hood, its vacant eyes staring, heavy tongue lolling. *Good Lord*, I thought, *little kids can't walk a dog in public but they can see this?* Heebie-jeebies skittered down my spine and Linus barked until the thing was well past.

I double-parked in the middle of town and turned on my

flashers, then ran through the sleeting rain to The Grind to grab a box of banket—a flaky Dutch almond pastry—for the office. Just as I opened the door, Red tumbled out.

"Hey, hi!" I said.

She grunted at me from behind shadowed eyes then stepped back into the covered doorway and hunched over her large to-go cup.

"Up early?" I asked.

"Let's put it this way. What time is it?" she asked.

"Eight thirty."

"Past lunchtime for me."

I made a sympathetic face and we stepped aside as a group of oldsters bustled into The Grind. "Not such a great morning?"

She slid glassy eyes at me. "You try standing around in the woods in the freezing rain at four in the morning because some scum is out there shining deer, trying to get a jump on the season." She sipped her coffee. "I may never be warm again."

Images of ways to warm her slipped across my brain but I ignored them. "What's shining deer?"

She explained that people went out in the woods with a million candle power spotlight and shined the beam on passing deer. This stopped them in their tracks. "Some people do this just to look," Red said, "which is fine, I guess. Some shoot them. Some take the animal away—feed their families this way. Especially in this economy. Some just leave the carcass to rot."

"Killing for fun."

She shrugged. "People do strange things in the woods." She melted her voice into mock innocence. "Oh, officer, I didn't bait deer with that pile of apples right there underneath my tree stand. I just came this morning and found it there.' Or, 'Oh, officer, I had to leave that tree stand up overnight in the park, even though it's illegal! Taking it down would have woken the baby that the young hikers had in a papoose pack—they walked through just when I was leaving.'" She shifted her voice again. "Oh, officer, I'm not hunting turkeys out here without a license, even though I'm sitting here blowing a turkey call and have three decoys set up. I'm hunting the coyote that ate my neighbors' pet rabbit.'" She laughed. "Of course, that guy didn't have a license for a coyote either. Not the sharpest tool."

"There must be some satisfaction in that." I shivered. Why was it that every time I talked to this woman lately we were standing in freezing cold rain?

She managed a weak smile. "We do get to whip through the woods on ATVs trying to catch the bad guys. That is fun. Beats the heck out of handing out tickets for those seven passages of Star's."

"Ah." I crossed my arms to keep the bone-nipping cold at bay. "You got official word on that?"

She nodded and rolled the warm cup against her cheek. "This morning. Warning tickets through Sunday. Real tickets starting Monday. Council final vote on exactly how many of those old laws to bring back into observation in November—the week after the election."

"Star has it all worked out, doesn't she?"

Red smiled. "Except you. I saw that news clip." She shook her head. "Jesus, Lonnie. Are you trying to start a fight?"

"Don't 'Jesus, Lonnie' me! She started it!"

Her eyebrows shot up.

"I mean, come on, everyone else is afraid to call her on her crap. I'm just pointing out the truth, you know? What she's doing is not about being a good Christian. Jesus didn't put the law above people."

"Or above dogs."

"That too."

She handed me her coffee. "You look like you're freezing." I took a sip. "Thing is," she continued, "Star's used to having more pull than anyone else in this town. Because she did. Until you came along and ruined her life."

I nearly spit my sip all over her. "Are you kidding me? I'm nobody in this town!"

"Are you kidding me?" She took the coffee back. "You are, as that reporter said, Sherlock Holmes with a collar. Jessica Fletcher as priest. Middelburg's Ecclesiastical Super Sleuth. "She took a sip. "Or MESS, as I'd rather refer to you. Given the situations you get yourself into. Like this one." She sipped again, studying me with shining eyes.

I knew I was being teased. "Right."

"Seriously. You got plenty of attention when you solved Vance's murder in the spring. But with the situation in August? Remember that full-page spread in the Grand Rapids paper? The special edition of *The Middelburg Review*? You see Star getting any of that? For being a hero?"

"But that doesn't mean I have any pull around here." I held up a finger. "I'm not Dutch." A second finger. "I wasn't born here." A third finger. "I definitely don't go to a CLOSER church." These were the three things required for acceptance in Middelburg. Believe me, I knew.

"You might not be one of us, but you get a lot of attention. And any attention that doesn't go to Star, threatens Star. Face it, Lonnie. She's afraid your light will outshine hers." She sipped her coffee again. She looked warmer, now, more awake than when we'd nearly collided. "So she's acting like a cornered animal." She blinked. "With rabies."

Evidently nearly everyone else agreed with her. From the Flashes to the folks at church to people I met later in the Grind, everyone I talked to on Wednesday and Thursday morning manufactured some excuse for not fighting Star's new initiative, even though they all professed to hate it.

"She's a good woman."

"Maybe we should be living better."

"Family and tradition is important."

"If I didn't like it, I could just leave."

This was the sort of thing I heard over and over. No one wanted to fight for justice because it just wouldn't be nice. But I wasn't going to give up. These people needed to learn a thing or two about standing up for themselves and others—about true niceness.

I had an idea while standing around in a misting rain Thursday afternoon, waiting for Linus to pee in the churchyard. He hated being on the leash and would never go potty when hooked up. So, keeping the letter of the law clearly in mind, I wove the leash carefully around his neck like a scarf and let him sniff free in the yard.

Within five minutes a sheriff's car pulled up and Red Carson stepped out.

I scanned the houses nearby. People stood in the windows of four of the six I could see. *One of you called the cops*, I thought. *But you'll see. I'm not breaking the law. You don't have to be so afraid!*

"Shouldn't you be out catching poachers?" I asked Red as she strode toward me, hands on gun belt.

"Not my afternoon in the woods," she said. "So, no. Unless someone calls about a deer hanging in a garage without a tag."

Linus ran up to her and circled her, wagging but knowing enough not to jump. Instead, he wiggled his butt on the damp grass.

Red patted his head. "What are you doing, Lon?" She didn't look in the direction of my neighborhood snitch.

"Are you mistakenly implying, Officer, that I am breaking the newly resurrected law that dogs must be on six-foot leashes at all times?" I grinned.

"No mistake." She pulled her ticket book from her belt. "Why are you doing this?"

I raised a finger to pause her. "You can't ticket me."

Red sighed. "Lonnie, eyes are on all of us. Literally as well as figuratively. People know that you and Star are going at it and they want to stoke the flames and sit back and watch. It's like reality TV come to their own backyard. Don't give them the satisfaction."

"Perhaps. But, Officer Carson, you can't ticket me because I haven't violated the law."

She shook her head. "I've been over this with a half dozen people today. It doesn't matter if it's your own property. You have to have the dog on leash or behind a fence." She looked weary and I felt sorry for her. Enforcing this crap must be just awful, especially on top of the weird hours of monitoring the woods for poachers.

"The law says he has to be on a leash. It doesn't say I have to be holding onto the leash." I pointed to Linus. "He's on the six-foot leash."

Red knelt to examine the dog's leash and Linus spazzed out, bouncing and licking her face. Finally, she looked up at me, her tired eyes giving nothing away. "Don almost shot you once by accident for doing something stupid on this dog's behalf. Are you going to make me sorry he didn't?"

I blinked innocently. "Just following the law, Officer Carson. And taking care of my dog."

She stood and clipped her ticket book back into place. "Okay. But I'm not sure every officer would agree with you. Now is not the time to fight. Stay out of it. Better yet, hide from her."

"Really?" I wanted to pump a fist at the onlookers. Word would spread that the laws could be interpreted in different ways. "Feels worth a fight to me. Feels like I might win."

Eyes narrowed, Red stepped toward me. "It isn't. It's a stupid pissing match the two of you have going. You want someone to fight? Take on your Aunt Kate. Go get her money."

Then she walked away.

That conversation bugged me so badly that Friday night I found myself at Marion's house, flopped over the loveseat in her home office, an ice bag on my knee and a Jameson's on ice in my hand. The chills between hand and knee connected somehow in my center, calming me.

Sort of.

"So what is it that makes everyone around here so complacent? So ready to just buckle and do whatever anyone in authority tells them to do?" I swept the glass around as I talked. The ice clattered.

"White sage'll cure what ails you," Marion said. She whirled about the room, her sunfire yellow caftan floating behind her upraised arms. She held two bluish-white smudge sticks, dried sage tied tight with white twine. She'd lit them and blown the flame out so that now each let off its own stream of white, distinctly pot-smelling smoke.

Linus, who slept on the floor by my side, sneezed without waking.

"Nothing ails me except people around here," I said.

"Maybe they are helping you see what ails you about yourself."

"Maybe they're helping me see that I don't really belong here."

I waited for a thunderclap. A gasp from Marion. Any sort

of cosmic reaction to my saying out loud what I'd been afraid to think all week. That I'd made a mistake moving back here. That I should leave.

Marion's only reaction was to twirl in the center of the room, circles of white smoke spinning around her.

"Did you hear me?" I asked.

"The universe hears you and always answers."

Marion was in one of those moods. I sipped my whiskey and watched Marion dance about the room. If I believed in reincarnation, I'd bet she'd been a shaman in a previous life. A moondancer. A medicine man. She turned a circle in front of a beaded cowhide drum, stepped across a handwoven Native American rug, and paused in the glow of her nineteen-inch computer monitor. "This will clear the bad energy hovering all over you."

I raised the glass. "So will this." I sipped again. "Actually, I have no bad energy." I felt relaxed and slightly buzzed, as much from the whiskey as the sage smoke. "Not any more. Because I have given up on everyone else."

"Have you?"

"Uh-huh. No one in this town except me seems to want to fight Star Hannes or the town council on this seven laws thing."

"I see." Marion waved the sticks in curlicue circles, like a kid waving sparklers on the Fourth of July.

"Even Red told me to hide from Star." I rested the cold round edge of the bottom of the glass against my forehead.

"Maybe that is the universe's answer."

"To hide? I wish. I'd like nothing better than a boring peaceful life."

Marion set the still smoking smudge sticks in a clamshell and sat in her high-tech desk chair. "I don't believe that for a second."

I propped myself up, knocking the ice bag to the floor. "Come on. I don't ask for trouble."

Marion pulled an African drum the size of an end table between her knees and rubbed her hands across the rough hide top. A steady circular rasp filled the room. Shish. Shish.

"Maybe you don't think so," she said. "But you're always standing up for some fight over something."

I stretched to grab the ice bag. "Over some lame principle, you mean? Like justice? Like democracy? Those kind of somethings?"

"Face it, Lon. At heart, you're a vigilante."

"Am not!" I balanced the ice back on my knee. "That's just mean."

"You're a kick-ass heroine in a priest's clothes." Shish. Shish. Shish. "Folks may think you're an Ecclesiastical Super Sleuth, but I think you're just Batman. So to speak."

I took a long swallow. The whiskey burned my gullet but I liked it. I liked Batman too. "I'd like a utility belt."

"Your Aunt Kate already gave you a Batmobile. Inherit the rest and you can build a Batcave."

"No." I swirled the ice again in time with her drum rubbing.

Shish. Clink. Shish. Clink.

"I'm not interested in Kate's games. I just want to live in peace."

Shish. Clink.

"I don't think you do, Lon." Shish. Shish. "I just don't think you do."

CHAPTER TEN

"If this isn't trouble, I don't know what is."

Marion nudged a shoulder into mine and tipped her head toward the other side of the ditch. There, four muddy, booted feet stood firmly in the spindly chicory. They belonged to the ninety-four-year-old Zaloumi twins who stood mute, watching the Hot Flashes gather, faces blank with innocence.

The thing was, Eddie and Leon Zaloumi, Middelburg, Michigan's identical twin bachelor farmers, were never silent. Or innocent. They were my parishioners, and frequent episodes involving garter snakes, wolf spiders and once a baby bat, had taught me that a silent Zaloumi was a Zaloumi waiting for something to happen, something he—or usually they—had planned.

I agreed with Marion. Trouble.

I scanned the scene, trying to guess what horror they were about to unleash in order to make my teammates scream. The morning blared with the clear blue sky of autumn. Crisp shadows outlined everything. Fourteen Hot Flashes milled along the ditch tying shoes and divvying up garbage bags and gloves. The berry bushes, empty now of fruit, throbbed with the deep wine color of fall in their leaves. Chicory grew knee-high along the five-foot-wide ditch, dotting the thick weedy green with periwinkle. A month ago, when it hadn't rained all summer, signing up for the Dainty Ditches Day cleanup seemed like a good idea. However, the parched ground hadn't kept up with the constant rain of the last week and today the ditch stood full of silent black water, clear for an inch or two, then opaque with the rich red brown of liquid tannin from the oak forest surrounding the field.

"Do you suppose they put something in the water?" Marion asked.

"No talking to the priest!" came a strident voice from behind. Everyone turned to see Star Hannes emerging from a van, followed closely by her entourage—camera crew and husband.

"It's ten o'clock," Star said. "Within twenty-four hours of Reverend Squires' church duties tomorrow. If you want to be faithful to our civic heritage—and obey our laws—you will not speak to her."

Marion slid a wide-eyed glance at me.

"It's not Sunday, Star," I said.

She shook her head. Her multicolored hair dazzled in the sun as she walked up to Marion, her lip curled the tiniest bit. "The law says within twenty-four hours of a church service. Either way."

I stepped toward her, rake in hand. "You mean no one can talk to me from Saturday morning until Monday morning? Forty-eight total hours? *Every week?*"

Star acted as if she couldn't hear me. She turned to the rest of the motley ditch-cleaning crew. "My people will be filming most of the event, and warning tickets will be issued to anyone who breaks any laws."

The crew members didn't look too happy about their role as creepy spy camera people. Artesia Collins actually scowled.

My brain scrambled across the laws. "Wait a minute!" I yelled. Everyone pretended to ignore me, but I could tell they were listening. "The law doesn't say anything at all about me not talking to you! I can talk to you! You can listen." I turned to Star. "Am I right?"

Her lips pursed. *Bingo!*

"Is she right?" Marion asked.

"That would be a violation of the spirit of the law, which clearly intends—"

"Oh, no!" I laughed. "Spirit has nothing to do with how you operate. So let's play by your rules—the letter of the law."

Artesia's mouth twisted into a badly hidden smile. Marion winked at me.

"These are some bad laws!" Romee said to Star. "Now when Lonnie speaks, no one can shut her up!"

"Exactly what are you doing here, Star?" I asked. She turned and walked toward her crew, but I followed, enjoying this. "Why bring the crew? Harassing us? Trying to catch people talking to me? Uttering a curse word? Afraid maybe we'd let a dog run loose?" I'd actually considered bringing Linus to do just that. Thank God I'd left him at home.

Star stopped in front of Artesia Collins. "Set up down at that end of the ditch, please, where you'll pick up some of these other women, but not all."

"Yes, ma'am," said Artesia, glancing at me.

"You are not to cover any issues with the seven laws," Star said. "Though, of course, any violations that wind up on film will be used to uphold the law. Understand?"

Artesia nodded.

Star reached into the back of the van and pulled out a set of enormous rubber waders big enough for two of her. I realized that this may have been the first time I'd seen her in anything other than a fruit-colored suit. She wore jeans and a plaid flannel shirt.

"We want to project me hard at work with community women. Rural interests. You know." She pulled a ball cap out of the waders and tugged it on. An arrow and a cross were embroidered on the front, along with the words Blessing of the Bows.

"Gil!" she shouted.

"Right here, darling."

She walked about ten yards away and began, with her husband's help, to pull on the waders. They came practically to her armpits.

Artesia stepped forward, microphone extended and asked about the getup.

"I borrowed these from a fishing friend," Star explained to the camera, "when I heard the ditches we volunteered to clean had flooded. A little water is no excuse to shirk one's duty!"

Beside her, Gil laughed too loudly. Clad in a light blue Oxford shirt, creased khakis and penny loafers (though no socks), he clearly had no intention of entering the ditch.

I looked down at my old purple high-tops and tattered sweats. When we'd heard about the flooded ditch, the Hot Flashes had decided it was time to celebrate our most grungy shoes and pants.

"Are we ready, ladies?" Star brandished a trash pick like Napoleon waving a sword. Like she was our leader. Like we had even invited her. We'd been the ones who committed to cleaning out a half mile of rural ditches. She'd just horned in when she realized that working with a group of women to help a set of nonagenarian identical twin farmers would provide her with a unique media opportunity.

"Ready!" shouted Mimi Manser. She'd arrived this morning as one of us, but defected as soon as Star showed up. She reminded me of Anakin Skywalker. Such potential too, but she'd gone over to the dark side. To Death Star Hannes.

Death Star Hannes. I hadn't thought of that before! I laughed.

Marion looked at me.

"Later," I told her. "It's hilarious."

"Point the sharp end away from your body," Marion said quietly, as she handed me a pointed stick and bag. She wore bright yellow plastic high-tops that looked like they hailed from the Seventies, bright red stirrup pants that I knew came from the early Eighties, and an oversized lime green sweatshirt proclaiming *If Ferris can have a day off, I can too!* "That way," she continued, "when whatever the Zaloumis are up to happens, you won't impale yourself."

The elderly twins stood, content as cows, watching us descend into their ditch. Star took her husband's outstretched hand and stepped gingerly down the incline.

Romee Vrooman, like most goalies a wild-woman extraordinaire, threw back her head with a whoop and long jumped in. The black water splashed across us, tingling cold. Star threw up her hands to protect her hair and took another careful step. Gil stepped back from the edge.

I snapped on my rubber gloves and stepped in beside Romee. The water bit into my legs with October chill, but it was still warmer than swimming in Lake Michigan most of the summer. The ground felt solid, not muddy, though a bit tangled with unseen weeds. I stuck my pick out and stabbed a Pringles short stack canister floating in a clear spot of water.

"Water bottles everywhere!" Marion muttered, grabbing two crushed floaters and tossing them into her bag. "A scourge to Mother Earth."

Movement on the edge of the ditch caught my eye. One of the Zaloumis—Eddie, I think—had stepped across from Gil, apparently examining the leaves of a blueberry bush.

"Heads up." I poked Marion. We both froze, waiting.

Next thing, Star's arm began to flail. Gil leaned forward to offer her a hand which she yanked, nearly pulling him headfirst into the ditch. She backed up the side of the ditch, slip-sliding around in those too-big waders. Her mouth gaped in a silent O. She shouted no warning to the rest of us, just threw herself into sudden reverse and scrambled to escape.

The red light burning on the T.V. camera swung toward her. This footage would not make the councilwoman happy.

"Snake!" Romee shouted.

Everyone screamed and froze.

Romee took a step toward it. "Cool!"

The beast glided low and thick in the smooth water, wriggling out of the weeds to get away from us.

"It's a hognose!" Romee could barely contain her glee.

At the edge of the ditch Star's waders slid out from under her.

She fell on her rubber-encased bottom in about six inches of water. The bib kept most of her dry, but her flannel sleeves blackened instantly. "Get me out of here!" she hissed at her husband, who bent to help as much as he could without compromising his own spotlessness.

Marion tossed a narrow glance at me and I could tell she was doing her utmost to keep from cracking up.

"Wait!" Romee said. "Check this out." All heads in Star's crew swung away from the candidate and toward our resident snake handler.

"Oh, great goddess," Marion whispered to the universe.

"Don't touch it!" yelled Annika. "It might bite!" Then she sneezed like a tornado.

Romee's hand hovered above the snake for a second, then snapped to grab the reptile. We all screamed when she held it aloft—a full four feet of thick black reptile.

"Rubber, ladies!" Romee tossed the snake toward Star who jerked back. "Attached to fishing line."

Above us, the Zaloumis pushed their dingy ball caps back from matching foreheads, grinned and shrugged.

Everyone moaned. A few splashed water at the old twins. Marion threw a water bottle at the brothers who now looked supremely proud of themselves. Hair mussed but I-can-do-it-all-as-your-next-congresswoman face firmly in place, Star clambered to her feet and returned to the water to spear trash with vigor.

For several minutes we chattered and cleaned, enjoying the joke, each other and the sunshine. The television crew filmed as we spread apart and waded slowly north. Annika kept sneezing, claiming the mold after the week of rain was tearing up her allergies. I said pretty much whatever I wanted, and with so many other folks around, it was easy enough for everyone to talk to me without actually talking to me. I was helping them see they could fight Star Hannes and still be nice. It was progress.

"Hey!" yelled Bets from the center of the ditch. "There's a tire or something over here."

The Zaloumis strode together toward her, bent with curiosity. Not one of their pranks.

"Come on," I urged Marion. "It'll take a few of us to move it."

We slogged through the chilly thigh-deep water toward our teammate, where Star had already assumed command. "What a dreadful shame," she said, tossing her voice toward the camera, "that people drive intentionally out to the country, our pristine God-given land, with the specific intent of discarding large items of trash instead of disposing of them in the proper way. We need to honor our existing anti-littering laws with more commitment. When I am congresswoman, I will see that we are better stewards of our planet. And we can do it without hurting big business or raising taxes!"

No one cheered. Romee poked her stick into the water. "I think it's a bag of trash. Maybe two. Not a tire."

Star stepped up beside her and poked her stick around as well. "By working together, by combining our efforts, we can handle this heavy weight. Like any heavy responsibility—the burden must be shared."

Romee rolled her eyes at me. Annika stepped forward, sneezing. "Here. If three of us—" She sneezed again.

Romee and Annika and Star grunted and levered, sought new purchase, tried again.

"More leverage here," Annika said. "It's giving way."

I tossed my stick and bag up to dry ground and stepped forward. I could grab whatever it was when they got it up close to the surface. I rolled up my sleeves and bent over, looking for a shape in the red black water.

For several seconds, nothing. Then a dark form, about as big around as a loaf of bread but three times as long, emerged from the murk. One end seemed lighter, both in color and weight, and moved upward faster than the rest.

A buzz zipped down my spine. Death.

I held my breath. A dead deer? Hit by a car? Shot in a shining and left?

"Can you grab it, Lonnie?" Annika asked me.

"Warning ticket!" Star said.

Then my skin jumped across my bones and I leapt with it, biting my tongue. I tasted blood. Then I yelled. I knocked Marion back into the weeds, then scrambled up the sides, tugging her behind me.

Star reacted to my terror and dropped her stick, stumbling backward, again slipping in her waders and falling, this time into thigh-deep water. She disappeared completely for a second, except for a float of tri-foiled hair.

"Help!" Gil Hannes slid into the ditch to retrieve his wife. "She'll drown."

Annika and Bets had already pulled the sputtering Star's head above water. Her waders had filled with water, though, and she couldn't stand.

"It's a person!" I croaked. I tried to swallow the blood I tasted, tried not to vomit for the nearness of the thing, the human hand emerging from a plaid shirt that I'd seen coming from the dark. I gagged and coughed.

Star, dripping, blackened with mud and leaves like the creature from the black lagoon, pointed toward the Zaloumis. "You have gone too far!"

No. Every cell in my body knew it wasn't a joke. "It's real," I shouted.

Artesia and her crew scrambled for a better angle.

"Everyone out!" yelled Wanda, defender of our zone and right now, of all of us. Everyone cautiously climbed from the water, whispering, watching me.

I started to shake. "Call the police," I managed. "Call Red."

"Yes," Star proclaimed from the other side of the ditch. "The full force of the law will descend on you two for such unseemly, unchristian action!"

The Zaloumis stood together, pale, ignoring Star and watching the rippling water.

"Look," one of them said.

Even though I knew, even though I didn't want to, even though I wanted to throw up and run like hell, I looked.

There, in the middle of the ditch, a man's hand floated. The cuff of a black and red flannel shirt just showed. The tilt made it clear it was attached to something in the deep, something that had once been the house of a living human soul.

CHAPTER ELEVEN

Bodies, emotions, bouncing off one another like we are all in a blender. Gil dragging his wife up from the water. The camera crew running, not toward Star, but toward the thick shadow in the black, black water. Chattering voices. Jittery colors. Sweeps of motion I can't quite follow. I hear my name once. Twice. Someone breaking the law. Water slides along my skin, which tries to crawl away. A clatter of sound.

"Lonnie, come on!" Marion's voice reaches me. I realize I'm shaking so hard I cannot move.

"Warning ticket!" yells Star.

The first cop arrives, a young, hazy boy who takes one look at the camera crew, fourteen hysterical middle-aged soccer players and one very pissed off congresswoman-wannabe and radios for backup. I'm not sure he even knows there's a body in the water.

I discover a blanket around me and don't know how it got there. I smell mildew and wet dog. Red lights strobe across everything, even in the noon sun. Blue chicory scratches my right knee. I sit on the slope, my feet inches from the ditch water. Artesia gesticulates wildly at a state police officer I don't recognize. Star pontificates to Don Loomis who towers over her, looking confused. Red chats with some guy in a turquoise golf shirt, yellow pants and blue surgical gloves. Flashbulbs glare.

Star turns from Don and smiles. She straightens her soaking shirt and jeans, then walks toward her camera crew. Artesia raises her mike and the big television light snaps on.

"If it weren't within twenty-four hours of Lonnie's Sunday service, I'd ask her if she were okay."

I open my eyes at Red's voice. She stands next to me, talking to Marion whose eyes are wide, wild.

"This is craziness! Talk to her for God's sake." Marion's hands flap. Her yellow nails aren't sunny anymore.

Red shakes her head. She kneels beside me. "At least not here," she whispers.

"Just as well," I say, remembering I'm allowed to speak. I fear what would spill out of me if I looked too deeply into those chocolate eyes and started talking about not being okay, about all the reasons that lately I'd not been okay at all.

"Later," Red says, looking at Marion.

I nod.

"In the meantime, I think a paramedic should have a look," says Red. Her voice is very close to my ear.

"I'm fine." I lie.

"Bullshit." Marion leans forward. "Write me a fucking ticket if you have to, Officer." As if Red is the enemy. "But get her some medical help now. She's in shock."

"That's three," I say. I don't think I can take any more.

I mean, of course, that this makes the third dead body I've found since I moved to Middelburg in the spring. Well, one had died in the hospital, but he'd fallen into my arms nearly dead, so I count him.

It seems a bad record.

CHAPTER TWELVE

My brain clicked back to normal as Artesia Collins knelt beside me. "Let them give me a warning ticket. I want to talk to you."

I wasn't sure how long I'd been out of it, grabbing only snatches of what had been going on around me. Blue lights flashed along the road. My clothes clung clammily.

"Can you answer a few questions, Reverend Squires?"

Marion stood huddled with the rest of the Flashes around the Zaloumis who, for the first time in the months I'd known them, looked upset. Star sat in the back of one of the police cars, answering questions. Gil stood beside her.

I stood, shaking my head. "Not now." My knee ached. I pulled the smelly blanket tighter. I needed to tend to the Zaloumis. They were my parishioners, after all.

Artesia stepped in front of me. "But it's news now. This is my chance. For heaven's sake, help me. Help me escape her." She raised the mike again. "I'm here with Reverend Lorraine Squires, Middelburg's Ecclesiastical Super Sleuth." She turned toward me, face set in newscaster seriousness. "Reverend, this is the third murder in Middelburg in the last five months. Will you investigate?"

"No." I sidestepped but again she blocked me. "Do we even know this man was murdered?" God, I hoped not.

"Shot in the back," said Artesia. "According to preliminary reports."

I took a deep breath but my brain filled with fuzz.

She pumped the microphone in my face. "How will you begin your investigation?"

"Warning ticket! Warning ticket!" Star charged toward us. "No speaking to the priest."

"Reverend Squires, why does Councilwoman Hannes want to make sure you are silenced, even after the finding of this murder victim?"

Star practically skidded to a stop on the gravel beside us. "Warning ticket! Officer!" She swung a hand at the camera. "Turn that thing off! Artesia!" She spun to her reporter. "You may not talk to her. You know that."

"This will be my break into real news!" Artesia squared her shoulders. "I'd be happy to interview you as well."

Star squared her own shoulders and smiled. "That would be nice."

Artesia glanced at the camerawoman and turned the mike toward Star. "Councilwoman Hannes, why are you so intent on keeping anyone from speaking to Reverend Squires? Isn't she the person in town with the best knack for solving mysteries?"

"No." Star stretched a thin smile in my direction. "She has the best knack for finding dead bodies. That's something you want to look into, Ms. Collins. Why, whenever someone dies as a result of foul play, is Reverend Squires right there on the scene? That is something worth investigating."

"That sucks." Romee Vrooman pointed a half-empty beer mug at the TV above Skinny's bar. "She's practically accusing Lonnie of being involved in all three murders!"

I don't remember much of Saturday afternoon. A long shower. Playing with Linus. Not much else. I know now I was in shock. Then it just felt like a weird dream. Shortly after five I found myself at a table at Skinny's with most of the other Hot Flashes. Marion had called us together to reorient our collective and individual auras. Pitchers and pizza will do that.

Of course, no one could talk directly to me. But after the surreal day, I hardly noticed.

"Middelburg's Ecclesiastical Super Sleuth didn't have much to say at the scene of Randall Koeman's death, Lloyd." Artesia spoke directly into the camera, wind whipping the yellow tape behind her. She was still at the Zaloumis' field. "Of course, we expect to hear much more from her in the coming days."

Cut to Lloyd Arands, local anchorman, complete with chiseled chin, high cheekbones, Ken-doll hair and perma-concern etched into his face. "A real live amateur sleuth, Artesia? Just like in mystery novels?"

Artesia laughed, well, artfully. "I've heard that a Hollywood studio has already offered Reverend Squires the rights to the story of her adventures!"

Everyone at the table looked at me. "So not," I said.

"Of course, thanks to seven laws newly enforced in Middelburg no one could legally talk to Reverend Squires today." Artesia explained the situation for the benefit of the perplexed Lloyd and their viewers. She leaned forward, her nose thrusting toward the camera like a 3-D effect gone flat. She had her dream and she was going for it full tilt.

Then the screen cut to the footage of me from last Tuesday's meeting proclaiming, "There's nothing Christian about this. It's idolatrous love of the law. It's false righteousness. It's stupid and dangerous!"

Cut to Artesia interviewing a twitchy Brady Wesselynk.

"The Word of God is absolute, yes," Brady said. "The Bible says what it says and our obedience must be absolute. No pussyfooting around there." He grinned his horsey grin.

I tried to hide my surprise behind my beer glass. Brady, taking me on through the media? Not like him at all.

Cut back to Artesia live at the crime scene: "There's more than one batch of trouble brewing in Middelburg, Lloyd."

I held my wet glass against my cheek and sighed. Everyone at the table sighed. A team sigh.

My cell phone rang. *Frontline Church of Christ.*

Marion put her hand over my phone. "Don't."

"Are you kidding? I'm dying to talk to him. Plus, think of the risk he's taking calling me. He's actually breaking that law!" Everyone watched. "Brady? Nice clip on the news just now."

"Lonnie, don't say my name. People will know I—Lonnie! I didn't know—" His voice broke in a hiccup. "Artesia didn't say anything about you. Just about the Bible, the absolute authority of the Bible." He sucked in air. "I would never, never have said anything to undercut you directly like that."

Actually, what he really meant was he wouldn't do it without a careful plan and backup from Star Hannes. He was freaked out now because he'd been tricked into it. He didn't have a plan to fend me off if I decided to engage in combat. Poor guy was hiccupping, he was so nervous.

"Put that in your message on Sunday," I said, "for all your hundreds of followers in the church and online. Say that you support me."

"Nice," said Bets.

Silence from Brady.

"When it shows up online," I said. "Then, I'll believe you." I hung up and looked at Marion. "There. My aura is realigned."

"Ladies, I've made an executive decision." Colleen sat straighter in her chair. I could tell from the looks that no one knew what was going on. "Though Lonnie's birthday isn't until Friday, we're giving her her present now." Grins spread around the table and that made me smile. "No laws against giving her a present."

"Keep the good energy flowing," Marion said.

Everyone clapped as Colleen pulled a bright pink gift bag from beneath her chair and slid it down the table. I rummaged around the fluff of tissue paper until I felt a box about the size of a deck of cards. I pulled it out.

It pictured hot pink lipstick. On a chain.

"Check out the look on her face!" Romee shouted with a laugh and everyone joined.

Bova leaned into the table, squishing the green and red parrots embroidered across the front of her orange sweatshirt. "It's not! Really! A lipstick!"

"Shush!" Wanda nudged her in the ribs. "Don't talk to her!"

"She could read the package instead of sitting there looking flustered," Marion said.

"Lady Chameleon Lipstick Taser," I read. "Three hundred and fifty thousand volts?" I absorbed their eager faces. "You bought me a stun gun?" I was afraid to touch it.

My cell phone rang again. Artesia Collins. I pushed the button to silence her.

"She's always getting hit on the head or poisoned or something," Wanda said, pulling the last slice of pizza toward her.

"Plus she lives alone out there in the woods," added Colleen.

"And it doesn't take up much room," said Bets. "She can keep it in that tote bag of hers."

"Or in a pocket," said Wanda, chewing, "so you—she—can find it quick if she needs it."

"Isn't it a riot?" Lucy said. "Jake told me he'd seen them in his hunting catalog. In camo!" She giggled wildly.

I held up the box. "Is this even legal in this state?"

"Don't ask, don't tell," said Trixie.

I made a mental note to check. I didn't want to actually break any laws when I was fighting Star on the stupidity of hers.

The pitcher went around the table and everyone filled up. "Anyone tries to talk to her on a Sunday," Romee said, "Lonnie can use that thing to keep 'em in line. Star will love it."

"Next she'll say we should all have them to make each other behave," Colleen added.

"And then," said Marion, "the town will be full of some real hot flashes!"

We cracked up as I pulled the thing out of the box. It looked exactly like a hot pink lipstick. "You people are lunatics." My chest swelled with love for these women and their goofy way of caring for me.

"Now she really is a Super Sleuth," Wanda said.

"A vigilante with a utility belt," said Marion.

"Will she withstand Hollywood's big money offers?" Romee's eyes twinkled.

"Please." I tucked the Taser into my pocket. "The only person offering me money is my great-aunt risen from the dead."

"A zombie aunt?" Romee leaned forward. "Excellent. Someone must tell us about the zombie aunt."

As I shook my head, Marion spoke up. "I will." And away she went, telling them everything about Maurice Brand, my Aunt Kate's will, the car, the trip, the unspecified estate.

"Half a million bucks?" Romee asked.

"And she's not going?" Rika asked.

I shook my head.

"Is she nuts?" Romee practically jumped out of her chair at me. "This is the opportunity of a lifetime! Of several lifetimes! Are you—"

"Careful!" Bova stopped her.

Romee sat back. "Is she afraid wealth will mess up her priestliness or what?"

"Vestry! Would! Give! Her! The day off!" Bova slapped her hand on the table.

Cheers from around the table.

"And I could watch Linus," Colleen offered. Others chimed in as well.

"I'm taking Linus," I snapped. "If I were going, I mean. But I'm not."

"Why?" several asked.

"It's all too weird," I said.

"It is weird," Wanda said. "Don't go. Stay here and solve the murder."

The others shot her down.

"I'll tell you all what's weird," said Marion. "Karmically speaking." She looked at Romee. "Lonnie's being here in this situation. I mean, she lives here summers as a kid, plays soccer with us, hates her great-aunt. Okay. But then, fifteen years later, after her great-aunt dies, she comes back to play soccer, winds up with a job as a priest and suddenly, for the first time in thirty-some years, we have a murder? Then another? Then another? Three in the six months after she arrives? And right before the third one happens, her dead aunt tries to get her out of town? On her birthday?" She leaned forward. "Birthdays are significant, by the way. All kinds of vortex energy centers on you on your birthday."

"God! Wants! To! Tell! You! Something!" Bova said.

"Yeah, like that haunted house in the movies." Romee made a monstrous face and spooky voice. "GET OUT!"

I shuddered. My fingers slid across my jeans to where I felt the lump of my bright pink Taser in my pocket. It actually felt good.

"Go!" Bova said.

"Don't," said Wanda.

"I'm going," I said, finishing my beer. They cheered. "Home." They booed. "I have a job to do here."

"That's right!" Wanda raised a glass. "Super sleuth!"

"My job as a priest," I corrected.

Wanda looked crestfallen.

"And that means I've got me a sermon to write."

As I walked to my car long stretches of blue shadows painted the ground in the orange evening light. The town seemed empty. I saw only one person, and she was leaning against my car, face tilted toward the sun.

"You looking for me, Officer?"

Red didn't move. Eyes closed, she spoke to the sky. "Too many eyes here. I'm going to the beach."

CHAPTER THIRTEEN

Ten minutes later we walked together in the golden light of the sunset. Red's curls tangled and spun in the wind. Her gun belt creaked. Her high boots left thick waffled impressions in the soft white sand. I was supremely buzzed and had a Taser in my pocket. It was illegal for her to talk to me.

Not what I'd imagined in my romantic fantasies. But it would do.

"You still on duty?" We walked south, me closer to the water, sneakered feet on firm wet sand.

"No. Just too damned busy to change." Red's boots slid a bit on the loose sand of the bluff. Her head was nearly even with mine because she walked on the rise.

"As if the poachers weren't enough, huh?"

Beside us the lake glowed midnight blue with streaks of orange. Tiny waves licked the sand.

"So," I said, "can you tell me what happened? Koeman looked familiar," as did everyone in Middelburg, "but I didn't know him."

Red turned toward me, hair crisscrossing her face. "Any chance you'll forget all about what happened today?" I said nothing. "Yeah, I didn't think so." She sighed. "I suppose if I don't tell you, you'll just go all over town asking."

"Pretty much."

"Randall Koeman was shot in the back, apparently from some distance. Rifle. Probably shot near where you found him, then just rolled in the ditch. They found some scraping, some blood in the gravel. It had been pretty thoroughly shoveled up and tossed in the water. There was some evidence of blunt trauma on his face. He may have been in a fight before he died."

"Was he the fighting kind?"

"More the drinking buddy kind, from what I can tell. Thirty-seven. Lifelong Middelburger. Married. No kids. Worked for Koontz Heating and Cooling."

"Ivor did it," I said, only half-joking.

"Yeah, I figured you'd say that. But happily you, Super Sleuth, are not investigating this one."

I held up my hands. "No way."

"Koeman hadn't been home since Thursday night, the wife says. She didn't call it in because she wasn't worried. Evidently he'd produced two plane tickets to Vegas last week and since she had them, said she knew he'd be back."

A white and gray gull swooped over us, hanging on a thermal, then dropping to the sand about fifty yards ahead. "Did he disappear a lot?"

"Wife said it happened. Always out Thursday nights, coming home late, drunk, or simply not until after work on Friday. She figured he had a mistress." Red pulled away a curl that had wrapped itself around her nose. "She says they didn't really think much of each other after the first few years of marriage, but decided it was easier to stay together and just roam a bit."

Divorce simply wasn't done in Middelburg. Affairs, on the other hand, if kept quiet, were.

"She have any ideas about who the lucky lady might be?" I asked.

"Said no."

"Believe her?"

"I do," said Red, eyes squinting in the sun.

"Because?"

"Because Mariette Koeman is terrified. She spit all this information at me faster than I could ask questions." Red half-smiled. "She thinks someone is going to shoot her next. In fact she wants you—" Red slid her eyes at me, "Middelburg's Ecclesiastical Super Sleuth—brought in to solve the case and protect her."

"Protect her!" I chuckled. "Does she know I can barely keep myself alive?"

Red shrugged.

"So what makes her think someone would want to shoot her?" I asked.

"Narcissism," Red said, then made a face.

I laughed. "She probably doesn't know anything about her husband's enemies, huh?"

"Nope. But according to the folks we've talked to, he was kind of a clown. A good-time Charlie. Big talker, good joker, everybody's buddy. But no one's friend. At least not that we've found yet. We'll talk to Koontz's crew on Monday."

"What do you make of the Vegas thing?"

Wind spun a curl around Red's temple. "Wife says he'd been promising it a long time. Got a lot of overtime from the rec center project. They both like the casinos—it's the one thing they still do together."

"Maybe Ivor didn't want to pay the overtime."

"Lonnie." Red sounded like I did when I caught Linus doing something bad.

"Find out what Ivor stands to gain with this guy being dead," I said. "He'd shoot someone in the back. He's low enough."

"There's probably a dozen folks with motives. That's what police investigation is for. Slow and thorough. We'll talk to them all. Don't worry."

"Why do you think I'd worry?"

Ahead of us, the gull hopped along the waterline, head darting as he looked from us to the dead fish he'd found. The sand under him glinted with water and light.

"Stay out of this case, Lonnie. Please."

I held up my hands again. "I'm out. Trust me. Star's crazy Faithful Heritage Initiative is enough to deal with. I don't want to get whacked, poisoned or shot. No thanks."

We walked in silence, but my mind took off noisily. The victim had worked for Ivor Koontz whom I knew to be violent. I also knew him to be a sneaky S.O.B. who'd do underhanded crap to anyone he thought had crossed him. Look at how Jack Putnam was convinced Ivor was sabotaging the security system at the rec center. And I remembered well how Ivor and Star had conspired to defraud the whole town last spring.

Ivor and Star. What if...what if they were up to something together? If Randall Koeman had found out? What if by checking out Ivor's involvement in Koeman's death I could discover something about Star, something that would pull the rug out from under her and her seven laws game?

The seagull launched, squawking from the fish carcass.

"Why are you grinning?" Red asked. "I do not like that grin."

I looked her right in the eye and lied.

Sunday proved one of the weirdest days of my life. Imagine, I went to church and no one could talk to me. Before the service, trying to set communion, coordinate the readers, double-check on the music, help a choir member find a missing pitch pipe—no one talked to me directly. It was like I'd had a fight with my entire congregation and we weren't on speaking terms.

"Tell Lonnie that her robe is hitched up funny in the back," one said.

"Tell Lonnie that Jack Putnam says the sound system blew a fuse and he can't find the replacements," said another.

My mood wasn't helped when Isabella Koontz arrived with her two daughters and no Ivor. He rarely skipped church, liking the patriarchal show of herding his girls around in their lacey dresses. A purple welt sprang from Isabella's left cheek.

Yeah, Red, I thought, *tell me again how Ivor Koontz isn't involved in this murder.*

At coffee hour, no one came within ten feet of me as if I had something catching. I wondered if the other ministers in town enjoyed this bizarre game. Brady Wesselynk in particular. He thrived on glad-handing his hundreds of parishioners after each megaservice, hobnobbing with his big money donors. How was he surviving this?

I'd just refilled my mug and snagged my third homemade windmill cookie and decided to head up the steps to my office when the front door to the parish house sprang open and Artesia Collins, carefully windblown, with jazzy scarf and bright blue mackintosh, pounced into the room followed by a camera crew.

At first, I thought Star Hannes' clan was invading my church like Darth Vader and his stormtroopers. But then I realized Artesia was on her own.

"Reverend Squires!" she hollered. The place went silent. Everyone stared. "I'm looking for the Reverend. Oh! There!" She pointed at me as if I were hard to spot halfway up the stairs, wearing my floor-length white alb and green stole. She snagged a mike from the cameraperson's gear bag and headed toward me. "I know I can't speak to her, but she can speak to me! The people want—they need—to hear what their Ecclesiastical Super Sleuth has to tell them. They need to know: when will this murder be solved?"

"No, no, no!" I said, barreling right back at her with my mug and cookie outstretched. "Not in my church. Not on Sunday morning."

"But the people—"

"Can wait until Monday." My coffee sloshed over the mug's rim as it met the mike in her outstretched hand. We stood like Rock'em Sock'em Robots waiting to battle.

Artesia glanced at my parishioners who watched, many with cookies or coffee cups in their mouths. "Evidently she can't speak about the investigation yet."

"You are welcome to join us for coffee hour," I said.

From her spot near the buffet table, Kitty Gellar, octogenarian Senior Warden of my church and a formidable presence in the best of times, raised a silver platter of windmill cookies like it was some sort of ninja weapon and smiled. "Cookie?"

Artesia blinked then turned to her crew. "We'll check in tomorrow afternoon." And like a bad odor, she wafted back out.

As soon as the door clicked shut behind her, everyone resumed chatting almost as if nothing had happened. I stood next to Kitty as she rearranged the platter. "Thanks."

"Hospitality is important here," she said to no one in particular.

"Run back to the Sunday school room and draw," Isabella directed her girls as she walked up beside me and Kitty. "Wasn't that terrific?" she asked Kitty. "The way Lonnie stood up to that woman?"

"Thanks," I said.

"I admire that," Isabella said. "You know. Fighting for what you believe in. Keeping things in order the way you know they should be."

"You could learn from her, my dear," Kitty croaked. Her crooked hands moved back from the tray and I saw she'd arranged the remaining cookies into a smiley face. "Off to clean up the kitchen."

Isabella and I stood next to each other facing opposite directions. I worried about that new bruise. What other ones lay beneath her clothes? I wanted to open the door for her without asking her directly if Ivor hit her. I didn't want to force her to lie to keep her secret.

"It's never easy. Standing up like that. Look." I held out my hand. It wobbled. "See? Even that little scene made my hands shake."

"Well, I admire it." Isabella took a step away.

"Wait," I said. "Where's Ivor today?"

She talked fast. "He didn't feel well this morning. Chesty cough. Under the weather. I told him it was better not to come to church and spread germs. He's had such a hard week. What with, well, the death." She breathed. "I'm not talking to Lonnie, you understand," she said to no one. "Just talking to myself. I do that sometimes. It can be annoying."

"One of his crew, I heard. That's tough."

"More overtime he has to pay someone else to keep up. He works so hard already. He's never home."

"Was he home Thursday night?" I asked. The night Randall Koeman was last seen alive.

Isabella's dark eyes flashed at me and I saw fear there. "Of course. He comes home to be a good father to the girls. A good husband to me. Every Thursday night. We watch television."

Obviously at least part of that was a lie—Ivor Koontz was not a good husband. But I wasn't sure how much else was also a lie. Because if one thing was certain, Isabella Koontz would cover up to protect her husband.

CHAPTER FOURTEEN

Monday morning I half expected to find Artesia Collins camped out on the parish house front porch. All was quiet on the parish house front, however, when Linus and I arrived.

When I walked through the door and greeted Ashleigh she exploded into tears.

"You gotta help me!" she sobbed. "I wanted to call you Saturday, but I knew we couldn't!" She sobbed and hiccupped. "I've been holding it in all weekend!"

Linus ran up to her, bouncing his front half into her lap. She buried her head in his neck.

I dropped my bags and went to her. "What happened?"

"That man—" she hiccupped, "Randy—head injury—I—I—killed him."

"Whoa, whoa." I stuffed a few tissues into Ashleigh's hand and she blew her nose. "What do you mean you killed him?"

Sobbing, hiccupping and blowing her nose, she managed to stutter the tale. Last Thursday night she'd been walking to her car from Skinny's and he'd followed her. Drunk. "I ignore him most of the time." She wiped her eyes. "But when I got to my car, he grabbed my shoulder, so I swung at him." Sobs burst forth again.

Linus rolled large worried eyes at me so I patted him too.

"You punched him?"

When she shook her head, I prayed that she hadn't picked up a brick or bat.

"My purse."

I'd seen it. A tiny thing barely big enough for a cell phone and a tampon. I'd always wondered why she bothered.

"And then my fist."

"Well, I doubt you—"

"But he fell! He was really drunk. Fell onto the car behind me. Hit his head. He was bleeding all over!" She blew her nose. "I wanted to call nine-one-one, but he just called me a bitch and said I'd be sorry one day and walked off. I figured he was probably okay." Her eyes dripped. "That was horrible, wasn't it? I should have called for help."

"You didn't kill him." I handed her another hunk of tissues. "He was shot."

"But he had head injuries! The news said. Maybe what I did made him do something stupid and get shot."

"Even so, you didn't shoot him. So you didn't kill him."

She studied me with watery eyes. "Really?"

I handed her another tissue. "Yes. If he was already drunk enough to hassle you, he'd already lost his judgment."

"Well..." She released Linus and patted his ruffled neck smooth. "I guess. Still, it's freaking me out."

"You could help the police. Call them and tell them this story. It will help them understand where the head injury came from."

She smiled a little. "Then I'd be sort of a Super Sleuth too, like you."

I smiled too. "More like a witness, really."

Her eyes rounded. "Will I have to testify at a murder trial?"

"Here." I scribbled Red's cell phone number on a sticky note. "You know Officer Carson."

She wiped her nose and studied the paper. "Okay." She shook her head. "God, if only he hadn't grabbed me, I would've ignored him like I always do."

"Like always? You said that before—that usually you ignore him. Was he often there?"

"Me and some of the girls, we go to Skinny's on Thursdays. Like, early TGIF, you know? Randy shows up about nine forty-five. Drunk. Leering after women in the parking lot. Most of us try to leave by nine thirty. Avoid him."

I wondered if Red had found this out yet. Maybe he didn't have a steady mistress.

"Anything different about this Thursday night?"

Ashleigh sniffed. "You mean, other than me socking him? And him being really really drunk? And then winding up dead?" Her pitch climbed with each question.

"Okay." I stood. "But yeah, other than that. Did he mention anyone else? Maybe someone from work? Or from around town?" *Like Ivor? Or Star?*

Ashleigh shook her head. "Here you are, sleuthing, and I'm not being any help. I should be of some help!" Water squeezed from her eyes again. "I'm sorry."

"It's okay. Just, if you think of anything, tell me."

She nodded and sniffed. "I think it's cool how you just started asking questions. Like a real detective. Except not. That's what's cool." She sniffed and smiled. "I work for a Super Sleuth. Oh!" She picked up three pink messages slips. "That reporter lady keeps calling."

"No matter what, tell her I'm unavailable. And call Red." She promised to do both.

CHAPTER FIFTEEN

Later I sat in my office and thought about it all. I didn't want to play into Artesia Collins' media fabrication of me. I didn't need to antagonize Star Hannes in terms of television coverage. And I didn't want to have anything to do with this investigation, not really.

I just wanted to stop Star's bullying of this town. Either to inspire people to stand up to her, or to come up with something that would force her to back off.

I turned options around in my head for about an hour while Linus snored. If Randy Koeman kept a regular schedule, got drunk a lot, hassled women and for some reason, last week, had gotten brave and more obnoxious than usual, well, then maybe it would be easier to find who'd killed him than Red thought. Maybe he'd "overstepped" as Ashleigh put it with one of his regular drinking buddies. Only instead of cracking him with a purse, the buddy whipped out a handy hunting rifle and ended the problem.

Cold-blooded, but possible if the shooter was drunk too. Or angry. Or afraid. Or just plain mean.

Which brought me back to Ivor Koontz. And maybe Star.

I chewed on that for a while. Thought about Isabella's many bruises in the last six months, about Ivor's conspiracy last spring with Star, about how much I couldn't stand the guy at my own deep gut level. Marion was always telling me to trust my gut.

In the end, I simply couldn't think of anything else to do. So I leashed the dog and headed back down stairs. "We're going for a walk," I told Ashleigh, "to the rec center."

"Are you sure you want to take him down there?"

"It'll be fine," I said. "I just have to run in to check the locker room for something I left last week. There's a bike rack out front. I can tie him to that and he'll be completely on the sidewalk. Totally legal."

And so we walked around the corner to Main Street and down the two blocks of shops, waving at Colleen in her Cuttery and at the folks in The Windmill Grind. I didn't see Marion, who was in the kitchen, no doubt, preparing for the lunch crowd. The sun shone with that particular graham cracker color of mid-fall, a color that meant rain was coming again soon. I could see the stacked clouds gathering out west over the lake.

At the rec center, I tied Linus to the bike rack where he could lie down in a sunny spot on the sidewalk. The muddy parking lot was littered with vans and pickups, including several marked Koontz Heating and Cooling. Everything was splashed with dried mud from the recent rains.

I wandered through the front doors. The glass and dark wood entrance sparkled. Pristine offices glowed on the left, shelves still empty and bare wires hanging from a few spots in the walls. Stairs curved up to the right, where a running track circled a multiuse basketball floor. To the right, doors led to what would be two indoor soccer pitches, like hockey rinks, but with turf. A center hall led toward the back, toward weights, classrooms and the main locker rooms.

I was not here sleuthing, I reminded myself. I was simply here to get a sense of things, of Ivor's situation. Of anything that I could use in my efforts to stop Star. Anything I found out, I turned right over to Red.

Definitely not sleuthing.

Rapid pounding drew me toward the office complex. In what would probably be a reception area, I found a thick pair of man's legs in grungy khaki workpants standing atop a stepladder. The rest of him was lost above the dropped ceiling tiles. The ladder shook each time the man hit whatever it was he was hitting up in the ceiling.

"Six goddamned inches," the man bellowed, beer belly bulging. Ivor Koontz. "I said six inches, Dale!"

I looked around and saw no one else in the area.

"You put eighteen inches up here, Dale," he muttered. "Measure this way all the goddamn time and no wonder it's all fucked up. Maybe it was you, not your buddy Koeman. Shoulda kicked both your asses."

I blinked. That seemed easy. Koeman had been screwing something up at work. Ivor didn't like him. What more did I need? Ivor had motive to get rid of the man. All done.

If I'd left right then, everything would have been different. Everything. Or, if you believe in fate, or Marion's karma, maybe it all would have turned out the same way anyhow. I guess I really don't know. But looking back, I wish I'd left.

I didn't of course. I wondered where this Dale was that Koontz was talking to. I wondered if I poked around just a bit more whether or not I'd find out what Koeman had done to screw up.

So I slid around Ivor's ladder and tiptoed back toward the administrative offices. I stopped in the hall and peered at an angle into the first office.

Inside the biggest paneled office, Gil Hannes sat at his heavy wooden desk. This must have been finished first, because he'd clearly moved into his new kingdom. Leather-bound books lined the shelves, an enormous computer flat screen glowed. A netbook sat next to the screen. An electronic whiteboard waited for action near a six-person conference table.

In front of him paced the spindly blond guy I'd seen arguing with Jack the other night. Dale. I remembered he was afraid of Ivor. Maybe, if he'd really been buddies with Koeman, he'd talk to me.

"You gotta protect me," came his deep voice. He wiped a hand across his splotchy yellow beard. "You're an attorney. You influence what goes on around here. Decisions made. You can do it, right?"

I leaned back against the wall outside the door, where I could hear without being seen. Did Dale need protection from Koontz? Gil did have a lot of influence on what sorts of decisions got made during the construction of the rec center.

"I don't have that much influence," Gil said.

"Maybe your wife." Dale's voice rose with desperation. "She has influence. She can talk to him."

"She has worked with him before, true," Gil drawled.

I resisted the urge to pump a fist. I just knew something was up involving Star and Ivor. Bonus if Gil was in on it too.

"I'll—" Dale hesitated. "After what happened last week, I'm afraid."

I wished I had a tape recorder so I could play this back for Red. She'd never believe it.

"You don't know he's responsible for that," Gil said.

"He has his eye on me now. You gotta help me!"

"God damn it!" Ivor's voice boomed from out in the reception area. I knew before I turned my head that he was out of the ceiling. "What are you—?" He held Jack Putnam next to the ladder and stared at me. "You too!" He shoved Jack practically into me, then shoved us both into Gil's office.

Dale shrank back against Gil's bookcase.

"This one." Ivor pointed at Jack. "I spotted headed into the center like a thief."

"I'm a contractor here, Ivor," Jack said calmly. "Like you."

"And this one." Ivor poked me with a finger covered in black hair. "Was just standing here. Eavesdropping." He shoved Jack's shoulder. "Hey, Putnam. Maybe Reverend Squires is the one screwing up your security system."

"Thank you, Ivor," Gil said. We waited until Ivor got the message.

"You! Zeerip!" said Ivor.

Dale jumped.

"I need your ass back out here to fix your screw-up."

Dale looked desperately at Gil, then followed Ivor out of the office. He looked like a man walking to death row.

"I have every right to be in this building!" Jack said. "Especially if you want me to figure out what's going on with the cameras!"

"Did they go out again?" I asked.

"Saturday night." Jack shook his head and his ponytail wobbled. "I'm rechecking the whole system today. I'll pull it all and start again if I have to." He rubbed his temples. "This is my first major job. I need it to go well."

"Perhaps it was too risky to leave your fine job with the local school in such an uncertain economy," Gil said. "If you can't figure out what's going on, I'm going to have to hire someone else to fix it." He waved Jack off.

"Just tell Koontz to keep his hands off my system. And me."

I'd never seen Jack so steamed. And both he and Ivor were my parishioners. Fantastic. I'd have to put something about reconciliation in my next sermon.

"Reverend Squires? Did you need something?" Gil's weak eyes blinked at me over his tiny mustache.

I wanted to ask him why Dale needed his protection. What Star and Ivor were up to now. How he was involved. I wondered for the briefest second if he, Gil, would jump at a chance to get out of that marriage if he had one offered to him. But I needed to cover my tracks, for now.

"I came back to find—" My brain scrambled. "My dog tag." Where had that come from? "You know, license. I got it last week, tossed it in my bag, can't find it. I'm worried maybe it fell out in the locker room."

"Well, nothing like that has been turned in." Gil rotated his chair to face his computer. "Go look. Then go home. This is still a closed construction site during the day."

I practically skipped out of there, circling around the entryway where two pairs of legs now protruded from the ceiling. Dale reached, his shirt creeping up to expose a big inny belly button coated in yellow hair.

"Do it right. Don't complain. Don't make shit up. Don't cross people," Ivor intoned. "Koeman never learned. He never learned."

"Nope," said Dale. "He didn't."

I couldn't wait to tell Red.

About halfway down the long hallway which led to the locker rooms at the back of the building, Jack emerged from a service room. He fell into step beside me, Birkenstocks slapping the floor. "So, Lonnie. What are you really doing here?"

"My dog—"

"Yeah, I overheard that load. So, for real. What are you on to now?"

"Nothing." I kept my voice low. "Really, I'm on to nothing."

"Look, I owe you. Last spring you saved my butt when Ivor and Star tried to tank my business."

I looked at him. "Do you think they're up to something again?"

He shrugged bony shoulders. "Someone is. There is nothing wrong with my system. The reports say it's clicking off and on. I think someone's doing it. But nothing changes. Nothing is missing, so no one believes me. They think it's a glitch."

"And you're sure?"

He nodded. "Do you doubt me too?"

"So what are you doing with it today?" We paused in front of the women's locker room door.

Jack grinned. "Putting in a second camera set. Totally separate. Motion detectors. If someone is messing around, I'll catch 'em in the act." He put a finger to his lips. "Don't tell anyone."

I zipped my lips.

He sighed and leaned back against the wall. "It's only been a few weeks and I already wonder if I should've stayed in the school. Maybe counseling—with a decent salary and benefits—was better than this."

Should I stay or should I go? I leaned back next to him. "Some theology holds that you can make no wrong decisions. That you are always on your path," I said.

He nodded. "You read the *Tao Te Ching*, Reverend?"

"Is it safe to admit it if I do?"

"Doesn't threaten me the way it would some around here," he said and we both smiled.

That gave me an idea. "Do you think Koeman might have spotted Koontz messing with your system? Threatened to tell? Or did the two of them hang out, buddies?" Maybe Koeman had gotten in the middle of one of Ivor's beefs with someone else.

"I never get invited to their parties, Lon. They cut me from their team long ago." He pushed away from the wall.

"You find what you're looking for?" Dale's shout echoed the length of the empty hall.

I raised my hands to show them empty as he approached. "Not in there."

Dale nodded and chewed his cheek. "Ivor asked me to show you out. Security. Construction zone." He pointed the way with fingers raw from being gnawed on. Nervous guy.

Dale said nothing as he walked me past the front offices where Ivor still pounded away in the ceiling. But as soon as the door closed behind us and we stood blinking in the sun, he turned. "Look, Reverend. We don't really know each other, but Randy Koeman was my friend. And someone shot my friend in the back. I'd like to know who. And why."

"A lot of people would." I glanced at Linus who leapt to his feet, but then sat, silently, waiting for me to come to him. "Good dog."

"You have any ideas?" Dale rubbed his hands together, then folded his arms, tucking his hands under his biceps. His blue eyes skittered from me to the dog and into the distance. "Used to be a nice place around here. Economy, everything." He scratched his patchy beard. "It's all gone to hell."

"Why do you think someone shot Randy?" I asked.

He tucked his hands away again. "Don't know. Keep thinking about it. He had a fight with Ivor last week." He shrugged. "Told Ivor something that made him really mad. Maybe overtime?"

Or maybe something about evidence that Ivor was hitting Isabella again?

"You think Ivor could be involved?" I tried to keep my voice

flat, not betray my eagerness. If Dale Zeerip had evidence against
Ivor…

"I don't know. I'm asking you."

Linus stood and barked once, unable to contain his puppy-
patience any longer. We walked over toward him. He greeted us
both and Dale pet him while I untied his leash. "Nice dog," he
said.

"You find anything else out," I said, "call me."

"Not the police?" He squinted at me in the sun.

"Yes, of course. The police." *Careful.* "Or me, if it makes
you feel more comfortable. Because really, I'm not investigating
anything."

He smiled. "Whatever. Television says you are. Folks say you
are. And this." He bent to Linus and gripped his collar. "This
says you are." He flicked a finger and Linus' license tag glinted
in the sun.

I didn't say anything.

"Makes me sadder to hand you this." He handed me a
crumpled yellow slip. "Found it attached to his collar before I
came back to find you. Grabbed it. Didn't want you distracted
until we talked."

I flattened it. A ticket. Signed by Deputy Don Loomis. Dog
off leash it said.

My temperature spiked. "He was on his damned leash!"

"Careful, Reverend. Don't want a second ticket for
swearing." He nodded toward the building and I saw a window
to the reception area cracked open. "Cops don't cruise by here.
Somebody called. And Koontz. Well, he's a pain in the ass." He
gave me a small wave and headed back toward the building.

"Does Koontz own a gun?" I shouted. I didn't care if Koontz
heard. "Does he hunt?"

Dale didn't turn but held his hands up in an I-don't-know
gesture.

I shoved the ticket in my pocket and stomped away from
the building. That son-of-a-bitch Koontz would pay for calling
the cops. Don would pay for writing a ticket. Star would pay
for starting all of this. I was calling someone. Red. The ACLU.
Maurice Brand. Someone. Someone would help me be sure

someone paid for this! And it was going to stop if I had to wring someone's neck to stop it.

Put a ticket on my dog, will you? I fumed. *Ticket me for not taking care of my dog?*

Linus' sudden yank backward on the leash brought me out of my fury in time to stop mid-stride and avoid stepping out in front of a little blue Dodge as it whipped into the lot. I held my hand up to apologize to the driver, who had her hand up to her face in a cough. When she waved back, I recognized the face of the girl who'd run me down on the soccer field last week. I watched her spin gravel as she drove around to the back of the building toward the fields.

Looked like she had lost something too.

CHAPTER SIXTEEN

"I'm telling you!" I shook the phone since I couldn't shake the person on the other end. "Ivor and Koeman fought. About overtime. Dale Zeerip saw it. You said Koeman came into extra cash because of overtime. Bought tickets to Vegas. Maybe he owed on the tickets and Ivor didn't pay. You have to bring him in for questioning."

I heaved out the rest of my air and tipped back in my desk chair. My stomach churned. Linus watched me from his bed in the corner, brown eyes alert.

"Lonnie, I'm exhausted here." Red sounded like maybe she'd shake me if she could. Good thing we were on the phone. "I know you're pissed off about the ticket."

"Oh, no," I said, my voice low and utterly controlled. "Trust me. This is not about that ticket. That is a whole other matter."

My body felt compact, still, taut—ready to fight. Someone was going down for that ticket. That had nothing to do with the murder.

"Okay, look. I'll have someone check around, see if we can come up with a reason to check into Koontz's pay records, okay? It might take a while, so don't hound me."

"You are not the one I'm going to hound."

Silence. "You don't sound like yourself." Red waited, but I said nothing. "You aren't going to do anything crazy, are you?"

"I like Don," I said. "So warn him if you want to. But the wrath of Lonnie Squires is about to get unleashed—no pun intended—and he does not want to be caught in the middle. If he gets called again to give me a ticket, he may want to be too busy."

"For God's sake! You can't threaten cops like that."

"I'm not threatening." Icy power flowed through my veins. Certainty. Resolve. I was going to end Star Hannes' reign of terror no matter what it took. No more Miss Nice Priest. Star— and whoever helped her—was going down.

"You know, Lonnie, really. This is a time to lay low. You can't just beat Star and her Faithful Heritage Initiative in a head-to-head battle. It's like that kid on the soccer field last week. Star has too much momentum. She has longer and stronger legs in this community. You need to just wait. Be patient. Something will change and your chance will come."

"My chance has come. I'm going to make it happen."

"You want my advice? Lay low. Hide. Stay out of her line of sight. For now."

"I don't want your advice."

I didn't even feel bad saying it. Not now. After all, I'd called her first. Told her what I'd learned at the rec center, about the ticket. She didn't have a single decent idea. Nothing better than *do nothing*. Bullshit. I was doing something. Now.

"I guess we're done then," Red said. She sounded angry.

Well, me too. I folded the ticket that lay on my desk precisely in half. Then into quarters.

"But Lonnie? Stay away from Ivor Koontz. Calling the cops on your dog is just his first swing. If he's really involved in all this, you don't want him any angrier at you."

After we hung up, I called the ACLU and left a message because I was crazy mad. Then I called Maurice Brand and left a message. I wanted to hurl the phone out the window. Where the hell was everyone when I wanted them?

Linus cocked his head at me from his bed in the corner. He sensed my rage.

"Oh, dog." I grabbed a bag of chips and sat on the floor beside him. "This isn't about you. It's about mean nasty people." He pushed his velvet nose against my cheek and puffed. "Dogs are so much nicer than people."

He agreed and suggested that since he was so much nicer he deserved chips. We both crunched thoughtfully.

Linus and I had found each other last spring when our lives had fallen apart. His owner had been murdered and I'd rescued him, nearly getting myself killed in the process. Later, when Jamie had ditched me, it was Linus who slept next to me, snoring warm breath across my cheek as I healed from a near fatal head injury. Since then, it had been Linus' limbs atop me in the night.

Now they were trying to use him to make my life miserable. Well, no way.

"You stay here." I handed him a few more chips and looked at the stack of unanswered mail on my desk. It had waited this long, it could wait a few hours more. I had a law book to read.

A few minutes later, as I walked through Middelburg's tiny, dusty library, shelves overflowing with worn paperbacks, looking more like a homespun used bookstore than a city library, I realized I didn't know exactly what I hoped to find.

But I knew this: when people like Brady Wesselynk or others threw out certain Bible verses they'd handpicked to suit their needs, the best way to fight them was by going to the Bible myself and looking for verses that contradicted them. That was the wonderful mystery of the Bible, and other holy texts. It contained so much that you could use it to prove just about anything. People used the Bible for decades to justify treating women and people with dark skin as less than human. They used it now to demonize gay people. And others used it to argue for the equality of all.

Well, I knew the Middelburg town charter was no Bible, but

I was willing to bet that Star had selected the seven passages that served her purpose and left plenty of others out. I wanted to have a look at those others and see how I might use them against her.

Bram VanRenselaar, the archivist and rare books librarian, didn't bother to hide his surprise when I walked into his tiny office. His hairy eyebrows crawled like spiders up his forehead when he saw me. He stood, unfolding a long frame from beneath a worn wooden desk, like a giant grasshopper come to life.

We shook hands. Even at my height, I had to tip my head back to look him in the eyes, which watered on either side of a hooked nose. Crow's feet lined his face, probably from a life spent beneath fluorescent lights in a room with no windows.

"To what do I owe this visit?" With two loping steps he crossed the room to a cabinet where worn books with crisp pages lay protected. "We have a vast collection of Bibles. In Dutch!" He held out a hand as long as a loaf of bread.

"Still can't read Dutch, I'm afraid."

He tsked at me, Adam's apple bobbing. "And you've been here six months already! That's just obstinacy on your part."

"And your Dutch is how good?"

"*Ja, ik kan heel goed nederlands praten, dank je wel.*"

"Impressive." Bram had helped me out once when I had to catch a murderer before getting caught myself. I saw him around town—he was hard to miss—but we hadn't talked much. He was the cousin of Rika VanRenselaar, Hot Flashes striker extraordinaire.

"Actually, I came to look at the original Middelburg municipal code. Or whatever it is Star is mining for her Faithful Heritage Initiative."

He nodded. "Foundations of the Municipality, Reformed Middelburg, Michigan." He opened an enormous drawer in a floor-to-ceiling cabinet.

You could hide a body in there, I thought.

Three intimidating tomes lay there, crusty, threatening, ready to rise from their resting places and point a bent and accusing finger at you. Zombie books, suddenly sprung to life and dangerous.

"The center volume holds the legal information I believe

you'll be interested in," Bram said. He reached out a sinewy arm to stop me as I stepped forward. "Not so fast, Reverend. You mayn't touch it without white gloves. Skin's oils destroys old paper."

"I haven't got—"

"Voila!" He whipped a pair of short-wristed white gloves from his jacket pocket. "Kept for seekers such as you."

I pulled them on as Bram donned his own. He lifted the book from the drawer and carried it to one of the long dark library tables in the center of the room. The book was two feet long and a foot across, nearly six inches thick, with heavy uneven pages stuck from between the cracked and graying black leather covers. I sat before it, alone in the center of three rows of tables, twelve chairs. Just me, the book and the book's guardian angel.

"I'm a little afraid to touch it," I said. "Though Star was manhandling it at the meeting last week."

Bram cringed. "I had nothing to say about that. Trust me." He bent and opened the book to its middle. He turned a cracked page or two, then stopped. "Start here. The beginning of the laws."

I looked down at pages, thin and stained. The writing was tiny and the print from the opposite page seeped through. This was going to kill my eyes. "How many are there?"

He shrugged his shoulders knobby even beneath his hanging jacket. "Take your time. Just be gentle with the pages. They're barely a hundred years old, but they're as fragile as some centuries older."

"Why?" I still didn't touch the thing.

"Because for the first fifty years this book was kept in the damp basement of the old courthouse. For the next twenty in some attic without temperature control. And it was printed on cheap paper with cheap ink to begin with. Ever thrifty, our Dutch founders." He stood, waiting. "Go on," he said quietly. "Turn a page. I'll watch so you can be sure you aren't hurting it."

I felt like I was handling someone's newborn as I turned the page. It rippled and fluttered with less substance than toilet paper, but didn't tear.

"Perfect," Bram said. "I'll just be here, if you need me." And he quietly folded his lanky self back behind his desk again.

After I trained my eyes to ignore the print seeping through from the back side of the pages, the reading went pretty easily. Except dull. Law after law after law without context or rationale or explanation. I found the seven Star had selected for special enforcement. But before too long I found others that interested me more. Laws that Star had decided to ignore.

•No children shall run free in public at any time.

•No child shall speak on the Sabbath except as engaged in worship or directed by a parent or minister.

•Women shall not engage in unnatural masking of their physical flaws to erect a façade of false beauty.

•No married woman shall drive a motor vehicle within the city limits except to attend a church function or if widowed.

To my delight, the litany of laws restricting women and children went on for a full two pages. No woman could own a pair of shoes made from leather other than that of a cow. A restriction against using goat's milk. It went on and on, the craziest stuff.

"Have you read this?" I asked. "Why do you think anyone would care if a woman's shoes were made of cow leather or not?" I asked Bram.

He looked up, throat working. "Well, a hundred years or so ago, there was a big cow farm owned by the VanOestermanns. Dairy and beef. Dedrick VanOestermann signed those documents, sort of like the John Hancock of Middelburg. He might have wanted to be sure he had a market for his hides."

"Seriously?" It was amazing how historical documents changed when you learned about the people involved and their real life goals and motives. Context was everything.

I thought for a few minutes, then changed my mind. Star hadn't conveniently decided to ignore these laws when launching her Initiative. Nutty as she was, she would never want to bring such things back under enforcement. She needed to wear fancy Italian pumps like I needed to play soccer. She needed to drive. She needed women to vote for her in the election.

She had probably sent someone—my bet was Mimi Manser—to look up laws that would make my life hell, started with those, and proposed the importance of living by the entire legal code without having a clue what was actually there!

I shouldn't have been surprised. People did this with the Bible all the time. Waved it around screaming about the seven passages against gay people and how we must live by the scripture, but without any clue about what else scripture really said.

"You got a piece of paper?"

I'd found what I wanted. Now, I just needed to call Artesia Collins and hope she liked my idea.

CHAPTER SEVENTEEN

That afternoon the spotty sunshine gave way to pummeling rain. I waited for return calls on the messages I'd left, and got some work done. I responded to a diocesan request for an outline of our children's education program. I got the agenda for Wednesday's Committee on Liturgy meeting finalized and e-mailed to the group. I managed a smile for the parishioner who dropped in to complain that I didn't visit Tri-Cities Hospital enough, even when I explained that no one had called needing a priest.

"How can you know," she'd asked, "whether or not there are Episcopalians who need a priest unless you go to the hospital and look?"

Evidently she thought I had nothing better to do than troll the hospital hallways checking the denominations of every admitted patient. Still, I managed to be civil to her and sent her out into the ripping thunderstorm with a smile.

I kept it together when Bova Poster came running over from the church and stood dripping in my office, bosom heaving beneath a powder blue sweatshirt embroidered with monarch butterflies, to announce that water was trickling down the walls in the sacristy. I didn't bother to ask her what she'd been doing back there. I just asked her if she'd be the one to call a few of the other parishioners and lead them in the cleanup. She beamed with responsibility and I stayed at my desk.

At 3:22, Artesia Collins finally called. We agreed to meet at The Grind. Marion's eyes widened when she saw me walk in and sit down with the reporter, but she knew better than to say a word. Just served us our thick black coffee.

Artesia looked ready for a safari in khaki pants, a khaki jacket with many utility pockets, a hunter green kerchief around her neck and a wide-brimmed khaki hat. Her eyes, a gold-flecked green, scanned the restaurant as I tossed the menu aside.

"Bring me whatever's best," I said to Marion.

"Nothing else for me." Artesia waved her away. "Diet. Television cameras add four sizes to your figure!" She laughed a laugh obviously orchestrated to tinkle like bells. She really was going whole-hog on this career move of hers.

Good.

"I have a story for you." I leaned over the table, my voice low. At this hour, The Grind wasn't crowded. But it wasn't empty. And everyone would know I was here talking to Artesia. Still, it seemed safer than having her to the church, where everyone would still know I was talking to her, but would assume I was trying to hide it. This would look more innocent.

Artesia leaned forward as well. "You've identified the murderer?"

I shook my head and her face soured. "As good, though. I've discovered a ton more laws on the books here in Middelburg. Laws that Star Hannes doesn't want made public."

Artesia sat back. "Aren't you even investigating the murder? Like a Super Sleuth?"

"Did you know that legally, children aren't allowed to play in public? In the parks? Or speak at all on Sundays?"

Artesia pushed her mug to the side. "Did you know that this Ecclesiastical Super Sleuth thing is grabbing a lot of attention as a human interest story? The network has expressed interest in a feature! You solve this murder and it could make both our careers."

I sat back. "I'm a priest."

She sat back. "A poor priest in a shithouse little town. You've got way more brains than that. I'm talking CAREER. National news features. A film-length treatment. Maybe a television series. The Midwestern Ecclesiastical Super Sleuth and the reporter who discovered her. We could be the next *America's Most Wanted*."

I couldn't help it. I grinned.

"I'm not joking." The fire in those green eyes made it clear she was, indeed, not joking.

"Nor am I." I leaned forward again. "A Super Sleuth works for justice. That isn't just catching murderers. It's stopping all kinds of criminals. Especially the kinds the law can't touch."

She considered this and then the light dawned. "You're a vigilante!" She grinned. "Don't suppose you'd consider ever wearing a mask or anything, just for the cameras?"

I pulled a few sheets of paper from my tote bag, the laws I'd hand-copied in the library. Duplicates, of course. "I'd like to make a deal with you. I give you some news, you help me out later if I need it."

Artesia's eyes glinted. "Let's see the news."

"These laws are also on the books." I passed them to Artesia. "Might make an interesting story to find out why Star Hannes ignored them. If she even knew they existed. What would life be like around here if that Faithful Heritage Initiative passed?"

"Or better, how she's violating them." Artesia studied the list. "Or how many people in town are violating them. What if everyone got held accountable to all these laws?"

"My question exactly."

Artesia folded the papers and pulled them into her lap. "What Star has said about observing her seven laws should follow for all of these, right?"

"Exactly."

Artesia sipped her coffee and studied me. "Glad you're on my side, Reverend." She sipped again. "It's going to be chaos."

I holed up that night in my cottage as the chilly wind and rain blew through the trees around us. I hunkered down at one end of the couch, covered in two thick fleece blankets, coddling a huge bowl of Beefaroni, my best nighttime comfort food. Linus curled at the other end, his lean body folded like a deer's.

The local anchors buzzed through the weather headlines and a story about a man in Kalamazoo wanted for armed robbery. Then they shifted to special correspondent on the lakeshore, Artesia Collins, for more on a developing story in Middelburg.

Artesia stood in the pouring rain in front of the lighted white spire of the First Church of Christ the Lord's Own Sainted Elect Reformed in downtown Middelburg. The drops flickered like spears of metal in the bright television lights.

"New laws on the lakeshore." Artesia hit every syllable like a jackhammer. "Creating better communities? Or more hypocrisy? More on this in a few minutes."

Nice. I raised a spoonful of macaroni in a salute to Artesia and her dramatic style as they cut to a commercial. The phone rang.

"Are you watching this?" Marion shrieked.

"If you mean Artesia, you bet."

Marion paused. "Great Goddess Gaia. You did this!" She laughed. "What have you done, Lonnie? Where is the hypocrisy thing coming from?"

"Watch and see." We hung up.

The story came out better than I'd hoped. Artesia even had statistics. "The actual ticketing system kicked in today, Lloyd," she explained to the anchorman. "Forty-nine people received tickets and four were jailed already."

The split screen showed the anchor looking amazed. "Isn't that about fifty percent of the entire population?"

Artesia chuckled a television chuckle. "Not quite, Lloyd,

but it's a lot. And that's after only seven of the laws have been brought back."

And on Artesia went. The other laws. Speculative questions on why Councilwoman Hannes and the rest of the town council had chosen to ignore these. More questions on whether or not one could, with integrity, pick and choose which laws one obeyed and which laws one ignored. "Especially if they're all still on the books, Lloyd."

Cut to Brady Wesselynk who looked flabby and nervous under the glare of lights in his office. Artesia's voice asked, "For instance, Pastor Wesselynk. When it comes to the Bible, is it acceptable to pick and choose which verses—or laws—you'll honor?"

Brady swallowed. "We must strive to follow all the laws of God, of course. But we're human. Fallible. Only through grace can we hope to attain perfection."

Artesia's voice again: "And the law about stoning adulterous women, Pastor Wesselynk. Is this a law you and your flock strive to follow?"

Brady swallowed again and looked nervously away from the camera. "Of course not. That law came from another time. Another place. A society much different from ours." The footage cut him off.

"Now that the full scope of the Faithful Heritage Initiative has been uncovered," Artesia said into the camera, "it remains to be seen how the town's populace will react."

Cut away to that same clip of me saying how this sort of absolutism was far from Christian. It didn't look so stupid now.

Back to windblown Artesia. "Councilwoman Hannes has been unavailable for comment. We'll have more tomorrow, Lloyd. From Middelburg, this is Artesia Collins."

I hooted and muted the TV as the phone rang again.

"How about that, huh?" I hollered into the phone, assuming it was Marion calling again. "All it took was one visit to the library. Why didn't anyone think of that before?"

"Because no one is quite as determined as you," said a man's voice.

I hadn't checked my caller ID. "Who is this?"

"Maurice Brand. I happened to see the news and thought I'd return your call. I understand from your message that you wish to sue Star Hannes? Or perhaps the town itself?"

"I do. These laws—they can't be legal. At least, only enforcing some can't be."

"Sorry to say, I only practice wills and probate. But I'm not sure you need to sue anyone to make your point, Reverend Squires. Artesia Collins seems to be handling that."

"Maybe." I wiped my finger around the inside of my bowl for the Beefaroni sauce. "Well, thanks for calling back."

"If I might ask—"

"Yes?" I held the bowl out so Linus could lick the rest.

"Why go after Star Hannes with such energy yet turn away from the idiosyncratic but essentially harmless bequest left by your aunt? I don't follow."

"I won't be manipulated." My hand jerked as Linus licked. "Even if my Aunt Kate is dead, her whole scheme is a manipulation."

"And devoting so much time and energy to defeating Star?"

"She doesn't want me to do it." I pulled the dish away. "She isn't manipulating me."

"I see."

He didn't. He didn't understand the difference between being manipulated by a crazy woman and fighting for justice against a crazy woman. It was so clear. It was—well, I'd had two beers. I couldn't quite see it now, but I knew it was clear.

"Well, Reverend Squires, I just want to remind you, the car is ready. As long as you leave Friday morning, you can still win the estate."

"No thanks."

"Well, it's there. In case you think a half million dollars is worth more than discrediting a local politician."

"I'm not trying to discredit her! I'm trying to get her to leave me alone! To leave this town alone! Before she really hurts someone!" Like Aunt Kate hurt me.

"Well, if I don't speak with you again, happy birthday."

I dropped the phone on the floor and lay back. Dang it, I'd been celebrating and now I felt like crap and I knew that somehow, my Aunt Kate was responsible. If it weren't for her Brand wouldn't have called and dampened my celebration.

It felt familiar. Like I used to feel all the time with Aunt Kate.

CHAPTER EIGHTEEN

I am fourteen. Almost fifteen. I should be home with my friends. Not stuck here in Podunksville with an old woman.

I watch my crazy Aunt Kate barrel down the boardwalk outside of Grand Haven, headed toward the lake.

I am way way way too old for sunset walks on piers with old women.

My knees hurt from scrubbing her tile floor. She made me do it if I wanted to eat. And I want to eat. But she still hasn't fed me.

My stomach grumbles.

"Move!" Kate shouts.

Dinner is after this stupid walk, so I move. I run past her. *Move, old woman*, I think.

I stop, though, when I get to the edge of the long, narrow

pier. It stretches out into the harbor, Lake Michigan in the distance. And the lake is boiling tonight. Gray and white and frothing. Waves punch the pier, curling fingers of slate water up and around. A few kids my age—maybe a bit older—laugh and chase each other in the closest section of the walkway. They look like they have a life, unlike me.

Still, no one, not one single person, is out on that pier.

I turn, grinning. "We can't go out there." Dinner that much sooner.

"Nonsense." Kate doesn't stop. Floppy straw hat tied tight beneath that loose-skinned chin, bony shoulders square, high-waisted pants billowing about her skinny legs, sensible shoes slapping in puddles left behind by the waves, she stalks right out past the warning sign. The warning sign that says adults drown here when the waves are high. *Extreme danger. Keep off in high surf.*

The teenagers huddle, watching her, whispering. Their tension makes me stop, grip the signpost with one hand. *Stupid adult.* "Aunt Kate, did you read this?"

She turns, walking backward. "So what? You don't get many chances to walk into energy like this. Come on. Feel it push against you."

She walks on, leaning her head into the wind while the kids whisper and stare at me. I feel sick. What if she falls out there? I can't just stand here—I have to stop her!

I run a few feet, clutching first one pole of the catwalk, then another. I look around, desperately hoping for a policeman to appear and stop her. Or for someone else to do something. But the wind has kicked up more. The other kids leave, casting me strange looks, like I'm the idiot. I feel my flesh burn.

"Aunt Kate!" My voice folds into the wind. "This is stupid!"

She keeps walking.

I run a few more feet, hunching against wind. Just as I grab the next catwalk pole a wave pounces over the rocks. I leap to the side, and the force hits me in the ankles instead of the knees. Spray shoots into the air.

My great-aunt, soaked, keeps walking farther out onto the pier.

My heart punches the inside of my chest. I swallow my pride. "Please. I'm afraid."

That stops her. She turns and looks at me. The narrowing of her eyes makes my knees weak with shame. She sees that too, and laughs.

"If you're that chickenshit," she says, "then I'm not wasting my money on soccer camp. If you can't face a force that wants to knock you flat, how will you be a decent athlete? Or human being, for that matter?"

Then she turns and keeps walking.

I cling to the post as long as I can before I follow. Water soaks my jeans and I become heavy and slow. Halfway to the end, a wave arcs over the pier and buckles Aunt Kate's legs. The water pushes her toward the edge, toward the sheer dropoff into the deep, boiling canal.

"NO!" I release my hold on the pole and run to grab her arm or leg. But she is too far. I can't reach her. She rolls half over the edge, then catches an iron cleat cemented into the pier and stops her own fall.

I grab the nearest post and watch her stand. Her linen shirt clings to her tanned skin and her wild brown hair droops around her ears.

She smiles at me. "You would have watched me drown." She wipes water from her face. "Because you were afraid. Think about that." Then she marches to the end of the pier.

I follow, my shame at having been too late to save her overcoming my fear. After about five minutes of standing, praying that another big wave doesn't sweep us both away, I feel her grab my arm. She smiles. "And now, here you are! You've conquered your fear."

She buys me anything I want for dinner. I eat steak so rare it's bloody. And that evening she enrolls me in soccer camp for the summer.

CHAPTER NINETEEN

The memory—almost a hallucination—of being with Aunt Kate on the pier twenty summers ago, coupled with the residual effects of a few too many beers, still had me in a foul mood Tuesday morning, even though the sun shone autumn gold in a crisp blue sky. At church I saw the morning paper featured a follow-up story on Artesia's coverage on the front page. Star Hannes' picture and the words "Heritage Initiative or Hypocrisy Initiative" in bold beneath it.

There you go, I thought. *Now you're getting more press than me.*

Maybe today I'd call Don Loomis and see if he'd like to reconsider that ticket he'd issued.

Ashleigh handed me a piece of paper. *Bishop Craig Tappen.* "He's called twice already." And it was only 9:34.

"I'll call him back. After coffee. You want coffee?"

I took Linus to my office and started my computer so it could warm up, then went back downstairs to make coffee. As it brewed I stared at my snack stash, contemplating if one could rightly eat Nacho Doritos at this hour and how they would taste with Fair Trade Ethiopian blend.

The slamming of the front door interrupted me. "Lorraine!" the voice boomed.

I turned away from the counter, shutting the cupboard on my stash as the bishop's meaty shoulders filled the kitchen doorway. I tried not to look as surprised as I felt. The man never left his diocesan house unless he absolutely had to. "Cup of coffee, Bishop?"

He glowered at me. "You have said, to the media—repeatedly!—that there is nothing Christian about loving the law."

"Actually, sir, I only said it once. The local television station just keeps replaying it."

His face reddened. "Are you aware of the effect this is having on people's perception of the Episcopal church?"

The Cap'n Crunch and milk I'd had for breakfast curdled in my stomach. "That we actually think about the impact our decisions have on real people before we start imposing—"

"Your remarks give the impression that we don't respect the Bible!" He stepped into the kitchen and I pressed back against the counter, trapped.

"Sure you wouldn't like a cup of coffee? As we talk?"

"No."

I reached into the drying rack near the sink for a mug anyway. "We keep those sweetener packets you like, just for you."

"I'm getting phone calls, e-mails. The letters haven't started yet, but I'm sure they will. 'How can you call yourselves Christians,' one asks, 'when you don't honor the law?'" He changed his tone. "'This explains why you let the homosexuals run your church,' said another. 'Is this how you disregard the Bible?' say others. And 'Fire that priest!' say an awful lot of them."

"I wasn't talking about the Bible. I was talking about seven old laws selected for attention because taken out of context they will make life miserable for some people those in power do not like!" I sucked in a breath. "I said it because I'm right—what Star Hannes is doing isn't Christian or even law-abiding. It's a mean-spirited use of law to hurt people. If anyone really honors the law, it's me because I want to see it used well."

He stepped toward me again, several steps, until he was only a foot or so from me. I could smell the pine in the soap he'd used this morning. Fingerprints cluttered on his pewter pectoral cross. He'd sucked a mint before coming here.

My skin pricked and I suppressed a shudder and the urge to push him away. Instead, I said, "She is a cruel bigot. It's our duty, as Christians, to fight for social justice."

He leaned forward, his face lower, closer to mine, his eyes dark and opaque. "Are you listening to me, Lorraine? Because I want to be very, very sure you hear what I'm about to say. Are you listening to me?"

"Yes."

"Do not engage with this woman. Do not break any of these laws. Do not do anything at all to stir up further media attention. Stay out of the spotlight. Do not speak to the press."

I blinked.

"You will do nothing to bring attention to yourself or, by association, me. You will not endanger the reputation of this diocese. It's hard enough staying afloat in this part of Michigan and during this economy as you well know."

Ah, so some big donor had written one of those e-mails or made one of those phone calls. Or maybe the bishop's marketing firm had advised there'd be trouble with the collections this Sunday as a result of my stint on TV. Suddenly I understood why he'd driven all the way here.

Money was at stake.

He studied me. "Why would you do something like this and endanger all your colleagues? It's so selfish."

I felt something solid within me, hard, pushing back, wanting to push him back, out of my face, out of my space. *Selfish? Screw you.*

I said nothing.

"That woman is hell-bent on winning that congressional

seat," he continued, his minty breath in my nose, "and would, I believe, delight in sacrificing you to that end. I'm doing you a favor here, Lorraine. I, as your bishop, *order* you to stay out of anything that this woman has to do with."

I kept my mouth shut, afraid of what might come out.

"Remember," he said, "I can bring you to ecclesiastical court and have your job. Maybe your ordination. For breaking your vow of obedience."

I remembered. And I understood who was selfish, who was honoring the Bible and exactly what I was called to do. I mumbled a lot for the next fifteen minutes, tried to remain monosyllabic and give the appearance of subdued obedience.

Between the Aunt Kate hangover I started the day with and mollifying my bishop, I didn't think the day could get much worse. Mercifully, it didn't. In fact, I got a ton of work done, not only for this week and next, but actually thinking ahead to Advent in December. I caught up on my mail, and even planned ahead for a baptism. The only interruption came when Marion called after the lunch rush to laugh about the press coverage I'd gotten for Star. "You are sure a brave one," she cackled. "Everyone's talking about it. Don't you go stand alongside a country road in the dark, young lady. Because if Star Hannes has access to a rifle, you're going to be the next one in a ditch."

Linus and I went home and had a long run on the beach. I worried that Red didn't call, either to laugh at the way I'd turned the tables on Star or to give me hell for it. I figured she was probably too busy chasing poachers. I wondered if she'd done any more looking into Ivor Koontz and what he had against Randy Koeman. But I promised myself I wouldn't call her until tomorrow.

Then came soccer. The sun shone and the Hot Flashes played great. The team was younger than us again, of course. But we tied. I ran like the wind and my knee only hurt a little bit. Don Loomis hovered around the benches, listening for curse words, no doubt, but we all managed to keep it clean. Even Romee, though she couldn't resist asking Don if he was going to ticket his own wife for driving her car inside the town limits. Colleen dragged her away before she could get into too much trouble. Skinny's was a blast. I drank too much beer and did as my bishop asked—I didn't talk about Star Hannes with anyone all day.

Wednesday morning dawned bright. Sunny, dry, with great Vs of migrating swans swooshing by overhead. A day of possibilities.

I loaded Linus into the car. The folks on my Committee on Liturgy loved him and protested any time I didn't have him around for our monthly meetings. Just before ten I had two pots of coffee brewing and stood arranging chairs in the meeting room when Bova Poster walked in carrying an enormous white box. "Saucey-ya-brood-ehs!" Her tongue tripped over the Dutch name for pigs in a blanket, but who was I to judge? If it weren't for Marion's tutoring, I wouldn't have a clue how to pronounce something spelled saucijzebroodjes. "From! The Grind!" She centered the box on the table and bent to rough up Linus, who had scrambled to his feet to greet her.

I handed her a mug of decaf. "How are you today?"

"Isabella! Can't come!"

I could tell by her actions that something was up, but I played dumb. "Is she ill?"

"Nope!" She placed her mug on the table and crossed her arms. The embroidered woodland creatures on her sweatshirt morphed into surrealist art. "Ivor! Won't! Let! Her!" She looked triumphant as she delivered this intel.

The whole thing irritated me. "Won't let her what? Come to a meeting? Out of the house? What?"

"Come! Where! You! Are!" Bova plopped her wide bottom down into one of the swivel chairs at the meeting table. "Says you! Are! Nothing! But trouble!"

"I've been called worse." I remembered how just a few months ago she had taken such delight in telling me that many Middelburgers thought I was an agent of the Antichrist.

She looked at me over her mug and snorted. Then she opened the box of pigs in a blanket and dug in.

"Hey, Reverend!" came a crusty-old-man voice. One of the Zaloumis. "Check this out."

"No!" Bova yelled swiveling so she could see them and trailing flaky saucijzebroodje crust after her. "You! Can't! Be trusted!" She looked at me. "Stop them!"

But I was too busy thinking about Ivor and Isabella. He knew how much she loved church. Was she safe in that house if he were pissed at me? Did he want to keep her away from me because I was on to something about his involvement with Koeman's death?

"Geez," said one of the twins as they rounded the doorway. "It's just a little spiderweb across the front window."

Linus went berserk, spinning with joy between the twins who poked and cackled at him, whipping him into a frenzy.

I hadn't figured my asking questions about Ivor would wind up isolating Isabella even more from her neighbors. From us. That wasn't good.

Linus yapped at the old men who wheezed and flapped their ball caps at him. He snapped after the hats, crazed with the fun.

"Stop them!" Bova pleaded.

"Okay, okay," I said, breaking up the children. I'd worry about Isabella after this meeting. "I'm going to run him outside quick for a break and then we'll get started." I clipped Linus' leash to his collar, wound it around his neck and tucked it in, and headed out into the yard. "Be right back."

We walked around to the side yard between the house and the church, Linus sniffing around for a good place to squat. I stood near the porch, watching, but giving him his privacy. He kept sniffing as Kitty Gellar slowly walked up to the house.

"Good morning, Father Squires," she cracked in a voice more delicate than the pages of Bram's rare books. "It's a good day to debate the issue of placing the Sanctus bell to the left or the right of the altar."

"Yes it is," I said. Such were the issues of church life. Change of any kind had to be debated, wrestled through. Sometimes—like today—it seemed a waste of time when we should be changing the world.

Kitty stopped, her veiny mottled hand resting on the porch banister. "Also, please lead a discussion on the supportiveness of the kneeling cushions in the pews. Some of our more elderly members have complained of sore knees after the communion prayer."

"You got it," I said. I'm sure Kitty picked up on my lack of enthusiasm.

"I'll see you inside shortly," she said and clattered into the house.

Linus squatted once, but I waited another minute. Boy dogs usually didn't empty themselves on the first go, and besides, Kitty could take time to get settled. I leaned against the house, watching him sniff, the light bouncing off his flexible body, the young muscles rippling under his shiny black fur.

I didn't notice anyone approaching me and in retrospect, I suspect it was because they didn't want to be noticed.

CHAPTER TWENTY

"This is your second violation," Don Loomis said from behind me.

I jumped as a yellow ticket swished in front of my face, but anger quickly took over. "Wrong, bud. He's on the six-foot leash." I called him and Linus bounded up to greet Don. I touched the leash. "And he was leashed—completely legal—the other day when you wrongfully ticketed him in front of the rec center."

"You have to be holding it," Don said, face locked. He held the ticket in front of me.

I refused to take it. "The law doesn't say that. You're out of line."

"No, Reverend. It's you who's out of line." A smoother voice. The voice of Satan, the fallen Star. She stepped from around the corner of the house. "If you don't agree," she smiled and flicked her hair back from her shoulder, "you can argue it in a court of law. If you can pull yourself away from the television reporters."

"Speaking of reporters," I said, "where's your crew?" It was just the three of us. No entourage. No cameras. I hadn't seen Star this alone in weeks.

Don looked nervously between us.

"Is that your way of thanking me for not recording your blatant violation of the law?" Star said.

I stepped toward her. "Your precious law doesn't say I have to be holding the leash."

She crossed her arms, pushing against her breasts, sharpening the cleavage exposed beneath the plain gold cross dangling from her neck. "Evidently you didn't take the first ticket seriously." Her eyebrows shot up. "A shame for you. More for your poor dog." She turned to Don and pointed a finger at Linus. "Impound him."

I threw my arm toward Don's chest. "You can't impound him. I haven't done anything wrong."

Star spun and the hatred glittering in her eyes stole my breath. "I will stop you from ridiculing these laws." She drew herself taller and half smiled. "If you have no dog, you can't continue to break them." She turned back to Don. "Take the dog, Officer Loomis."

She was serious. Fear squeezed my throat. I yanked Linus so hard he lifted off his front feet. I shoved him behind me. "Arrest me. I'm the one breaking your precious laws, not him."

"No, no, no." Star smoothed her hair, though it was not out of place. "It would be inappropriate to rob this struggling congregation of its spiritual leader. They shouldn't have to suffer for your inability to legally care for your dog. Of course, if they chose to remove you because of your blatant disrespect for the law..." She shrugged to indicate there would be nothing she could do.

"You're crazy!" I yelled. "This is crazy! Don!" I turned to the big man. "Don, you know what she's up to. You can't be a pawn in all this."

His face remained immobile. "A judge can sort it out." He reached around me toward Linus.

"NO!" I squared myself. "This is why you didn't bring your cameras. You don't want footage of you stealing my puppy." I pointed my finger and screamed. "Star Hannes is stealing my puppy!"

"Get the dog!" Star shoved Don toward me.

"No!" I screamed so loudly that my own voice rang in my ears. I threw my arms up to stop Don's movement. "Get out of here!"

"Now, Lonnie," Don started.

I grabbed Linus' collar and yanked him backward as I stepped back. "Get out! Help! Help!" If the people inside heard, if they came out, Star would have witnesses. She might stop then.

"Do you want to go to jail for obstructing justice?" Star asked. "You'll never get your dog out of the pound if you're in jail."

"Lonnie, I have to take the dog. It's the law." Don stepped toward Linus.

My voice roared forth from deep within me, a voice I didn't know, a voice I'd never heard before. "Do *not* touch my dog!"

Don froze.

Every part of me vibrated on the same note, a high pitch of rage I didn't know I had in me. "I'm not kidding." I stared at Don. "Leave or else I'll—"

"Reverend Squires." Don cut me off, unsnapping the leather strap from across the Taser on his belt. "Step away from the animal, please." I didn't move and he stepped closer. "Step away from the animal."

"Lonnie?" Ashleigh's voice from above, up on the porch. "What's going on?"

"Get the camera," I said. My voice came slow, thick, utterly plugged into the energy—of fear, of rage—coursing through me. "Take pictures. Film it all."

She ran into the house.

"Get the dog!" Star shouted.

Don lunged for Linus' collar and I screamed, rushing full force into him, smacking his chest. He pushed me aside, back against the rough peeling paint along the side of the house and stuffed his meaty hand between Linus' collar and neck. Then he yanked. Linus spun his butt, aiming his head toward me, eyes round, white-rimmed, afraid.

Looking to me to save him.

I screamed something—I don't know what—and flew across Don's back, hooking an arm around his neck, kicking, screaming. My voice beat him too. I don't remember the words. I just remember exploding, expecting my bones to shoot out of my body like poisoned arrows, singing with rage.

He flailed. Yelled. Tried to get a hand on his Taser. I punched him in the ear. He moaned and nearly fell, but I held on to him and started swinging my feet at Star.

Suddenly hands were on me pulling me off the big man, pushing me back against the house. The Zaloumi brothers stood there, spittle on their lips, holding me with unsteady hands. Bova Poster screamed from above us on the porch.

"What! Are! You! Doing!?"

"You've assaulted a police officer!" screamed Star. She swung her arms toward my parishioners. "You are all witnesses. And that dog will be impounded for evidence. *For months.*" She narrowed her eyes at me. "Maybe destroyed."

I pushed against the twins, but they were wiry and tough. "Let me go," I growled at them. "I don't want to hurt you!"

Don grabbed Linus' leash with one hand and rubbed his ear with another. Then he shot me a wounded look and led my dog away.

"No!" I screamed and flailed again. If I could get free, get to Don, I'd go for his gun. I could use it to slow them down, make them leave us alone, until I could get out of here...

Linus looked up at the big man he knew so well and cast another worried glance at me.

"Leave him alone!" I begged. "Don! Please!"

But Don walked away and my puppy, my innocent, confused puppy, followed.

I shook my head hard, thrust myself to the side, screaming, but I couldn't break free.

"Lonnie!" Bova's voice grabbed me. My face was hot and wet from tears. I thought my heart would shred itself. "Lonnie." She appeared beside me, touched my cheek. "You have to! Let them! Take! Him!"

"Yes, you do," said Star. "We're taking him because you blew it, Reverend. You could have kept him safe. But you blew it."

And as they lifted my dog into the back of the sherriff's car, I fell to my knees and sobbed.

CHAPTER TWENTY-ONE

I ran two blocks after Don's car until he shot out of town toward the pound. Then I ran straight to the courthouse to get my dog released. I started politely and ended shouting at everyone. Finally a guard threatened to jail me if I didn't leave the premises. I was daring him to do just that when Marion showed up and dragged me to her car.

Seven hours later I sat on my bed and stared at the carpet. Patterns swam across the Seventies-vintage mottled shag.

My heart had broken. I had nothing left. I had done this, by pushing Star.

What did justice matter if they could take my dog?

I should have made keeping him safe my first priority.

Even Red had told me that. I called her, of course, left panicked, pleading, sobbing messages begging her to help. She hadn't called me back.

I couldn't bear the thought of Linus locked in some cold concrete cage with a million other dogs barking, frantic, terrified. He wouldn't know what was going on, or where I was. Why I wouldn't come and take him home. He wouldn't know.

I wanted to go to the pound, or back to the courthouse, or to Star's offices—somewhere to do something. But Marion had taken my car keys. "Lon, you'll do more harm than good for that dog. Just stay put until you settle down."

It nearly killed me. I sobbed and sobbed. I think Marion tried to get me to eat something but I just screamed her away. I wanted nothing in me, nothing to interfere with the hate that filled every atom of me—all the space between the subatomic particles that made me. Hate.

Finally I realized that the patterns of the carpet had stopped swirling and descended into shadow. It was after five o'clock.

"Go home to your kids," I yelled to Marion who I knew sat at the kitchen table.

"Are you kidding me?" The chair scraped and she appeared in the doorway. "With your soul shattered like this? Honey, you are in a fragile state. Evil energy could seize you now and we might never get you back."

I stared at her from beneath hot lids heavy with self-loathing. "Too late."

She sat on the bed next to me and stroked my head. "All's not lost, Lon. It's awful, but he's just in the pound. He's safe and—"

I pulled away from her. "Just shut up."

She stared at me. "I'm going to go get some sage. This place needs a smudging. Right now."

I didn't care what she did. Smudge me. Drum around me. Paint me blue and toss me in Lake Michigan. None of it mattered—unless it got my dog back.

Soon the weedy smell of burning sage scratched at my nose and throat. My eyes watered and I sneezed.

"I'm calling Artesia Collins again." I stood. "I want that bitch Hannes' move all over the news tonight."

Marion blocked the doorway. "Not such a good idea."

Last bits of energy flickered in my chest, nearly exhausted. "Why not?"

Marion waved the smoking wand of sage over my head. "Great Goddess Gaia, protect this wounded soul with your white light. Mighty warriors, angels of the land, protect her—"

"And her dog." I sat back down on the bed. "Ashleigh didn't get any photos of them dragging Linus away, did she?"

"Honey, from what Kitty Gellar told me, they were so busy holding you down, no one had time to turn the camera on. She said it took four of them to hold you back."

"Two were in their nineties."

Marion leaned against the doorway, holding the smudge stick high. The white smoke wafted across my ceiling. "Just as well that there's no footage of you jumping Don. Their word against yours on the assault thing." She watched me for a minute. "Did you really bite his ear off?"

"I should have," I said. I didn't mention to her my fantasy of taking the gun, of holding them all at gunpoint while I escaped with Linus. If only I'd gotten my hands on it when I first jumped Don, instead of wasting my time jumping on him. I'd be— where?

In jail for sure. For what? Shooting somebody?

I expected a flutter of fear, a punch of revulsion. Some reaction to the idea that I might have shot someone to protect my dog. But instead, I felt only leaden certainty. If I'd had a gun in my hand right then and if shooting someone would have stopped them from taking my dog, I'd have shot it.

This should horrify me. But it didn't. Probably it would later. When somehow, this was all over and I looked back on it, my dog asleep by my side. I'd work it out then.

"I promised I'd keep you here," Marion said.

"Promised who?"

In response she just waved the smudge stick and headed toward the front room.

I crawled into my bed and lay down. I needed to rest. "Keep smudging," I said. Maybe if I died right here and now, beneath the white smoke of smudge and Marion's love, at least I wouldn't go straight to hell.

"Wake up, Lonnie."

I crawled back out of the deep and my eyes pulled apart slowly, focusing on the dim shadows. *My bedroom. Night. A little light from the next room. The kitchen. Home. Middelburg.*

Star had stolen my dog.

All the pain of the day tore me apart once again, like sharks in a feeding frenzy. Plus my head clanged with pain. I moaned.

"Wake up," Marion whispered. She sat on the bed beside me. "The police are here."

I pulled myself to a sit, rubbing my face to try to get it to move normally. "What?"

"A sheriff's car just pulled up in front and I came to get you." She spoke in a tight whisper.

"Who's in it?"

"I don't know!"

Loud pounding came from the front door and Marion jumped. "Shit! Should I tell them you're gone? Left town?" Her head swung. "Where can you hide? Is there a back door?"

"Whoa." I put a hand on her thigh, still holding my head with the other. "I'm not a fugitive."

"What if they're coming to arrest you for assaulting Don?"

"Then call Maurice Brand and get him to bail me out."

Pounding came again, this time louder. I stood, ran fingers through what I knew would be awful bed head. My mug shot would look like hell. But didn't they all? I debated if I should wet my hair down, put on a clergy shirt and collar. That would make a heck of a shot, wouldn't it?

Screw it. I headed for the front door. "Call my parents too, would you?"

Marion followed me. "Don't answer it."

I rolled my eyes at her. "Please. Me? A life on the run?" After all I'd done, I deserved jail. Maybe if they had me behind bars someone could get Linus out of the pound.

Red Carson stood outside in her uniform, hands raised as if she were about to pummel the door with her fists. Or perhaps she was about to pummel me.

"Are you out of your fucking mind?" Though she was a good foot shorter than me, she pushed me aside easily and banged into the living room where she spun on me. "Is that what's been going on for the last five months? You always sticking your nose in where it doesn't belong? Investigating murders—violent murders? Making yourself the target of killers? Is it all *because you are out of your fucking mind?*"

"Maybe an insanity defense is a good idea," Marion said quietly.

"Shut up!" Red held a hand up as if to catch a softball, then took a deep breath. "Sorry. I'm not mad at you." She turned back to me. "You need a psychiatric evaluation."

I didn't say anything.

Red paced into the kitchen. "Why, Lonnie? Why did you push the limit with Star? Even though you knew she could take your dog!" She blinked rapidly and I realized she was fighting tears. "Tell me why you did it!"

"I don't know."

"Bullshit! You're not that stupid." She paced back and stood in front of me, nose inches from my throat. "And I want you to say it. I want to hear you say it!"

"It wasn't right!" I shouted back, fighting my own tears. "Star is using the laws just to be evil. To frighten and control people in town who are too weak to stand up to her. I wanted justice."

"Sometimes," she said, her voice tight and flat as a metal band, "justice is illegal."

"Unjust laws shouldn't be observed," I said.

"And that is why you lost your dog. You really care more about justice in this town than you do your dog?" She flung her arms wide. "No one—and I mean no one—in this town cares as much about Star's crazy games as you do. So what did you sacrifice your dog for, Lonnie? Huh?"

I opened my mouth, but she stopped me.

"And don't give me that justice bullshit again. You did it for yourself. So you hate the way she operates? Ignore her. Stay out of her way. But no. You." She poked a stiff finger into my breastbone. "You have to get in her face. No matter what you say, it's really all about you and your own goddamned ego."

She spun and paced toward Marion who danced out of the way.

"I tell you what." Red turned back. "You owe God and your Great-Aunt Kate about forty days and nights of on-your-knees prayers of thanks. Because they have given me an idea that might get you out of this mess."

I didn't know what to say.

"Linus too?" Marion asked.

"*Linus mostly*," Red said to her. "I could care less if this idiot goes to jail for assaulting my partner." She ran her hands through her curls and looked at me. "Get dressed. Wash your face. And practice puckering. You are going to kiss Star Hannes' ass."

CHAPTER TWENTY-TWO

"The best thing you've got going for you," Red whispered as we climbed the stairs to Star's downtown office, "is that I know—and you know—that Don Loomis is never going to press charges against you. You saved his life this summer. But that doesn't save Linus."

We paused in front of the wooden door with a frosted glass window. The brass sign had recently been changed and now contained only Star's name. No need for her to share with Gil now that he had new digs at the rec center. "If you aren't scared," Red said, "and you should be—well, at least act it."

"Red, I'm—"

"Shut up." She knocked on the door and we went in.

Star sat behind a heavy antique wooden desk. A brass lamp with green shade tossed a circle of golden light onto some papers there. She looked up, frowning when she spotted me.

"You didn't mention that Reverend Squires would be coming," Star said. "I thought you were bringing Don. To talk about the incident."

"We're here to talk about the incident," Red said. She pointed to a chair and looked at me. "Sit."

I did. I could tell Star was impressed. I stared at the floor, trying to look scared. Really, I was just trying to keep myself from sailing across the desk and throttling her.

Red sighed. "The problem here, in the legal sense, is that we are an understaffed community smack in the middle of hunting season with an open murder case on our hands. And there are seven new laws that need to be carefully enforced."

"Not new laws," Star said, voice cold. "Foundational laws no longer ignored."

Red swallowed. "We all want to do well by the law here. But the way things are going, we can't."

I said nothing.

"When I'm elected to Congress," Star said, "I'll make better policing a high priority. I mean, when we can't even rely on our clergy to uphold the law—" She let her voice trail away. "Christianity itself is in danger here!"

"Read your Bible," I said. "Jesus was a hell-raising lawbreaker. At least, that's what people in love with the law thought of him."

"Reverend Squires." Red's voice warned me to shut up. Then she sat in the other chair. "I think what we need here is a treaty. Some sort of deal that keeps you out of each other's way, at least until—"

"Until the election is over!" Star said. Her hands rested on the desk.

Red nodded. "Until the election."

Star smirked. "Why would I engage in any sort of agreement? Reverend Squires is well out of my way right now. She can't break the law with her irresponsible dog ownership any longer."

"I didn't—"

"Lonnie!"

I clamped my mouth shut.

Star liked what she saw going on between me and Red. "As I said, with the dog in the pound indefinitely." She paused to lick her lips. "And with Officer Loomis contemplating assault charges, I don't feel any need to reach any sort of agreement with Reverend Squires." She sat back, satisfied as a cat.

I half rose. "Let's get out of here."

"Sit. Down." Red said without moving. I sat. "I was thinking," Red continued, staring into space, "not so much about today's unfortunate events, but the future. Your future." She looked at Star. "As you said, the election season."

Star blinked. Interested.

"I was thinking that Lonnie might be able to help you, for instance, pick up your standings in the polls."

Star and I both snorted our surprise.

"In what way?" Star asked. Her hand swept across the room slowly. "She'll dust my office? That sort of picking up?"

"I can't help her," I said. "I can't."

"Your Aunt Katherine can," Red said to me. That caught me off guard.

Star leaned over her desk with slow deliberateness. "I've heard about a bequest." Her eyes locked on Red. "Are you talking about the bequest?"

I turned to Red as well. "I told you. I don't want my aunt's—"

"Nearly half a million dollars," Red said to Star. "Plus a car worth another hundred thousand."

"Only eighty—" I interjected, but Red cut me off.

"Money that only Reverend Squires has the power to get." She made a teepee of her fingers and waited.

Star's eyes narrowed as she studied Red.

But I'm not getting that money, I thought. *Especially not with Linus in trouble.*

"I wouldn't want it publicized," Star said.

"Understood," said Red.

I didn't understand.

"The car." Star raised relaxed fingers and wagged them. "Not my cup of tea. No offense."

"None taken," said Red.

"And the Reverend." Star even glanced toward me. "Not one word about this to the press, to the congregation, to an old man over coffee. Not one word to anyone."

Red nodded.

I wanted to ask if they remembered I was in the room. But something—probably my guardian angel—kept me silent.

"And not one word," Star said, "not one, you understand—against me or my initiatives. Not one law broken. Not one insinuation made."

"Done," said Red.

A smile snaked across Star's face. "I admire your confidence, Officer Carson. However, one thing I'm sure of is that no one controls Reverend Squires. I'm not even sure she can control herself. So along with your word, I'll need hers."

Slowly they both turned toward me. Red's eyes burned like lasers.

"It's your choice, Lonnie," Red said. "Things as they stand. Linus in the pound indefinitely. A potential assault charge. Yourself stuck here in the middle of a heart-breaking mess. Or." She leaned over her knees. "You agree to the conditions of your great-aunt's will. Call Maurice Brand. Go on that trip. Get that money. Then donate it all—"

"Except the car," Star interjected.

"All of it except the car to Star's campaign." Red waited, almost daring me to react. "And then, you heard the Councilwoman. You stay out of sight until after the election. No comments to anyone about anything." She clenched and unclenched her hands, her eyes never wavering from mine. "That's your choice."

"And no," Star said, "she can't think about it. We agree now, or there's no deal."

"How about if instead," I said, "I simply tell people about the little conspiracy to defraud the town you and Ivor Koontz put together last spring?"

Star didn't flinch. "Your word and Jack Putnam's against mine? Your credibility is shot, Reverend. And given the sorry performance of his security system at the recreation center, his is too." She traced a finger along the wood grain of the desk. "Funny thing about the pound. They get so overcrowded. Not all the animals can be kept."

"You—"

"Lonnie!" Red's voice stopped me.

My hands shook. "I want my dog now," I said. "And it's a deal."

Star barked a laugh. "Are you kidding me? Please? This isn't some television cop show, Lonnie. You don't make demands. I'm not doing anything for you or your dog until that money is in my election account." She waved me out of the room. "Go on. Get the money. Show me a check and proof that it will clear and we'll talk about releasing your dog."

I lurched to my feet, headed for Star, but Red stepped in front of me so fast her shoulder punched my ribs. "Done," she said. Then she slowly pointed a finger at Star. "That dog's well-being is your concern, Councilwoman. The minute he's out, he's going to a vet. If he has lost one pound, has one wound, so help me, I will personally destroy more than your campaign."

Star smiled and picked up a pen. "The dog will be well-kept. I'll see to it myself." She shuffled her papers into a stack. "Now I have work to do. Leave."

CHAPTER TWENTY-THREE

At 5:57 a.m. Friday morning, I raised a silver travel mug of scalding black coffee over my kitchen sink, toasting the sky where the palest pink light ribboned through the purple morning sky.

"Happy birthday to me."

I didn't mean it.

I stared at the tattered black suitcase. Silver duct tape held one seam together. I felt about the same. I hadn't had my dog for two whole days.

I grabbed a plastic grocery bag to fill with the road food I'd promised Marion. My cell phone rang as I raided the cupboards. "I won't forget your Pepsi." Who else would call at this hour but Marion?

"Happy birthday!" Marion sounded too cheery for my stomach. "Let's go take a trip in a super-keen race car."

"Look." I grunted as I filled the bag with Pringles, rainbow Gummi Bears, Three Musketeers bars, peppermint gum and a six-pack of Pepsi. "I'm doing this for one reason only. Get the money, give it to Star, get my dog back. There's nothing happy, super or keen about it."

She puffed into the receiver. "Oh, come on, Lonnie. We've got to spend the next three days in the car together. Aren't you going to enjoy it even a little?"

"No." I double-checked the deadbolt on the back door.

"Well, I am."

"Fine." I cast a glance around the kitchen to make sure I hadn't left anything out to invite mice. "But don't expect me to."

"Well, listen. I called to remind you to pack that little stun gun the girls got you."

I grabbed my raincoat from the closet and tossed it onto the pile by the door. "Why would I?"

She sighed her exasperation. "So you can tell the friends who love you that yes, you took it. You cherished it because they gave it to you. You felt safer with it."

"I'm about to leave the house. If I can find it, I'll toss it in." I stared at the electric lipstick in the bowl next to the door. Right where I'd put it. Right beneath the spot where Linus' leash usually hung.

I stuffed it in my pocket and headed off on my Great-Aunt Katherine's wild goose chase.

At her house, Marion threw more luggage into my old Honda than I thought the car could hold. We arrived at Carson's Car Care at 6:27. Right on time. About a hundred people milled around the parking lot in front of the old building.

"Everyone's here to see you off!" Marion said.

"Great." I didn't mean that either.

"I'm surprised there aren't more, what with all the 'Amazing Race to the Pearly Gates' coverage yesterday."

Artesia Collins' newest story. She'd jumped all over it as soon as word got out I'd decided to pursue Aunt Kate's bequest. Though I couldn't imagine anyone really cared about a priest in rural west Michigan driving an old car around the lake, the catch phrase caught. Journalists from Detroit and Chicago had called me yesterday for quotes. I'd blown them off. Told them to call Artesia. Of course, I'd blown her off too.

As I struggled with my stuff and half of Marion's, she plunged into the crowd, high-fiving people and waving to others. She was way too bright this morning with an orange fleece big shirt over a purple turtleneck, purple spandex pants and orange sandals with her usual four-inch spike heels. The nails on both hands and toes had been redone in orange with a purple spiral. A silver pendant of a flaming sun hung from each ear. Still, it made it easy to follow her in the crowd.

Smells of perfume and aftershave pressed against me as we walked.

"You go, girls," said a woman with coffee on her breath.

"Come back rich!" The man who patted my back had eaten onions for breakfast.

"Don't screw up the pictures, Marion!" Romee shouted from a cluster of uniformed Hot Flashes. Frozen breath hung in the air before them. I waved and mimed putting on lipstick, then patted my pocket. They laughed.

"Can I have a ride, Reverend?" I couldn't see the child who'd yelled it.

I won't be here long enough to give anyone a ride, I thought. *Get the money. Pay off Star. Get my dog back.* That much I'd told Marion.

But I had more planned: *Sell the car. Quit my job. Get the hell out of this crazy crazy town.*

That was my whole plan.

"Reverend Squires! Lonnie!" Artesia Collins shoved and wheedled her way through the press of bodies. I recognized a black-haired woman—Isabella had come. She stood next to Ivor, who stood next to Dale and the Zaloumi twins. Gil and Star were conspicuously absent.

Artesia bumped up against me. "You didn't call me back!"

"Been busy." I shifted one of Marion's giant totes on my shoulder, shoving her back accidentally on purpose.

"But we have a deal, right? I took that law story public. You're investigating the murder for me, right?" This quietly, under her breath.

"As best I can," I said. "But now, leave Star Hannes alone."

She looked stunned.

One of the Zaloumis slapped Marion on the back. "Can't believe that car's actually going somewhere after forty years!"

"More'n can be said for you," said the other twin, who slapped his brother on the back.

"Yeah, we never leave town either!" said the first twin.

"But wait!" Artesia trailed me. "What about this story with your aunt? The trip. The money."

"Great-aunt." I said. We'd almost reached the garage doors.

"They say that car's worth a lot," said Zaloumi Number One. Eddie I think. Because he didn't have a scar above his left eye.

"Yep," said Leon.

"Imagine something worth that much stashed away in a garage," said Eddie.

"Kept it safe," said Leon.

"Safest place in town," came Dale's deep voice. He waved. "Travel safe!"

Artesia kept following. "It's a blockbuster!"

"Go ahead. You have my blessing."

Marion had reached the door. She tried the handle, but it was locked. She knocked.

"Even bigger combined with the Super Sleuth thing. I think we could land a national feature. Network news." Artesia said.

I shifted my bags while Marion knocked again. "I'm not solving anything for anyone any more. Really. Artesia. I wish you luck. But I just can't help you."

"You'll change your mind!" Someone shoved her from behind and she tipped into me. "Call me when you do."

"I won't."

Her bottom lip poked out as the door swung open. Marion and I dove into the yawning black. Red clicked the door shut behind us and my body settled into the cold quiet. Dark stained tools lined the cinder block walls. One half of the room yawned empty except for a ramp and oil stains. In the other, a bright circle of light shone around the upraised hood of a vintage green speedster of some kind. The place smelled of oil and spent electricity, like my dad's old antique Lionel train when it shorted out every year underneath the Christmas tree.

"I don't see any car worth eighty thousand dollars." Marion's voice echoed. She nodded toward the speedster. "That's cute, but I hope that isn't our car, because the luggage won't fit."

"Yours is in the back."

Red led us through a padlocked door in the far wall into a separate, single stall. The roof slanted away from the main building, nearly hitting my head. A shaft of light beamed through a smudged window in another, external door. Dust danced in the light above a large car covered with soft cloth.

We dropped our bags as she lay her hands on the covered roof of the car. "Get the lights, would you?"

As the fluorescents buzzed and brightened, Red circled the car untying the cover. "Grab that other end," she said. "We'll lift together. Don't want to scratch the paint."

"Is it new paint?" Marion grabbed a corner.

"Factory original," said Red.

"That's sort of the point, Mare," I said, grabbing another corner. "Vintage car."

We lifted the cover and there it stood. A white two-door sedan with black interior and black tires, its chrome flickering.

"Welcome to The Pearly Gates." Red grinned and placed gentle hands on the hood.

"That's it?" Marion asked.

Red drew her face tight, like she'd sucked a lemon. She rolled the cloth cover tightly against her body as she spoke. "*That* is a 1966 Ford Fairlane factory-produced 427 500 XL. It has a four-twenty-seven cubic inch, four hundred and twenty-five horse-power dual four b.b.l. solid lifter engine, a side oiler, medium riser V-eight, four-speed big spline top loader, and fiberglass hood. It's a super stock racer."

She might as well have been speaking Martian.

"The engine," Red continued, "is an R code, prepped for drag racing by Holman-Moody. It has less than seven hundred miles on it. Everything about this car is factory original and you can prove it. The numbers all match. And it's virtually unmarked."

Marion circled the car. "I can't see how any car worth eighty grand isn't red. Or black. Or some rockin' color. This is just plain old white." She bent and looked inside. "Plain old black on the inside. Bench seats." She stood and banged on the roof. "Not even a convertible."

"This is Wimbledon White." Red tossed the cover onto a workbench. "An original hue made only for this model."

"I guess it's a little pearly." Marion sounded doubtful.

"It wasn't named for the color." Red glanced at me but I shrugged. "The Pearly Gates was her racing name. You know, the entrance to the promised land—the winner's circle."

"Oh." Marion stopped next to me at the front of the car. "I like the stacked headlights. And the big grille. And you don't see shiny bumpers much anymore." She nudged me. "Real metal, no fiberglass."

I slung a bag toward the trunk. "Let's get this show on the road."

"Not a word of appreciation?" Red asked.

"What's that scoopy thing on the hood?" Marion asked. "That looks pretty cool."

Red shot me a look before she walked to the front of the car to answer Marion. "That's a functional air scoop. Whole hood is fiberglass. Light enough to lift off."

"So, does this go fast?" Marion asked.

"Like a bat out of hell," said Red. "It has a trap speed of 101 miles per hour."

Marion smiled. "Speed trap?"

"She said trap speed," I said. "Can you open the trunk please?"

"Trap speed is how fast a car can do a quarter mile from a stop," said Red.

Marion smiled. "I'm liking Pearl better!"

"And that was with the car's age and the original tires," Red said, "which were nothing compared to what we have now. This car has amazing engine potential." She put her hands on her hips. "You have new tires."

"Cool." Marion tapping the wheels, again channeling her inner mechanic. "Check it out. The wheels are painted to match the car."

Something struck me for the first time. I turned to Red. "How did my aunt keep this thing a secret? And why did she bother?"

"My dad just let people think it was his, I guess. He didn't talk much about it. I know your aunt would sometimes meet him out of town, late at night, so she could drive it fast on empty roads." She shrugged. "You know your aunt better than I do."

"I was hoping for an answer better than 'she was nuts.'"

Red handed me a key ring with two keys on it. "Have a look."

Marion glanced at the keys. "No clicker. That will take some getting used to."

I slid the key into the door lock, turned it and the button popped up on the door.

"And you have to reach over to let me in." Marion waited by the passenger door.

I slipped my hand around the silver door handle and pushed the knob with my thumb. "I don't think I've opened a door like this since I was a kid." I tugged at the door and it barely moved. I took a better hold, leaned away from it and slowly it creaked open.

"Big doors. Heavy construction. " Red sounded a little like a salesman.

I stuck my head in. "Leather?"

Red patted the inside of the door. "Best pseudo-leather vinyl money could buy."

"And windows you have to roll up and down!" I slid into the front seat and glanced over the dashboard. "This is like entering a time machine."

"Will you open my door for the goddess' sake? I want to see!" Marion pounded a fist against the window.

I leaned to reach the other door's lock and the gear shift handle jabbed me in the ribs. "This car's a boat."

Red squatted beside me just inside the door. "The regular version of this car was marketed as a family car. You know, lots of interior leg and luggage room. But I'll tell you what. These seats," she slapped the side of mine, "are damned uncomfortable after an hour. And the backseat is even worse."

The car bounced as Marion tested her seat. "It's sort of like sitting on a foam block."

"Well, street races were usually pretty short. And no matter how Ford advertised them, even the family version of this was a thinly disguised racer. So if you find an empty highway in the U.P. and open her up, call me. I'd love to hear how fast she can go."

"You got it!" Marion grabbed her open door and pulled. "Urgh! It's practically impossible to pull this shut." When she did, the car rocked with the slam. "Still, it has good energy." She ran her hands over the expansive black dashboard.

"No radio," I said.

"Yeah, but check out that the speedometer." Marion pointed an orange nail to the speedometer, which filled most of the horizontal space on the dash.

I gripped the black steering wheel tightly. "This feels too close."

"You can't adjust it. That's a later luxury." Red pointed to several knobs on the dash. "Lights. Windshield wipers. No intermittent, remember. Cigarette lighter."

Everything was covered in shining chrome.

Marion popped open the glove compartment. "Whooee! You could keep a twenty-pound turkey in here."

I settled my hand across the large chrome T that was the gear handle. It felt cool.

Marion snapped the glove compartment shut and turned toward the backseat. "Plenty of room back there for the pup."

I froze.

"You know. When he's back," she said.

"Let's load up," I said.

Marion struggled mightily to open her car door. "This must be why my mom would never drive a two-door." She swung her legs and gently kicked the door open. "It would be easier to get out of a lunar capsule, she used to say."

"Just be careful with it," Red said. "Any damage will lower the value of the car."

"Typical Aunt Kate crap." I looked at Marion. "She's probably hoping I'll tell you not to drink Pepsi or eat Pringles in the car.

That I'll never let my dog ride in it. That I won't have the dash altered so that I can at least listen to some decent music."

Red winced.

"She wants me to fuss and feel guilty and anxious the whole time I'm on this birthday trip of hers."

All three of us stared at the car. The fluorescent lights buzzed.

"She's dead, Lon," Marion said.

Somehow, that didn't matter. "Let's get going," I said. "I want my dog."

We tossed all of our luggage—my suitcase and soccer ball and Marion's half dozen totes—into the cavernous trunk.

Red handed me a small plastic tool box. "Most of what you might need is in there. A few specialized tools. Duct tape."

Marion slammed the trunk shut. "Atta girl, Pearl!"

Red and I walked back toward the driver's door.

"Hang on," said Marion, bending by the back bumper. "Just one finishing touch."

"What are you—" I started.

"No bumper stickers!" Red shouted.

We rushed back. There on the shining chrome of the back bumper was a sticker for Woman at the Well Episcopal Church, with a cute little drawing of a church.

Marion beamed. "Kids and I drew that in permanent marker for the car."

I swallowed.

Red bit her lip.

Marion laughed. "Oh, for the sake of the good goddess, look at you. It's a magnet!" She peeled it off, then stuck it back on. Red didn't laugh.

Marion got into Pearl, situating her purse, small cooler, and tote bag with camera, maps, guidebooks and a clipboard of information she'd gotten from Brand. "Let's do this, RevLon."

I slid in.

"One last thing," Red said. "Pearly Gates takes super premium only."

"Yow!" shrieked Marion. "Doesn't that cost like four bucks a gallon?"

"More up north," said Red.

I gripped the steering wheel. "I suppose the car gets about fifteen miles to the gallon too."

Red grinned. "You wish. More like eight in the city, twelve or thirteen on the highway."

"I brought my charge card."

"Then we've got to make it around the lake and get your aunt's money so you can pay off the gas bills," said Marion.

"Not my money, remember?" I had, of course, told her about the deal with Star.

"Where are the cup holders in this thing?" Marion held a can of diet aloft.

"Got to hold it the old-fashioned way," Red said. "Between your thighs."

Marion winced. "Oh, I remember that. Warms your drink up way too fast." She shoved the can between her round thighs and looked at me. She braced an arm against the dash. "Ready, Batman."

Red hit a button on the wall to raise the back garage door. People peered around the opening to get a look at the car.

Red bent through the open driver's window, her face electrically close to mine. "Tell me you know how to drive a stick."

I nodded.

"Atomic batteries to power," Marion chanted.

"If you run into trouble, just call. I know the car like the back of my hand. I grew up helping Dad tinker with it." Red looked us up and down.

"Turbines to speed!" Marion yelled.

"I know you don't want to hear this— "I began.

"You're welcome," Red said.

I looked at her. "It's about the case. Dale Zeerip. He works for Ivor Koontz. He's convinced Ivor's involved in Koeman's death. And he's afraid to talk to you."

Red frowned. "When did you—"

I held up my hand. "Last week. But I saw him outside and it made me think I should mention it to you. Just in case."

She studied me. "Okay. But no more!"

"Nope. Just want my dog back." I checked that the car was in neutral, then turned the key. The engine rumbled and the car vibrated underneath me.

"Woot!" Marion shouted over the engine. "My girl Pearl rocks!" She started shouting the theme song from the Sixties Batman TV series.

"One last thing," Red shouted. "Sometimes the accelerator pedal falls off. Don't let that scare you."

Just the thought scared me. "Are you kidding?"

Red shook her head. "Just stop the car and slip it back on. You'll see how it fits." Red patted the door twice.

Well, Aunt Kate, you got your way. I pressed in the clutch and shifted the car into first. I eased the clutch out until the gear caught and lurched the car forward.

"Here we go!" Marion drummed her hands on the dash. "Here we go!" Then she thrust both her arms out her window and waved at everyone.

A glance in the rearview mirror showed Red leaning in the garage doorway, waving slowly back. Maurice Brand stood next to her, looking tight but happy. Everyone else milled around waving. I felt a little like Dorothy leaving Munchkinland for Oz.

Saving our dogs. Appeasing the witches.

"Ding dong, the witch is dead," I whispered under my breath. Not yet. But I could hope.

CHAPTER TWENTY-FOUR

After a few minutes, I realized driving Pearl wasn't going to be easy. Shifting went okay, but turning was nearly impossible. I pulled hand over hand against the tires. "I'll have bulging biceps by the time we finish this trip."

"No power steering. No power brakes either." Marion sipped her soda. "If you have to stop fast, remember to pump 'em."

I hoped we wouldn't be stopping fast, or doing anything even remotely exciting with this car. I wanted to sell it to some rich collector. Take my money and run.

"Oh, goddess," Marion mumbled, rotating her head to look at the window beside her. "Where is the seat belt?"

"Shit. I never forget my seat belt." I slid my hand along the crease between the seat's back and bottom.

Marion pulled two ends of a lap belt from either side of her square seat. "Just like in an airplane."

I found the ends of my belt, but couldn't snap them with just one hand. On the first straight stretch of road out of town, I steadied the wheel with my leg and clicked the belt together.

"You're driving with your knee," Marion said. "Where'd you learn that?"

"My first boyfriend. High school."

First and last boyfriend, I almost said.

"It's tough to get a date in Middelburg," Marion said. "I was lucky to find Denny. You want me to get some friends from Holland to help fix you up?"

I swallowed. "I'm fine. Where to first?"

Marion glanced at her clipboard. "Grand Haven and the world's only musical fountain!" She read silently for a minute. "It only plays at night, though, so we won't get to see the synchronized light show."

I glanced at the dash where a clock should be, but there was none. So I checked my watch. "We should be there before eight. Get the photo, keep moving."

Marion glanced at me. "Are you going to be any fun on this trip?"

"No," I said. "None."

We drove north on U.S. 31 for about twenty minutes in silence. "There!" Marion pointed to a beached U.S. Coast Guard craft sitting in the median. "Left. There."

Grand Haven's downtown was bigger than Middelburg's, but not big by any other definition. A county municipal building sat atop a hill, all whitewash and Greek columns. Neon "Open" signs flashed blue and red in the front windows of a brightly lit diner. One shop had kayaks in the front window, joined by a yellow banner announcing a Fall Clearance. Nine black mailboxes poked off the front of a three-story Victorian house, sky blue with white gingerbreading. The mailboxes didn't belong, like zits on a chin. Clearly the old beauty had been chopped into apartments.

I braked as the street narrowed to a one-lane road in a three-block shopping area. The buildings lining the street were perfect rectangles, most brick, many with concrete ornamentation on their facades.

"Where's the fountain?"

"The map says straight."

The road ended in a T and the only thing I saw ahead was an old railway station of red brick and leaded windows and the channel, its water thick and gray under the morning sky.

"Hey, look!" Marion tapped her window and waved. "They're checking out Pearl!"

Sure enough, a few people on the street stared at us as we passed. Marion waved. One woman with an infant strapped to her chest waved back. Behind her a well-tanned redheaded farmer in a green John Deere cap turned to watch us pass.

Marion waved again. "Everyone loves Pearl."

I stopped, though the light was green. I didn't see a fountain and I didn't know which way to turn. The black SUV behind me honked.

"Turn right into this lot," Marion said. "We'll find it."

I hauled the steering wheel to the right and puffed. "No one told me I needed to bulk up for this adventure."

Marion leaned forward and tapped the windshield, pointing toward the nearest building. "There's a coffee shop over there."

"You're drinking soda." I hauled on the wheel some more. "Get the picture. Get out—puff—of here."

"There!" She pointed to the first non-handicapped empty spot in the lot closest to the coffee shop's door, between a van and a hulking SUV.

"I don't know if I can swing the car in there."

Marion wrinkled her face. "The goddess and I provided you with a perfectly good spot. Envision yourself pulling in."

I sighed. "I'll try."

"Only do. But let me out first," Marion said, grabbing her purse, "so I don't have to try to squeeze out this door in that tiny space."

She kicked and heaved her way out of the car then waved me on. Even if I'd been driving Pearl for years and knew exactly where the enormous body started and ended, I couldn't have gotten it into that parking space on the first try. Today, it took me five.

Marion applauded when I finally turned the engine off. "You did it!"

A polished young woman, her blond hair drawn back into a pony tail which bounced against her hunter green sweater, slid against Pearl to enter the SUV parked next to it. As I pulled myself out of the driver's seat, the woman opened her own car door. "Maybe next time," the woman flashed perfectly even and blindingly white teeth, "you shouldn't use your husband's car."

"I gotta pee," Marion said, "so I'll order. Double mocha latte?"

"I want a photo of the fountain. That's all."

She pouted, but followed me as I turned back toward the water. Though larger, Grand Haven reminded me of Middelburg. Clean, beautiful trees and flowers. Newly painted shops with bright signs. Young mothers jogging with all-terrain strollers, their tots wearing thick sweaters with fall leaves or schoolhouses or boats knit into the designs. All were Caucasian; most were blond and well-tanned, even in October.

The old train station bore a hand-painted sign, black on white, that proclaimed it the local museum. It wasn't open until noon.

"The Musical Fountain ought to be right here." Marion stood, one hand on a hip, facing the channel. "That's what the map said."

"Not Kate's map," I said. "Right? I mean, we did double-check that this stuff all still exists, right?"

"Brand did." Marion stepped around the building. "There's a whole lot of bleachers back here."

Empty bleachers that faced nothing except the flat surface of the channel and the blank hill of long brown grass across the water. "Bizarre."

"Maybe it's in the channel," Marion said.

"Oh, please," I said. "A fountain's a fountain. You know, concrete. Water shooting in the air." I wanted to kick something. "First stop and we're already screwed."

"No, look." She pointed to a blackboard with white removable letters. *Grand Haven's Musical Fountain*, it said, with show times on Friday and Saturday, all after dark.

"Where?" I flapped my hands, exasperated.

"Hey, hey!" Marion flagged down a lanky teenaged boy

gliding a longboard toward us. He wore a backpack that must've weighed forty pounds. "Excuse me."

He jumped off the board and scooped it up, then tugged on his baggy camo pants. "Hey, it's after Labor Day, okay? And I only rode about ten feet, okay? Lighten up." He ducked his head to walk away, but Marion stopped him.

"No, wait, please. We need your help."

The boy slung his eyes toward us, then pulled silver and black headphones from his ears. "Okay. What?"

Marion pointed to the sign. "This says there's a fountain here, but we can't find it."

The boy scanned Marion, then me, evidently deciding we weren't joking. "The water squirts up over there." He pointed to the hill on the other side of the water. "From a couple of places, okay? Lights over there." He pointed to two tall light towers near the bleachers. "Sit here." His thumb jerked toward the bleachers. He shrugged. "People like you love it. Summer, not everyone can even get in 'cause of the crowds." He dropped his board, steadying it with one foot.

"How can I get a picture of it?" I asked.

"Come back at night." He pulled his headphones back over his ears and pushed himself away.

I had to find the fountain. I needed it. I needed Linus. "I need that fucking fountain."

Marion studied the hill. "Since we can't see a fountain, maybe this sign, with the bleachers would work for the picture."

"How we gonna get the car in the picture?" I asked. "The old train station's in the way." I rubbed my face. I realized with a horrid sinking feeling that I had to rely on my Great-Aunt Kate's planning to save my dog. I thought I might throw up.

"What if we just jumped the curb for a second, pulled up here, took the photo and drove away?" Marion held up her coffee cup like a surveyor's tool. "It'd only take about thirty seconds. Worst we'll get is a ticket."

I shot her a look to let her know the crack about tickets was not funny. "This should be easier."

Marion stood in front of me to grab my full attention. "Rev, this is not hard. You jump the curb for thirty measly seconds. I take the photo and we're gone. Look." She waved her hand at the sidewalk beneath us. "We won't even smoosh any grass."

I watched the steady stream of traffic. "I don't know."

"So a few people honk. We can survive that." She paused. "Star isn't here."

Maybe, I thought. But Aunt Kate was. Kate and her demands. "Okay," I said. "But do it fast."

Marion slapped me on the back. "Kick ass."

CHAPTER TWENTY-FIVE

It took me three tries to get the car out of the parking place and then, suddenly, we drifted toward the plaza. "I don't know about this."

"Nonsense. It's an adventure." Marion poised like a runner in blocks, her hand on the door. "I'll be really fast."

A glance in my mirror revealed only three cars behind me, none cops. "Here we go!"

With a push on the gas, I popped the car over the curb in a series of solid thunks that lurched everything in the car.

"Hey! You dumped my bags!" Marion bent her not insubstantial torso to gather the stuff that had flown about the floor and seat.

My stomach clenched. "Leave it! Get the picture!"

"I can't!" Marion thrust the camera at me. "I haven't put the memory card in yet. It was in my bag."

Behind us a car honked. Sweat stuttered onto my forehead. "Come on!"

Pencils, tissues, gum, a compact—it all flew past my head as Marion's hands flashed across the junk from her purse in search of the memory card.

Another honk.

My stomach bolted. I regripped the wheel. "I'm getting us out of here." I shifted into first.

"No, no!" Marion unsnapped her lap belt and reached up to the edge of the floor mat. "Got it." She held the tiny plastic-cased card up like a fine diamond. "Just let me snap it in."

I waved meekly at the snarling lip of the woman who drove past, staring. But I didn't take it out of gear.

"Okay, okay!" Marion unlatched her car door, and leaned against it. "Damn thing's heavy." She jammed her shoulder into it. The door lurched wider, then swung shut again.

The sedan that had been behind us stopped in the road next to us, the driver holding her hands in the air in disgust.

My pulse pounded in my neck. "Quick, before someone calls the cops!"

Marion swung her legs and kicked the door open. "My shoe!" She bent forward to retrieve the orange sandal, effectively mooning me through purple spandex. The car honked loudly.

"We're okay," I waved, pretending I thought the other driver was worried about us. "Marion, forget it!" I yelled to her. "We'll think of something else."

"No way." Marion hopped around the back of the Fairlane. She waved the camera at the other cars. "We're tourists. From out of town!"

I shifted into neutral and sunk in my seat. *Damn it, Aunt Kate, this is not funny.*

Marion suddenly stood by the driver's window. "Hold your head up, Rev, or I won't see you."

I watched her try to frame the picture. Then she lowered the camera. "Won't work. I'm too close to get the sign too. Gotta go into the street." She held up her shoe like a traffic cop and confidently stepped into the street.

A red pickup stopped and let her walk in front of him.

"Okay, Rev, smile!" Marion held the camera to her face. Then she scowled and pulled it away. "It's all dark."

It was all I could do not to drive away and leave Marion standing there, a redheaded woman wearing a flaming orange shirt carrying one matching sandal, trying to get a digital camera to work in the middle of a street in Grand Haven, Michigan.

"Just press the button," I said, "to turn it on again."

Marion scowled at the camera, then grinned, nodding.

Cars behind her began to honk short, polite honks. The young man driving the pickup rolled down his window. "That's one boss car, lady. Sixty-six or sixty-seven?"

I forced a smile at his stubble, at his camo ball cap with a deer head embroidered on the front. At the NRA sticker glinting from his side window. "Sixty-six."

Marion dipped and bobbed in the middle of the street like a disco dancer. "Can't quite get it all in. Just one more sec."

"Cool," the young man said. "It looks cherry. Hey, you want me to take a picture of you and your friend?"

"No!" I held up my hand. "Thanks, no."

"Got it!" Marion looked at the camera's small screen. "Yep, it's a keeper." She hobbled back to the Fairlane, waving her shoe at cars in both directions. "Thanks. Thanks so much."

"You ladies have fun," the young man said, grinding his truck into gear.

I waited just long enough for Marion to plop into her seat before I gassed Pearl out of there. An unsmiling mustached man paused his Saturn and waved me into traffic.

"Hey! I haven't got my seat belt on yet! Or my shoe! Plus my stuff is all over!"

"No more stopping traffic for photos," I said.

"What are you fussing about? We got a great picture. And that young man liked Pearl." Marion patted the dashboard. "Pearl likes to hear a compliment or two, don't ya, girl?"

"I don't care what Pearl likes to hear, I—" I stopped myself. Why the hell was I arguing about what the car liked?

"Ah, but look, Rev. You broke a law and nothing bad happened. The world outside of Middelburg is normal."

I looked at her, my skin sweaty, my stomach sour. "Nothing's normal, Marion. I still don't have my dog."

She nodded. "I know, hon. But we are going to get him back." Then she waved her clipboard like a call to arms and shouted, "Next stop, a submarine!"

It didn't take long to get to Muskegon. I had a momentary glitch—a breath-holding, eye-closing moment when the highway crossed a drawbridge. It bucked as Pearl and other heavy traffic crossed it. My stomach climbed into my throat. But I said nothing and breathed my way through it. Marion didn't even notice.

The road into Muskegon sure differed from Middelburg or Grand Haven. Here, Sixties-era shopping malls, boarded-up buildings, construction equipment dealers and a few questionable-looking motels lined the street.

"Check that out!" Marion pointed to a restaurant called The Cherokee. Its hand-painted sign announced "Good Food," though you had to walk through a shingled teepee to get it.

"You know where we're going, right?"

Marion pointed to a small brown sign for the USS Silversides National Monument. We followed it and many identical others, winding through increasingly nicer neighborhoods until we reached the flat, sandy, wind-whipped Lake Michigan shoreline. The fine white sand spread thick fingers across the road as we curved north along the edge of the gorgeous state park.

"I read online that they use bulldozers to keep the sand off the road here," Marion said.

The beach looked lonely. Regularly placed metal barrels had tipped in the wind and the black trash bags lining them lashed against their openings. One couple wrapped in wool blankets meandered near the waterline. In the distance, a pier jutted out into the whitecaps. On our right, small cottages with enormous porches sat empty, shuttered for the winter. They had no yards, just sand.

We drove more than a mile before the road turned to follow the channel, a lane of water lined with huge white boulders and bright blue railing. Soon, the submarine appeared, tied to the channel wall.

I pulled us into the empty gravel parking lot right next to the sub. We took a minute to finish picking up the stuff that had flown all over the car when we jumped the curb in Grand Haven. Then Marion leaped out, her hair whipping in the lake wind, snapped the photo and slid back in. "Can I drive now?"

As I walked to the other side of the car, I noticed the nearby trees hung with aging green leaves, yellowing at the tops. The ship hulked above us, gray, pocked and empty. Tiny replicas of the Japanese flag lined the control tower, like notches in a gun. Kills. I imagined most of the men who lived and worked on this weren't killers. But when threatened, you did things you wouldn't normally do. Like Ashleigh slugging Randy Koeman. Me attacking Don Loomis. We all needed to survive, to protect our loved ones. Maybe Koeman's murderer had done the same.

I got into the car and Marion revved the engine loud and long.

"Try not to use up all the gas in the parking lot, okay?" I pulled the Pringles from my tote and tossed them onto the seat between us.

Marion woofed as she hauled on the wheel to turn us out of the parking lot. "You weren't kidding about this building up your muscles."

I munched a Pringle in reply and watched the sand folding over itself in the wind.

"So," Marion said. "You want to talk?"

"'Bout what?"

"Oh, I don't know. Girl talk." She sounded suspiciously chipper. "You know, secrets."

I leaned away from her. "Secrets?"

"Sure." Marion kept her eyes glued to the road. Not typical. She was one of those hands-flying, never-look-at-the-road drivers. Something was up. "You know, stuff you never get to talk about at home, 'cause, well, it's home. But here, anything goes. You know. What happens in the Pearly Gates stays in the Pearly Gates."

I recognized the tactic—I used it with Isabella Koontz when

I tried to reassure her it would be okay to talk about the abuse at home without directly asking her. Marion was asking me if I was gay!

"There's nothing I want to talk about," I said. "Thanks."

"Okay." She shrugged with overstated vigor. "Next up, the world's largest crucifix."

CHAPTER TWENTY-SIX

Since we had a good three hours to our next destination according to the itinerary Brand had given Marion, I decided to work ahead a bit on next week's sermon. The New Testament reading came from the middle of Matthew 22. The Pharisees are trying to trick Jesus by asking him if taxes should be paid to Rome and he utters the famous line about giving to Caesar what is Caesar's and to God what is God's.

There was something there that applied to the whole Faithful Heritage Initiative in Middelburg, I just knew it. I'd gotten about three sentences down when my cell rang. I hoped it was Red. Caller ID said it was my mother.

I tapped my pen against my teeth.

It rang again and Marion's eyes slid toward me. "Aren't you gonna answer that?"

"I'm writing. I can talk to my mom later."

"But it's your birthday." Her hand shot for my phone. I tried to stop her, but too late. "Hel-lo, Missus Squires. It's Marion Freeley."

I tossed my pen at her shoulder.

Marion stuck her tongue out. "Good to talk to you too."

"Give me that phone," I said.

"Ye-e-e-s," Marion said. "You'd like to speak with her?"

I grabbed my pen and pretended to jab her.

"Yep," she said. "We're up and out early celebrating her birthday." Pause.

"Don't tell her what we're doing," I whispered. "Just give me the phone."

"Ooh," Marion said, still to my mother, "that sounds nasty." A long pause.

What on God's green earth was my mother telling Marion now? The story of my surprise birth, four weeks early, in the lingerie section of Marshall Field's? My fifth birthday party when she freaked out after I, having been forced to wear a dress, had reasoned I could wear pajama bottoms instead of underwear so I could play football with boys? Any other of the many traumas that occurred annually in conjunction with the anniversary of my birth?

"Seven stitches?" Marion glanced at me.

That would be my third birthday, when Cassie, then five, had fallen and cut her head on the brick patio wall. My party got canceled in favor of an afternoon in the ER.

"Give me the phone." I held out my hand. "Please?"

But Marion seemed to be holding her breath, her cheeks puffed and reddening, her eyes wide.

Suddenly she let out a burst of laughter and arched her eyebrows. "You're kidding me!"

"Give me the phone," I said.

"And everyone saw it? Was she in huge trouble?"

"Give me the phone!" I snapped my fingers.

"Uh, Mrs. Squires, Lonnie would like to speak with you." Pause. "Yes, ma'am, I'll keep a close eye on her." She handed the phone to me and whispered, "She loves you."

"Hap-py birth-day, sweet-ee!" Mom always sounded like she

was singing for a children's album whenever she talked to me or my sisters. It was even worse with the grandkids.

"Thanks. Couldn't celebrate it without you." I pushed the tiny phone between my ear and shoulder and picked up my pen.

Mom giggled, high-pitched and childlike. I heard the clatter of pans in the sink in the background. "Without me or the Marshall Field's lingerie department. That lovely assistant manager, Derrick. He gave me that Dior nightie to—"

"I know, Mom, I know." The phone had slipped down my cheek, away from my ear and Mom's voice had become a tin buzz.

"Or Cassie's exceptional behavior for a two-year-old. Everyone said how—"

"How exceptional she was while I was being born. Yeah, Mom, I know." I heard it every year.

"You're exceptional, too, honey." Then came the deafening grind of the garbage disposal—my mom never talked on the phone without running appliances at the same time. "In fact, I was just telling Cassie how proud I am of you."

"For what?" I drew my version of an ancient Roman coin and outlined Caesar's profile on it.

Silence. "For being—well, for being you."

I did love my mom. "Yeah, Mom. Thanks. It is nice to hear from you. How's Dad?" Since they'd remarried my father almost never came to the phone.

"Fine, of course." She paused during unidentifiable pounding. "You didn't happen to hear from your Aunt Katherine today, did you dear?"

I nearly dropped my pen. "Aunt Kate?"

Marion lifted her eyebrows.

Mom sighed. "When you were little, she always so looked forward to your thirty-fifth birthday. And giving you a present. Too bad she died first."

I didn't remember this.

"Uh-oh, sweetie, you're silent. You are thirty-five today, right?" Mom sounded genuinely worried. "My math isn't off, is it? You know I'm not good at math."

"Your math is fine. I was just wondering about the Aunt Kate thing."

"Oh!" I could feel her relief through the phone.

"What did she say about my birthday?"

"Oh, honey, it's not important. Did I tell you that your father says happy birthday too? He—"

"Mom! It is important!" I exchanged a glance with Marion. "What did she say?"

Now it was my mom's turn to be silent. Water rushed in the background.

"Mom! Quit cleaning the kitchen and talk to me."

"I think she first mentioned it when you were sixteen or so. You'd been visiting her for a few years. One time when I dropped you off. Or picked you up. I'm not really sure."

"You knew about all this?" I couldn't believe it. I smacked Marion's shoulder. "She knew about this. Mom, what did Kate tell you?"

"I don't—except she—" Her words began to beep out. "I think my call waiting's buzzing, dear. I'll call you later."

I gripped the phone to keep her with me. "No, Mom! Tell me what Aunt Kate said."

"Lonnie, honey, it's Cassie—kids calling from Texas."

"MOTHER! Why did Aunt Kate do this?"

"I don't know—wanted you—invited to party—be left out. So she—your own party—Bye-bye, Lon." She made a smooching sound.

"Mom!" When she clicked off I threw the phone in the glove box. "Damn it. My entire family, dead and alive, drives me nuts."

"Everyone's family drives them nuts," Marion said. "It's part of the definition of family. What'd she say about Kate?"

I scribbled on my pad. "I don't know. Something about me not getting invited to parties or having my own party or something. She kept cutting out."

Party, I wrote. *I never get invited to their parties.* What did she mean? Whose parties? Who did Aunt Kate think was cutting me out?

I stared at the words. I'd heard them before.

Jack Putnam. Jack had said it about Ivor. Or Randy. Someone. I couldn't quite remember. But he'd been hiding something when he said it, my gut told me.

I pulled my phone back out of the cavernous glove compartment.

"Calling Mom back?" Marion asked.

"No." I searched for Jack Putnam in my contacts.

"Oh, no." The car swerved onto the gravel shoulder as Marion lunged for my phone. I yanked it away. "No calling home. No investigating that murder."

"It's not about the case. I have to make a few—uh—pastoral calls. I'm still a priest, you know."

I could tell by the thrust of her lower lip that Marion didn't believe me. "You promised Red."

Indeed. But this wasn't really investigating. It was following up on something I'd already heard. Something that could help Red. I wouldn't bug her with it unless Jack gave me something that could help. I owed her that much.

Jack answered on the first ring.

"Last time we talked," I said, "you mentioned something about not getting invited to parties with Ivor and Koeman. Being cut from their team. Did you mean they partied together?"

"This doesn't sound like a pastoral call to me," Marion grumped.

"I'm a little too old to fuss about getting left off some party list," Jack said.

Are you? I wondered. *Are any of us?* "None of us likes to be on the outside looking in."

"Get used to it if you're going to stay in Middelburg, Lon."

Mental note: yet another reason to move away as soon as I got my dog back. I didn't want to wind up like Jack.

"I heard that Ivor and Randy Koeman got into a bit of a fight the week before Randy died. At work. You around to see that?"

"Hang up," said Marion.

Jack seemed happy to change the subject. "Something about overtime pay rates is all I heard."

Something wasn't right. "How come you didn't mention this when we talked before? At the rec center?"

"Didn't know it then. Just found out yesterday. One of the guys on the crew mentioned it, you know, after Randy's funeral."

I'd skipped that, what with getting ready for this trip and the bad publicity. "Anybody else complaining about pay?" I asked.

Jack laughed. "Would you?"

"So look, Jack. About the party thing. Why protect them?" It was a shot in the dark, but it must have been in the right direction, because Jack was silent. "You are protecting them. Why?" I remembered what Ashleigh had told me. "Was it on Thursday nights?"

Jack sighed. "Look, Lonnie. I was never part of it. Talk to someone who was."

"Who? Jack, who? Give me a name, please."

"I can't Lonnie. I don't want it on my head. It isn't my business."

"Please, Jack! I—" He had clicked off.

"End of phone calls." Marion grabbed for the phone. I yanked it away and Pearl spun tires on the gravel strip along the road.

"Careful, Marion! You're going to ditch us!"

She bumped us back onto the pavement. "You're the one who needs to be careful, Lon. You're way out of bounds here."

I studied my phone. "One more call, Marion. I'm onto something. One more call. In case it's something Red can use."

Marion didn't like it, but she let me call Isabella Koontz. I knew her kids would be at school and her husband at work. I hadn't spoken to her since she'd missed the meeting. I had every good reason to call her cell.

When she heard my voice, Isabella sounded both happy and not happy that it was me.

"I've missed you at church," I said. "Honestly missed you."

"Thanks," Isabella said. "Things have been so busy. With the kids."

"You be nice to her," Marion whispered.

"I thought you were on that trip?" Isabella asked. "After all that money?"

"I am. But Marion's driving so I could call you."

"Where are you?"

I looked at the expanse of grass and trees and fields on either side of the highway. "Where are we?" I asked Marion.

"North of Big Rapids," said Marion, loud enough for Isabella to hear.

"Beautiful there," Isabella said. "I camped up there when I was a girl."

"Life was simpler then, huh?" I waited while she waxed on about her father's love for camping. "Isabella, are you okay? Is there anything you want to talk about? You know, while we have some time, just the two of us?"

"What happens in the Pearly Gates," whispered Marion, "stays."

"No," Isabella said. "Everything's fine. I'll be back to church soon. Just a few things to get taken care of first."

"I'm sorry if I upset Ivor the other day," I said. "You know, showing up at the job site. Talking to people."

"You shouldn't do that, Lonnie." Isabella's tone was urgent now. "Just stay out of his line of sight. You can't beat him. He's too strong."

I wondered if that's what she told herself. Her girls.

"I'm sorry if that made life harder for you." Maybe it couldn't get much harder, I thought. "I need to ask, about Thursday nights. Ivor wasn't home with you last week Thursday, was he?"

"Lonnie!" Marion stuck out her hand. "Give me that phone!"

"Isabella? It's okay. You won't get in trouble for covering for him."

"I don't need to cover for him!" Isabella's voice caught with a sob. "He didn't do anything wrong. I was confused. You confused me. Ivor says you are always confusing me. Messing with people's minds all over town."

"Where was he, Isabella?"

"It was Thursday." She sounded angry now, defiant. "He was at Bible study, okay?"

Woman at the Well didn't have a Bible study on Thursday nights. "But we—"

"He goes to a men's Bible study at Frontline, okay? That's why I didn't want to tell you. Why he has me keep it a secret. So we wouldn't hurt your feelings!" A sob hiccupped across her breath. "He doesn't fit the Episcopal scene so well. He just comes because I love it. The girls love it. He comes for us, Lonnie. *For us.*"

I didn't quite know what to say, so I just thanked her and wished her well.

"Give me that damn phone," Marion said and I did. She tossed it under her side of the seat. "You are done. You are on a trip with me. We are going to get you rich and save your dog. And between now and then, we are going to have fun. Right now. In this moment. Seize the day. Live in the present. No more worrying about the crap going on back home. Got it?"

CHAPTER TWENTY-SEVEN

Pretty soon the rhythmic ka-thump of wheels over sections of highway knocked me right out. When I woke up, we were pulling onto a two-lane road and my knee was killing me.

"Where?" I mumbled.

"M-55," Marion said. "Getting off soon. I have to pee. And the gas pedal fell off back there so it's a little hard to drive."

I rubbed my eyes. "Me too." Then I replayed what she'd just said. "The gas pedal fell off? How're you—?"

"The stick thingy's still there, so I'm pushing on that, but it isn't too comfortable."

I stretched my leg to ease the throb and looked around. The trees here had leaves so dark green they seemed almost black, spotted with deep reds and oranges. An occasional stripe of white, the bark of a birch tree, stood out among all the color.

I looked for a dash clock, but of course, there wasn't one, so I glanced at my watch. "Marion, it's only nine forty-five! Did you drive ninety miles an hour?"

Marion shrugged. "Would it be a sin if I did? Pearl's a race car after all."

"Well, evidently she's also got a cloaking device."

"Nah. I have cop karma."

We followed a pickup truck pulling a flatbed trailer filled with three old washing machines held on by day-glo orange straps. "Don't get too close," I said, "in case one of those things falls off."

Cornfields spread out from the road, the stalks chopped and bent. The ground rippled with great puddles of gray water. But as we passed, the gray puddles lifted—morphing before my eyes into hundreds of Canada geese. At the end of one field a billboard declared, "Adoption=Life. Abortion=Death." Tacked onto it, a hand-painted sign said, "Sugar Beets."

"What's with the beets?" I asked.

"Cheaters use them to bait deer," Marion said. "Feed them, tame them, then shoot them when they come to eat."

Talk of deer and hunting made me think of Red. How angry she'd been at me. How hard she'd worked to help me. Or, I had to admit, to help Linus.

After a few miles Marion turned Pearl into the lone gas station amidst the fields. She scooped up three empty Pepsi cans from the car floor.

I shoved my shoulder into the door to open it. "You want to pump or pee?"

"Pee." Marion wagged the Diet cans at me. "And restock."

"Can that much pop be good for you?"

Marion ignored me. "You want anything?"

A shiny black banner with day-glo orange letters flapped from the side of the station, welcoming hunters. Nothing else about the place looked new or well-kept. "I'll come in and check it out myself after I pay." I just hoped the bathrooms weren't gross.

I'd just finished filling Pearl's enormous tank with super expensive super premium gas, when Marion returned with a purple soft-sided cooler dangling from her shoulder. "Check it

out. Only two bucks with a six-pack of Pepsi!" She flipped the
keys in the air and caught them. "I'm still driving, right?"

"If you want." I watched a giant red truck—the kind with
four full-sized doors—pull up to the next pump. It had window
stickers of antlered deer and Calvin peeing on something. A
red and gold NRA sticker flashed from the bumper next to an
oval "Sarah! Palin/McCain" bumper sticker. Three enormous
unshaven young men tumbled out of it. Their jeans and field
jackets were covered in dirt. I felt for my wallet.

Marion reached into the backseat to position the pop. "Hey,
I asked the lady in there and she said the sun sets about five. So
we should be at the crucifix place in plenty of time, as long as we
don't get lost."

In the station, while the attendant ran my credit card, I
glanced around. Live bait shared cooler space with homemade
ham sandwiches shiny with plastic wrap. Handwritten labels
identified clear containers full of "goolash" and "toona salad."
My stomach gurgled with hunger, but I wasn't sure.

"Add two bottles of juice onto that too, please." I grabbed
one bottle each of apple and grape.

Outside, the young NRA Republicans huddled by the
side of their truck, sharing what looked like chewing tobacco
and sneaking quick glances at Pearl. Marion was in the trunk
rearranging her luggage. Trouble just waiting. But I had to pee.

I used the toilet, which was surprisingly clean, thank God,
and got back to the car as fast as I could. But not soon enough. By
the time I got out there, the three men had surrounded Marion
near the trunk of the car.

Be cool, I told myself. "Hey, guys."

The tallest, skinniest guy turned. He wore a gray T-shirt
with a decal of an American flag draped on crossed rifles. He
looked about twenty and stood well over six feet.

"Yeah, this is the priest?" he asked.

"Honest." Marion leaned against Pearl, unconcerned.

I extended my hand. "Reverend Lonnie Squires."

"Kyle Johnson." He motioned a thumb toward the man to
his right, a blond with bulging biceps and a macramé necklace
with a seashell pendant. "Brucey D." His thumb jerked around

to the other man, a shorter, darker, pudgier guy in a torn red shirt, dirty jeans and a ball hat with a colorful patch of a rainbow trout. "Gumbo."

I shook each hand in turn keeping my gaze steady. I'd seen looks like theirs before. Young guys with a secret. Up to something.

Three big guys, two women alone, a remote area. It made my stomach jump. "Nice to meet you. But we gotta hit the road."

Marion didn't budge. "These guys were telling me about our next stop."

"World's largest crucifix." Kyle rested his hands in his pockets. "Yeah, surprised you don't know about it, being a priest and all."

"Cool. A priest," said Gumbo. He swept a shock of black hair back from his forehead.

Brucey D. said nothing.

I smiled. "Well, I'm not Catholic or from around here."

"So, uh, yeah. What kind of priest are you?" asked Kyle.

"Episcopal. Marion, let's go."

Gumbo pushed his hair back again. "I thought priests always had to wear collars."

My knee throbbed which made it even harder to look relaxed. "Don't want to wear working clothes on vacation, right?"

Brucey D. nodded.

Gumbo laughed. "That'd be like wearing a suit when I run the combine. Don't want to do that shit."

Kyle smacked him in the chest. "Language in front of the priest, jackass."

"Nice meeting you," I said, but Marion didn't move. I grabbed her arm. "Come look at this a minute, would you?" I pulled her a few steps toward the building, where a hand-carved wooden three-dimensional map of northern Michigan took up much of the wall. "Are you nuts?"

"We were just talking." She looked genuinely surprised at my concern. "They're cute."

"Have you seen *Thelma and Louise*? Do you know what happens when they talk to a cute guy? Disaster!"

Marion yanked her arm from my grasp and headed back to the car. "These young men were just admiring Pearl."

"Yessir!" Kyle grinned, stepping closer. "Saw it when we pulled up. My God, I thought to myself—" He winced and nodded. "Sorry about the language, Reverend."

I held up my hand. "Really, it's okay."

"You should hear her when she's mad," Marion added.

"Yeah, that's a race car." Kyle rubbed his stubbly beard. "And I'm kind of a car guy."

"He's a total car guy," said Gumbo. "Likes 'em more than girls." He laughed and his hair tumbled into his face again.

Kyle smacked him in the chest again. "Jackass."

I bet that plenty of girls fell for him, whether he paid attention to them or not.

"Yeah, I just wondered what sort of engine was in that car, if you knew?" Kyle's gaze wandered toward the Fairlane. "Or, maybe, if I could have a look at it?"

"Sure you can." Marion headed for the front of the car.

I followed her. "Marion!"

"Relax, Lon."

"You'll get to the crucifix before sunset," Kyle offered.

As if that was what was worrying me.

Gumbo sidled up to me. "We're going up north tonight. After work. To hunt."

"Yeah, meetin' the dads," Kyle added. "Right near Indian River. Been doing it since we could drive."

"Before!" Gumbo laughed and swatted Brucey D.

"Yeah, maybe we'll see you up there," said Kyle.

"Oh, right," said Gumbo. "Like, we're with the dads in the tree stands at five a.m. We won't see these ladies."

I marveled again at the vision of my friend. Marion strode forward, her orange heels digging into the gravel, three hulking farm boys trotting along behind her.

"The parts are all original," Marion explained as she touched Pearl's fender. "Something about a wedge and a side oiler."

"You don't suppose it's a 427 R-code?" Kyle said to Brucey D., who just ran his hand across the fender.

"That sounds like something somebody said to me," I said.

"Holman-Moody?" Kyle's face lit up and he looked like a little kid.

I nodded. "I think that's it."

"Kick ass!" said Gumbo.

Kyle pulled back his arm to swat his friend, but before he could, Gumbo saluted in my direction. "Sorry, Reverend."

Marion bent in front of the car. "Now, if I can just find the hood release."

"Oh, no ma'am." Kyle ran his hands lightly over the hood scoop now. "It's held on with these four pins at the corners. You just lift the whole thing off to work on the engine. It was a feature designed for NASCAR racing."

He gazed at the car the way Linus gazed at me—pure love. I felt a little guilty. Maybe they really were okay. What could it hurt for him to have a little look? "Go ahead. But quickly, okay?"

They had the hood off the car in seconds and stared silently at the engine until Brucey D. whistled.

"Yeah, uh, how many miles has this got on it?" Kyle's voice was as hushed as if he were approaching the world's largest crucifix.

"Less than seven hundred." I felt a little wave of pride.

Their silence continued for seconds.

"She's clean as a whistle," said Gumbo.

"Mario Andretti won the Daytona 500 in nineteen sixty-seven driving one of these." Kyle kept gazing. "Did you know that?"

"No," said Marion and I together.

"I think they made less than sixty of them." He dropped his hand into the engine to touch a pipe. "Yeah. This must be worth a fortune."

"Well, not really—"

"Over eighty-thousand dollars," said Marion.

I wanted to slap Marion in the chest.

Brucey D. whistled again. Gumbo took one giant step back then reached out and slapped Kyle. "Dude. You got that?"

"It costs a fortune in gas," I said, as if that would dampen their enthusiasm.

"But it sure is fun to drive," Marion said.

The men were practically salivating.

"Well, we have to get moving now." I looked at Marion. "I'll drive."

Her eyebrows lowered. "You said I could drive."

I held up my hand to indicate I would not be deterred. "Keys." Then I looked at Kyle. "If you could put the hood back on please."

The three men stood staring at the engine.

"This thing still have the original drive train?" Kyle rubbed his stubble.

"It's all original," Marion said.

"Marion," I said through clenched teeth. "Now."

She heard my unspoken threat. "Hey guys, we have to go now. Off to the shrine."

Slowly, their loving gazes fixed on the engine, the three men put the hood back on. Kyle then double-checked each pin. "Don't want it flying off when you drive."

As we got into the car, the guys lined up at a respectful distance.

"You ladies spending the night in Indian River?" Gumbo asked.

Before I could answer with something noncommittal, Marion spilled it all.

"Nah. Driving out to Cross Village for dinner at the Legs Inn, then I booked us at some little motel in Bliss."

"Hey, no shit." Gumbo sidestepped out of Kyle's reach.

"Yeah," said Kyle. "We always eat at a place near Bliss, The Purple Slipper." He stepped up to Marion. "Give me your cell, I'll put the number in."

She handed it to him.

"I'll put my number in too," Kyle said.

"We'd meet you for breakfast," Gumbo started.

"Yeah, but we'd have to meet you at like three a.m.," finished Kyle, "in order to meet the dads on time." He shrugged. "Tradition. Yeah, important to them. You know, a dad/kid thing."

The other two nodded. "Maybe lunch," Gumbo said.

Marion looked like she might cry and invite them all home with us after the hunt.

"We have to be on the road before that, but thanks," I said. "Nice to meet you."

"Okay, then," said Kyle. "Hope you enjoy seeing The Man on the Cross."

That was a sentence I never thought I'd hear.

"Nice boys. College kids." Marion cracked her soda as we drove away.

"Next time, maybe don't get so cozy with three big, armed men, okay?"

"They were frat brothers, they said. Home this week on a break helping Kyle's dad pull corn out or something. I didn't quite follow the farm talk." She cracked a soda.

"Just next time, don't get involved. Promise me."

She took a gulp. "Is there some reason they freaked you out? I mean, they were teddy bears. You on edge about something else? Something you want to talk about?"

There it was again! The second time this morning she was poking me for some sort of revelation.

"No," I said.

She accepted that. "Well, you gotta put out some good energy, Lon. Relax." Which is exactly what Marion did, because within minutes she was snoring. A chance to do a little more follow-up. At a stop sign in Lake City, I dug around under the seat until I found my phone, and called the Frontline Church of Christ.

CHAPTER TWENTY-EIGHT

I wasn't really investigating. Just following up on a thing or two so I knew if it was worth turning over to Red.

"Well, Reverend Squires!" said Brady. I could just see him, sitting on the corner of his desk, swinging a leg, casual and chummy. "How's the pursuit of filthy lucre going?"

When I first met him, I wrote Brady off as a dim-witted Bible-slinger. Then I realized he was actually a decent guy, just misguided as hell when it came to theological reflection. Lately I'd realized I never could entirely tell when he meant the stuff he said and when he was joking.

"On angels' wings," I said.

"I can't say I'm inspired to wish you good luck," he mused, "since you cannot serve both God and money, but as a Christian, I won't turn away a sister in need. How can I help you?"

"I'm calling because I'm hoping to piggyback off one of your successful ministries. Maybe start something like it at Woman at the Well. On a much smaller scale of course."

"Happy to help! Happy to help any way I can, Lorraine!" The music in his voice betrayed how easily I'd puffed his ego.

"Great. I'm wondering about this Thursday night men's Bible study you run."

It took him just a second too long to answer—a second that told me whatever he said next wouldn't be the truth.

"A small but vigorous ministry, yes. Quite private. Dedicated members."

"Sort of a private party, huh?"

"It is a small group. I have other studies, of course. Much larger. You'd be welcome to come! Monday and Wednesday we meet at—"

"No, thanks. It's the Thursday event I'm particularly interested in."

He waited too long. "Why is that?"

"Because it connects to Randy Koeman. Who got killed after your meeting let out."

This was all true, but didn't mean a thing. I was hoping, though, that Brady would assume I knew a lot more than I said.

"As it says in Proverbs, 'A gossip betrays a confidence, but a trustworthy person keeps a secret.'"

One thing about me and Bible-slingers. I can't keep up with them because I don't memorize verses. So I almost never get involved in a slinging match. "Tell me about Randy Koeman."

"He wasn't one of my flock."

A definite nonanswer.

"Neither is Ivor Koontz. He's one of mine. But he attends your little Bible study, doesn't he?"

This caught Brady off guard. "How—" He caught himself. "I certainly hope you don't begrudge him work through our church that—"

"My people are free to attend whatever churches they want. But neither of these guys seems like the Bible-study type, if you ask me. So what was going on at your little parties on Thursdays?"

The road traveled along a beautiful flat gray lake lined with tiny cottages and removable boat docks. No one out in this weather.

"Pastoral confidence, Lonnie."

Yeah, I'd used that one myself now and again. How was I going to get out of Brady what I knew he was hiding? I didn't know enough to get a purchase, to pry the information out of him.

"Lonnie," Brady said. "Are you having second thoughts?"

"About what?" I pulled up to a stop sign, nodded at a guy on the corner who grinned at Pearl.

"About chasing the riches of the world instead of staying home and caring for your flock. For love of money is the root of all evil."

This from a guy whose church had professional grade ball fields and a Broadway-style theater for a sanctuary. Still, I wanted to keep him talking until he told me about Thursdays. *Help, help, help,* I prayed. "Why do you ask?"

"Because you're off on this great adventure—the stuff of road movies, really. Wacky aunt. Odd tourist stops. Dream car. Best friends. But instead of enjoying it, you're still thinking about what's going on here at home. You are sleuthing. Which, as I understand it, you are not supposed to be doing."

"What do you think I should do?" Like I cared. But it would keep him talking.

"As it says in Hebrews, *'keep your lives free from the love of money and be content with what you have.'* God wants you home."

Interesting. Whenever Brady said God wanted something, it meant Brady wanted something. So this meant Brady wanted me home. But why?

"You should be home living out the gifts God has given you," Brady said. "Whatever that may be. Whatever the risk."

It's the murder. My internal voice. *He wants you to come home and solve the murder.*

Badly enough to use the Bible to convince me. Which could only mean he was scared.

"Well, I can't come home," I said. "But maybe I can live out my gifts from the road." I paused, pretending to think. "Maybe you can help me discern God's will?"

"Happily, Reverend!" I imagined him leaping off his desk, high-fiving an imaginary Jesus right there in his office.

"If only I knew more about how Ivor and Randy and you all fit together," I said, "then I could pray for guidance."

I heard him suck his teeth, something he did when thinking. I had him between a rock and a hard place—not wanting to tell me anything and wanting me to do something for him.

"Why would you think I—" He sucked his teeth again. "What are people saying?"

If Brady feared one thing as much as the wrath of God, it was poor public opinion.

"That you know quite a bit. Maybe who killed him and why." Okay, so I lied. "Your church—" I let my voice fade away.

"The church has no connection to Randy Koeman! To any of it!"

"Brady. You say I have gifts from God. Isn't it your duty to help me use them well?"

I could practically hear his brain chewing on that.

"Brady. Serve God. Tell me." I only felt a little guilty about using the Divine this way.

He sighed. "It's nothing really. They had already made up the Bible study excuse before I learned about it. That's how I got involved. To stop them from using my church as camouflage."

"What are you doing? Going to a strip club?"

Next to me Marion snorted and rotated, her head lolling against the window.

"Good gracious, no! Nothing depraved!"

"People will talk, Brady. If they know you're doing something secret, they'll make up the worst. Trust me, I know."

He mumbled something.

"I can't help you—God can't help you—unless you tell me." This was dirty pool and I knew it. *Sorry*, I thought, glancing at the sky. It floated low and gray, unbroken clouds as far as I could see over the undulating dead fields.

"A poker game," Brady said finally.

"Really?" I struggled to keep from cracking up. In ninety-nine percent of the world, no one would care. But in Middelburg, a poker game was about as close to a sign of eternal damnation as liquor sales on Sunday. Plus it was illegal. *"You* play in a poker game?"

"Lonnie, as a fellow minister, you understand. I couldn't just abandon them in their sin."

"No, of course not."

"It is our duty to walk with them, like Jesus," Brady said, "to break the rules now and again so we can break bread with sinners and hope to pull them once again into the light."

Oh, man. I couldn't wait for Marion to hear this. But she snored away, her mouth open.

"You play Thursdays? Ivor, Koeman, you, and who else?"

"You'll keep this confidential, right, Lonnie? I mean, professional courtesy. You can't let on I shared this information with you. Right?"

"I would never reveal my source," I said. *Except to Marion.*

He listed eight men total. The Zaloumi twins traded out a seat. Lex Brenninkmeyer, Provost up at Five Points College. Jake Vogel, husband of Lucy from the Hot Flashes. Bram VanRenselaar. Ivor. Dale Zeerip. Koeman. Himself.

"Did Koeman owe anyone a lot of money?"

"Randy Koeman owed everyone—every single one of us— money." Brady sighed. I could imagine him running his hands across his thighs to smooth his pants. "When he told us about the overtime he'd been earning, that he'd bought tickets to Vegas, well, there were some tempers, yes. But no one wanted him dead. They just wanted their money."

"So, Brady, I'm confused. Do you want me to come home and work on this case because you think someone in your game killed Koeman?"

"I want you to solve this case before the police find out about this game. Before it gets made public. My involvement—I can't tolerate the negative publicity, especially after your little battle with Star about the law. Lonnie, you have no idea! You have a denomination to protect you. But me. This church is everything. If I slip in the Lord's sight, the whole undertaking could collapse!"

"If it did wouldn't that be God's will?"

"No!" He collected himself and said more quietly, "No.

People make incorrect assumptions. Nothing Godly in that."

I found myself agreeing.

"Find out who did it. Quickly," he begged. "Before a worse scandal erupts."

In other words, he wanted me to save his butt. Again.

"What about Gil Hannes? Does he play?"

"As if he could get away from his wife two nights a month?" Brady snorted. "He's never even tried to join."

I decided to take a shot. "How much money did Koeman owe?" A green sign indicated that my turn onto I-75 was coming up soon.

"Me, about three hundred dollars. I have no idea how much he owed the others."

Ivor was violent. A few hundred could have been enough to motivate him to kill.

"Tell me about the others. Their relationships to Koeman."

"Lex Brenninkmeyer is a man in complete control. Exactly two drinks every evening. Precisely two hundred dollar limit to his bets. Out the door at nine fifty no matter what's in the pot. He never ever exceeds the rules he sets down for himself. He loaned Randy some, but not much. Probably fifty."

That matched what I knew of the man from some investigating I'd done about poisons kept in the chem labs up at the college. "Okay. Bram?"

"Bram loves three things: the archives, some game he plays on the Internet and the poker game. He doesn't care if he loses or how much. He just loves playing and hanging out with the guys. I think we're the only actual people he knows well."

"How about Dale, the guy who works with Ivor?"

"He still lives with his parents. He comes to the game to blow off a little steam. Better with us than with dubious women, I figure."

I tried to remember what I'd seen of Dale at the rec center. "Is he hotheaded? Strapped for cash?"

"Opposite, really. He doesn't brag, but he owns two houses in Holland. Income property he fixed up and rents. He's putting money away to help his parents in retirement. They're both in ill health. He's a good son."

I knew the Zaloumis hadn't killed anyone, so I didn't bother to ask. "Jake Vogel?" I hoped to God Brady didn't have anything creepy to say about him.

"Good guy. Patient. Generous. This is why I—why we all—need your help, Lonnie. None of these guys did it. We need you to find out who did before anything more comes out."

I still put my money on Ivor Koontz. "What if one of you did do it? Would you help me prove it?"

"Thou shalt not kill, Reverend. If one of the players did it, I would not hesitate to turn him in." He sighed. "I suppose, in any event, this will be the death of the game."

He sounded about as sad as I'd sound if someone told me I could never play soccer again. It made me actually feel sorry for him.

"I'll do what I can," I told him.

CHAPTER TWENTY-NINE

I drove for nearly an hour thinking on and off about the poker players. All men. All from different strands of Middelburg society. Meeting to play their secret game, blowing money, lying to their wives. Then meeting in public and pretending not to know each other's truth. It reminded me of being gay.

Somewhere along I-75 Marion woke up and I told her the whole poker story, leaving out the names of most of the players, except for Ivor Koontz and Randy Koeman. She yelled at me for making the call, of course, but admitted it might be important information.

We stopped for gas in Gaylord and decided we had made such good time we could afford to stop for lunch. Marion picked Arlene's Diner on the main drag because it reminded her of The Grind. "Always want to see how folks run things," she said. "Pick up a few new tricks."

Then we hit the road for the last few miles and at 1:03 we pulled off I-75 at Indian River to find the crucifix. The road through Indian River passed the Tiki Fish Market Specialty Store and Gift Shop, Tomahawk Trails Canoe Rental, hand-painted billboards, and a sign with Smokey the Bear assuring us the fire risk was low today. Since it had started raining not long after we passed the 45th parallel ("halfway between the equator and the North Pole" the sign had told us), I wasn't surprised at Smokey's declaration. This far north, the pine trees glowed a ruddy green mixed with maples gone pure red and yellow. Still, in the drizzle, everything looked grayed and flat.

"There." Marion pointed to a dripping sign with white letters, a reverse silhouette of Jesus. "The Cross in the Woods."

We drove around the nearly empty parking lot but couldn't see any crucifix. We pulled up beneath the sign and Marion swooped her raincoat over her head. She cuddled the camera to keep it dry until she got the photo and climbed back in. "Ready, Batman."

I paused. It seemed silly not to go see the world's largest crucifix when you're already sitting in its parking lot. Especially for a priest. Plus, we were making good time and though we'd been in and out, we hadn't really stretched our legs since this morning.

"Let's have a quick peek," I said.

Marion, clearly surprised, hopped out of the car before I could change my mind. We walked through the drizzle to a long, low-roofed porch. Hundreds of red glass votives glowed with the flames of small candles. Golden and dark-colored icons hung above them in a jagged row.

I felt strangely at home. I liked the art and flame. I loved that this was outside. Already it felt like all the good things about church.

Maybe that was what I needed to get my good energy flow back. Once I had Linus, I could just hunker down and focus on the good things about church, my job, my life in Middelburg. I mean, somewhere else, it could be much, much worse, right?

I just needed to adjust my thinking, to focus on the good.

"The shrine is back this way." Marion headed past a post

of signs pointing in various directions to bathrooms, gift shop, indoor pews, shrine and The Nun Doll Museum. She tapped the dripping museum sign. "I'm visualizing Barbie dressed as Sister Bertrelle."

We walked down the stairs and along a meandering sidewalk through deep trees. I nodded greetings at statues of St. Francis, Our Lady of the Highway and St. Peregrine. The rainy afternoon light and the statues' widespread arms and compassionate gazes made me want a few seconds to pray. To kneel in a quiet hut. To breathe and rest a bit from the mess that had been the last few days. It was the best of church. Peaceful, loving, serene.

Yes. I felt it. This was the right path. I just needed to find it at home too.

"Check it out," Marion said, pulling my gaze to row after row of sturdy pews just visible between the trees. They looked uncomfortable, square and heavy, built from lumber like railroad ties.

I imagined sitting under a soft evening sky, surrounded by the compassion of God. Perhaps we should find out the service schedule, stay if we could. Or I could come back some other time.

In front of me, Marion stopped so abruptly she almost tottered off her heels. "Holy—"

I pulled up short behind her and we both stared into the clearing at the horror that hung there.

A brown body loomed in the sky. Thunderclouds hulked all around, threatening to split and fall.

Something reached down my throat and pulled the air from my lungs. "It's horror—" I swallowed. "Horrible."

In front of the field of pews a concrete platform rose, holding up a marble altar, marble pulpit and marble priest's chair. Behind that arched a green hill and from it thrust a cross fifty feet in the air, black square wood, dripping. A giant bronze Jesus hung, ribs exposed beneath rippling muscles, drooping head, all of him pouring downward into limp, dripping toes.

"Oh my God, oh my God," I said and it wasn't a cry of devotion.

Marion heard my despair. "You don't like it?"

"No!" Tears burned as the creeps skittered up my spine. "It scares me to death."

"I think we can walk up there," she said and started toward it.

"Closer?" I stood, eyes riveted on that thing. I followed her to the side of the hill. Gazed at it in profile. Wounded side, fingertips, stripes of ribs. Those limp toes.

"How much does it weigh?"

"Seven tons, according to the file." She rushed up the wet steps on her tippy toes.

This suffering was enormous. If He fell, we would die.

The stairs that climbed the hill split in the middle. Marble on the left if you cared to approach on your knees. Concrete on the right if you wanted to walk.

For me, each step up felt like a descent into the belly of some enormous beast. I cooled my palms on the slick metal banister and pulled off my hood so the light rain would find my burning scalp.

The sculpture was a terrible beauty. The bones and muscles squared off at the edges, the same Byzantine look of the icons near the parking lot. The hair hung in clumps that zigzagged like lightning bolts.

A few feet behind me an older lady appeared wearing a garbage bag-type poncho that said "Six Flags." I didn't want to block the stairs, so I sped up to join Marion who stood right beneath the behemoth.

I looked up at the bronze feet. They dripped onto me as they might have onto his mother Mary, only I got cold rain on my face, not blood. Each foot was as large as my torso and I could see the lines on the heels, the curve of the toenails, the edges of the cuticles. Another drop fell, almost in slow motion, and I blinked as it hit my forehead.

I wanted to open my mouth to catch the next one like a snowflake, but I clamped my mouth shut. My Aunt Kate's voice reminded me that rain is dirty, containing who knows what poisons.

I thought again of Jesus' mother, Mary, who didn't know the miracle to come as she stood beneath this broken body. I thought of my own despair just a few days ago at losing Linus, when he got dragged away, all innocence. Rage flamed from the center of my chest. I thought the rain on my skin might steam away in its heat.

"The story doesn't end here!" I shouted, as much to myself as to Marion. "This isn't truth. This isn't the end!"

From my pocket, my cell phone rang and I nearly jumped off the hill. The bronze body above me seemed to buzz with it.

CHAPTER THIRTY

The lady in the Six Flags poncho glared at me as I scrambled to silence the ring. Of course, in my fumble, I answered by mistake, so I had to say something. Sadly, it was my bishop.

"Where are you, Lorraine?" he boomed.

I cupped my hand around my mouth and walked to the top of the stairway. "Gazing on a very large crucified Christ."

"Contemplate the vision of His suffering while we talk about the suffering you are causing me."

I tilted back to look all the way up the statue. "But suffering isn't the end of the story, sir. It's just a step toward the end. The triumph." A fat drop fell from the sky and touched the center of my forehead.

"I'll bear that in mind when I try to explain to my standing committee the behaviors of one Lorraine Squires, rogue priest!" He paused. "I told you to stay out of the news, yet the newspapers, blogs and television are plastered with you chasing your aunt's money!"

"Why do you think Christians always focus on Christ's suffering?" I asked.

"Because that sacrifice is the point, Lonnie. It saved us all."

"Wasn't it the resurrection that really saved us? I mean, that's way bigger than everything here." I turned and looked at the sea of pews. "The victory trumps all of it."

"And you should honor it by honoring your vows of obedience, Lorraine. But you couldn't stay out of the news!"

"I don't think Jesus' point was that we owed him because he suffered so," I said. "But that does seem to be the point of this place."

The woman in the poncho watched me. I smiled. She wore a pink plastic rain cap beneath the poncho hood. Her blue eyes shone from layers of soft aged skin, her lips thin, her cheekbones flushed.

"Come home now, Lorraine," said the bishop, "and I will discern whether or not forgiving you is the best way to serve you in Christian love."

He sounded puny. Whiny. A mosquito in my head.

"This Jesus," I gestured toward the bronze body above me as if the bishop could see, "is too dead. Why always big and dead? Why victimization? Why make fear the point of the story?"

"Christ died for you." The bishop spoke now as if I were a tiny child. "He suffered a bloody, painful death. You'd better fear that sort of sacrifice. And know what he could do to you if you fail to live up to your side of the bargain."

"But Christ lived in compassion and love. He accepted everyone. He wasn't about physical strength." I looked upward again and shook my head. "Wouldn't this have been more beautiful if it was seven tons of resurrection? Seven tons of Jesus the winner instead of Jesus the loser?"

"My dear," said the woman in the poncho. She stood only inches from me now. "Do you ever attend church?"

I gazed at her. The blue eyes held only the open question. "Yes, ma'am, I do."

Marion stepped forward and slapped her arm around my shoulders. "Let's go."

"Lorraine, if you know how displeased I am by your failure of obedience to me and to the scriptures, you know the Lord's wrath is one hundred times that wrath."

"So little?" I asked, shrugging Marion away. "Jesus isn't puny like that," I said. "He didn't want us scared by his suffering." I continued, almost not knowing where the words were coming from. Or the urge to fight. "He wanted us scared by the magnitude of suffering in the world. He didn't want us to worship Him. He wanted us to live like Him. Justice. Tolerance. Loving our neighbors."

Bishop Tappen lowered his voice. I could almost see him fondling the heavy cross around his neck. "The church has rules you must follow, just like parishioners must obey your authority as priest."

"We're just people with lots at stake, just like everyone else." And as I said it, I wondered if I could believe that and still be a priest.

Can you still be a priest? came that voice.

"No. Ordination is a sacrament," said the bishop. "Priests are more than just people. And bishops are more than priests."

I looked at the marble altar below. The surfaces gleamed in the rain and setting sun. One chair only on that stage. For the priest.

"The church is about separation." I looked back at Christ. That was about separation too. "But Christ came back. He's about inclusion." I sighed. "The church is wrong."

"Hang up now, Lonnie," Marion said.

This time when she pulled on me, I didn't resist. "Bye," I said to my bishop. "Don't worry. I'll call you when I get back."

Pain spiked through my knee as Marion sped me down the stairs. I nearly slipped on the last marble step. "Can we slow down, please?" But she plowed ahead.

As soon as we entered the trees we stopped and I bent to rub my knee. "Whew. Sorry. This really hurts."

"Yeah, you're hurting." Marion kept walking. "Do you want to lose your job talking to your bishop like that? What's with you?"

I just rubbed my knee.

She shook her head, wiping water from her nose. "You get yourself together and I'll meet you at the car in five."

I nodded and watched her go, then wandered back to St. Peregrine's hut. It still looked warm and dry, but now I just couldn't go in.

I stood on the sidewalk and pulled my wet hair behind my ears, exhaling like a pressure valve. I'd heard it, the scary tiny voice asking me if I really should be a priest.

As pissed as I'd been at the church, I'd never questioned that before.

If I wasn't a priest, who was I?

I followed Marion around town while she shopped. Even the retro wonders of rubber tomahawks and genuine arrowheads and leather moccasins to fit any taste and budget couldn't distract me from the rat of doubt gnawing in my gut.

If I wasn't a priest, who was I? If I didn't live in Middelburg, where would I live? If I didn't have my soccer team, who—beside Linus, assuming I got him back—would always be there for me?

Just after six we ended the hour-long cruise to our next destination, The Legs Inn in Cross Village which, ironically, is not where the cross was. We pulled into the parking lot and stared at the building.

Marion whistled with admiration. "What's it made out of?"

"Everything."

The Inn stood between the street and a high bluff overlooking Lake Michigan. Stones, rough-hewn timbers, driftwood and what appeared to be cast-iron stove legs all formed part of the multi-level, many-roofed structure. The parking lot was jammed.

"Reservations?"

"We got 'em," Marion said.

"Good." Because I needed a beer.

The Legs Inn dining room lived up to the building's exterior. Roaring fires tossed dancing shadows across sculptures made from roots and carved branches. The service was fast and friendly and the food Polish and fabulous. In less than an hour we settled back in our chairs and stared at the empty plates that had held veggie nalesniki and golabki with pierogi.

Life felt immeasurably more tolerable after such an amazing meal.

After dinner we took our picture, which ate the better part of a half hour while Marion learned how to use the nighttime flash function on the camera so that the picture showed the car and the inn behind it.

Then we drove east, again through rustic utter darkness, toward a town called Bliss. The blackness was empty, not even the distant glow of a town in the night's horizon. Maybe the dot of white light from a farmhouse here and there. So when the hand-painted, dimly lit billboard appeared, we both studied it carefully.

"Man Killing Giant Clam," Marion read. "500 lbs. At Sea Shell City." A childlike painting of a clam, its maw yawning for blood, filled the board.

"Do you think the clam killed the man or the man's killing it?" I asked.

"And which one weighs five hundred pounds?" Marion added.

We discussed the virtues of purposely—or not—ambiguous advertising until we neared I-75 again, and wove past it to a squat white building with ten red doors and a sign proclaiming "Zineski's HAH" in blinking pink and blue neon.

"HAH?" I looked at Marion.

"Home Away from Home. And before you say anything, everyplace else was booked with hunters."

I cranked the steering wheel to guide the Fairlane into the only open space in front of door number ten. Marion pushed against her door. "I'll check us in."

I set the first two bags outside of the car. Dark pines surrounded the motel and they made it smell like home. In the distance, through the trees, I saw a light. A brightly lit hand-painted sign of a purple Arabian nights-type slipper.

The Purple Slipper. Of car guy fame.

I grabbed my soccer ball and spent a few minutes juggling, trying to work out some of my road kinks. Normally I could do a hundred easy, but tonight, I couldn't get past twenty-five kicks in a row. I tossed the ball back into the trunk and pulled out the last of the bags.

Marion grabbed her leopard print bag and shoved it back in. "I don't need that one tonight. It's my just-in-case stuff. You know. Extra shoes. Stuff."

I locked Pearl and headed for door number ten.

"This way, honey." Marion pointed down the building. "Door number one."

I trudged behind her. "Where's your parking karma now?"

"It's twenty yards, champ. You can walk it."

I decided to keep my tired and strung out thoughts to myself. No one likes a whiner. I was, after all, looking for the good, not the bad. The resurrection, not the crucifix.

The room was clean and smelled only a little musty. A tiny TV hung in a corner. Faded prints of sunflowers clung to all four dark paneled walls.

"Comfy enough." Marion dropped her bag on the far bed and headed to the bathroom.

Some birthday. My mom never called back, my sisters didn't call at all, I nearly got arrested in Grand Haven, I got called out by my bishop while standing beneath a statue of the crucified Christ, I was following my dead aunt's orders to earn money to give to a woman I despised and I was having the mother of all identity crises.

I wanted Linus to jump onto the bed beside me, stick his nose against mine and lick me until we had a wrestle.

Soon, he will, I told myself. *Soon.*

When Marion emerged wearing bright yellow fleece pajamas with red smiley faces and slippers to match, I took my turn. I slid into a purple Episcopal Women's Caucus T-shirt and gray soccer shorts. In bed, the pillow was flat and hard, but the sheets felt clean.

"I set the alarm for five thirty," said Marion in the dark. "Time to wake up, eat somewhere and get on the way by seven."

"M-kay," I managed. Sleep touched me like a warm sun.

"Happy birthday," Marion said. "I had fun."

"Me too," I said. At least, I think I said it. I'm not sure. I was half asleep.

I drifted back to the woods at Indian River, swirling in the dark beneath the cross like Marion's voice around my ears. The cool air touched my suddenly naked skin. I heard rustling around me, listened as it developed a rhythm like many bodies breathing. Though I could see nothing, I knew it was Jesus, Mary, Francis, Peregrine, Bishop Tappen and all the rest of the spirits of that place, alive in the chilling October air. In the dream, I searched for my puppy, but he wasn't there. The dark swelled around us as night creatures crept forth to move boldly about in the dark, and then I drifted away from that too.

I'm not sure how long it was before I heard Marion's voice again.

"Lonnie, you've got to wake up!" Marion's voice pulled me up from some deep, dark, quiet space.

It cannot possibly be five thirty already.

"Wake up! Pearl's gone."

CHAPTER THIRTY-ONE

I tried to lasso consciousness and pull it forward, but I couldn't hold on. I began to slip back into the dark place again, now surrounded by giant man-eating pearls.

The dream disappeared when Marion raised me by the shoulders. "Lonnie, for goddess' sake, wake up."

I sucked a deep breath and forced my eyes open. "What?"

"Pearl's gone." Marion's voice shook.

I tried to see her face in the darkness. "What do you mean, gone?"

"I mean she's not in the parking lot."

I looked at the alarm clock. 3:57. Everything she'd said clicked. "Jesus Christ!" I yanked the covers back and leapt to the window. I couldn't see the spot where I'd parked the car on the end of the building.

"Are you sure?" I fumbled with the chain and deadbolt.

I barely heard Marion's "yes" as I ran barefoot down the concrete. No Pearl. Only the space where my car should have been.

My car. My ticket to getting my dog out of Star's control.

"Oh, shit. Shit, shit, shit." I ran around the building, through calf-high grass, across sticks and stones. But it was just woods behind the building and darkness everywhere except for the Purple Slipper across the street.

Marion drooped in our doorway.

"How could someone have driven it away?" I asked. "We would have heard."

"We were pretty tired and—"

"Wait." I ran back to the motel office—well-lit, but empty. "Hello?" I tried not to sound too panicked. Panic was not good. "Hello? Someone?"

A fiftyish man resembling the Michelin tire guy, except for dark hair stuck up at odd angles, wobbled into the room, blinking fast. "Fire?"

I forced myself to take a breath. Probably a simple explanation. "No, no fire."

His body sagged with relief.

"My car's gone. Did you move it?" *Please God, please let him have towed it for some ridiculous reason.*

He rubbed his shadowed cheeks. "Ya sure?"

"Of course I'm sure!"

He walked around the desk to peer out the front window. His quilted flannel shirt, jeans and thick socks reminded me I was standing here in a T-shirt, shorts and bare feet. And I was freezing. "You had that old Ford, didn't you?"

"Yes. Do you—"

"And it's gone?" He turned back to me and rubbed his face, still waking up. "Your friend go out in it?"

A vast pit had opened in my stomach. He didn't know anything about it. I'd lost the car. *The car I needed to get my dog back!*

"Loan it to anyone?"

"No!" I screamed.

He nodded solemnly. "Want me to call the cops for ya?" He went back behind the desk, nudging the phone.

"Yes." I shivered. "No. Wait. Let me dress first." I ran back to the room. This time, the stones bit my feet and the near freezing temperatures prickled my skin.

Marion looked up with hope but I shook my head. "Get dressed. He'll call the police." I collapsed on the bed. "I can't believe it. Now, how am I going to get Linus out of—"

I couldn't say anything else. It was too horrible to speak. *Help, help help.*

Marion bit her lip. "Maybe we don't need the cops? Maybe someone borrowed Pearl and will bring her back?"

I sat up. "Those car guys you buddied up to! You think they took it!" I leapt up, buzzed with certainty and hope. "Where's your phone? Call them! Get that car back here now!"

She shook her head, eyes wide, hair askew, fleecy red smiley faces contorted across her body. "Not them. No way."

"Who else?" I dug through her purse looking for her phone.

"Lots of people know where we are. From the publicity. And what about that secondary beneficiary thing?" She sat up straighter. "Remember? That person would stand a lot to gain by stopping your trip. All the money!" She bobbed her head up and down.

I dropped her purse and yanked my shorts off. "Get dressed. We might as well not freeze to death while we talk to the cops." I snagged my jeans from the back of the chair and tugged them on. "They'll find Kyle Johnson and friends."

"Maybe we should rent a car and go look for her," Marion said.

"Maybe next time you'll be more careful about who you chat with about that car!" I zipped up my jeans.

"Well, Pearl would stick out, right? She'd be easy to spot."

"Then the police will find her."

"We can't call the police."

I turned. Her mouth buckled, quivering. "What's going on, Mare?"

Marion sucked in so much air her bosom rose a foot. Then she sighed it all out, along with some silent tears. "You know that leopard bag I left in the car? I have a little—" Marion paused. "Lonnie, I never meant for this to happen. It was just for fun, you know, away from the kids and all. It's not a usual thing, and—"

"What's in the bag, Marion?" My mind had begun to reel through possibilities.

She rubbed her knees as if they were magic lamps that could transport her away from here.

"*What* is in the bag?"

Her eyes slid to mine. "Marijuana."

I heaved a sigh of my own. "Shit."

"Not much!" Marion buried her face in her hands. "Forget it. Call the police. You have to get the car. You have to get Linus. I'll just tell them it's mine."

"But it's in *my* car." I sat next to her. And I didn't want her arrested on drug charges for God's sake. Not with kids. Not in Middelburg.

"Lonnie, I'm so so *so* sorry." Marion put her hand on mine. "I screwed this up."

Yeah, but I wasn't going to agree. My aunt had screwed this up. Star Hannes had screwed it up. I had screwed it up. "The only one who isn't a screw-up is Linus."

We sighed in unison.

"So, what're we gonna do?" Marion's voice was quiet.

Ten minutes later we sat in the screaming brightness of the Purple Slipper Donut Den, contemplating plastic-coated breakfast menus and wishing—hard—for coffee. My stomach gurgled as much from the smells—coffee, bacon and baking donuts—as from the anxiety about my dog.

The Purple Slipper Donut Den's owners took the name seriously. Purple slippers stood, flopped or spun everywhere. Above the white framed windows a purple shelf ran around the top of every wall, loaded with slippers of all kinds. Slippers sat on windowsills. The service counter held a glass case full of miniatures. Faded poster art in thin purple frames featured slippers from around the world. Foot-long purple shelves on the walls behind the cash register were filled with fuzzy slippers shaped like farm animals. Above us, a colorful mobile of high-heeled slippers swayed in the circulating air. Trying to figure out how many slippers there were in the knotty pine dining room would be like guessing the number of jelly beans in a giant jar.

Normally it would have amused me.

"Lonnie, just call the police," Marion said.

"If we involve them, we'll never make it around the lake on Aunt Kate's schedule anyhow. There will be reports on the car, the drugs. Publicity."

I leaned back as the fifty-something woman in an old-fashioned black and white waitress uniform expertly flipped two heavy white mugs from her hand onto the purple plastic covered table.

"Hey, gals." Her nametag said Paula. She didn't ask if we wanted coffee. She just poured then put the thermal pot on the table. On her feet she wore terrycloth slippers, lavender, topped with a bright yellow three-dimensional sun. She pulled out pad and pen. "Take your orders?"

Though the Purple Pancakes stuffed with blueberries and topped with warm blueberry syrup tempted, I felt too agitated to eat a thing. We both just stuck with coffee.

Marion shook sugar from a baby food jar with holes punctured in the lid into her coffee. "What if we act surprised about the drugs? What if we say the thief planted them?" She tilted her head in a look of inquisitive hope, rather like Linus anticipating an outing.

"But isn't it in your bag?"

"The thief planted it there, to keep himself clear, in case he got caught with the car." Marion grinned. "Yeah!"

I swallowed coffee which burned a track down my throat. I watched Paula talk to someone else, presumably the cook, through an old-fashioned window behind the service counter.

"Look," Marion said, "if someone stole Pearl, you can't possibly lose your inheritance, can you?"

I grimaced over my mug. "You don't know my great-aunt very well, do you?"

"Maybe we should call Brand. Find out who—"

"Call Kyle Johnson, Marion."

She winced.

"I know you hate the idea of finding out your intuition misguided you on something, but face it. You were wrong about them." I held out my hand. "I'll call him."

Behind her Paula delivered heaping plates to a clean-cut dark man who sat with a woman in a raincoat. He had on a Race for the Cure T-shirt and black suspenders connected to his jeans. Behind them two middle-aged men, one African American and the other white with bright red hair and a broad-brimmed leather hat, wore camouflage pants and shirts. A man who looked to be in his seventies sat at the counter, joking with another younger waitress.

"Oh, Frank," she laughed, "you're just a freak of nature."

I wriggled my fingers. "Phone."

Marion dug in her purse. "I just don't think—" As she pulled it from her bag, it rang. Marion jumped like it was a snake then stared at me. "Who would call—what if something happened to Cam or Mitchell?"

She answered, her expression shifting from worry to puzzlement as she listened. "She's right here." She held the phone out to me. "It's Kyle Johnson. He says it's about Pearl."

CHAPTER THIRTY-TWO

I resisted the urge to start by swearing at him.

"Kyle, do you have my car?" I watched Paula refill the camouflaged men's coffee.

"Yeah, well, no," he said. A truck rumbled in the background. "Your car's by the side of the road. We didn't see you. Brucey D. said it wasn't right and we ought to call. Make sure you're okay."

I didn't believe him. But it didn't matter if they had taken it or not if they could help me get it back. "Where is it?" I asked.

"Where?" Marion asked.

"You at the Slipper?" Kyle asked.

"Where's my car?"

I heard muffled voices, then a new voice spoke.

"Reverend? Gumbo. Car's about five miles south of The Slipper. You need a ride?"

"Unless you can bring it to me," I said. "Or is it wrecked?" Maybe that's why they were calling. They'd missed a curve and run Pearl into a ditch or a tree.

Marion grabbed my forearm. "Wrecked?"

"Not wrecked," Gumbo said, "but I don't have the key."

Like that had stopped them from taking it in the first place. "I'll get a cab."

"We'd come get you but it's the dads. We're damn near—" He stopped himself. "Sorry. We're darned near gonna be late meeting them as it is."

Steals a car but still worried about meeting his dad on time. Cute.

"Tell me exactly where it is."

"Behind the counter," said Gumbo, "there a young girl chattin' up an old dude named Frank?"

I swung my gaze back to the other waitress and her freak of nature. "Yes."

"That's Shirley. She'll loan you her truck. She's my cousin."

At his request I gave Shirley the phone and the next five minutes unfolded like magic. After Shirley gave Gumbo an earful for not stopping by for breakfast and exacting a promise that he'd bring himself, Uncle Jim and the rest of the boys in after the morning hunt, she said sure, she'd loan her fiancé Joey's pickup truck to me, if Gumbo said she should.

She clicked the phone off and handed it to me. "Gumbo says you need a truck for a bit, no questions asked."

Marion and I looked at each other. "The universe is on our side," she said and grinned. "Kick ass."

"No celebrations until we're back on the road in that car," I said as Shirley led us through the steaming kitchen and out into the frosty night.

A few minutes later I drove a rattling pickup south on some unnamed county road. I'd turned left at the Peterson's Orchard sign, so I guessed we were on the right track.

Marion sat stiff-armed against the dashboard. "Should you slow down?"

I checked the speedometer. Seventy. "The faster we get our hands back on Pearl, the closer I am to getting my dog back."

"Hoo-ee!" Marion slapped the dash. "Can you feel the good

energy, Lon? The goddess wants us to get her back from the sons a bitches that stole her." She sounded like she might actually bare her teeth. "And to save Linus! We're gonna do it."

I still wasn't convinced that Kyle and company hadn't taken the car for a joyride, then called us to pretend they'd spotted it. But if I got Pearl back in decent shape, I didn't care.

We'd barreled south about four and half miles from The Slipper. "Gumbo said the car was right here." I slowed to a respectable sixty as I followed a curve to the right.

"Deer!"

I kicked the brake. "Where?"

Marion pointed up ahead. "I saw a flash on the side of the road."

Shirley had warned us to scan the side of the road for reflections of our headlights in deer's eyes. "This time of the morning, huntin' season. They're running."

I slowed, saw two flashes up ahead, unmoving.

"Great goddess, blessed be!" Marion's shout echoed wildly in the truck's cabin. "It's Pearl!"

I slowed to twenty, drove past the car. She tilted sideways into the ditch at a precarious angle and her trunk was wide open, but otherwise, she looked unscathed.

"What are you doing?" Marion asked.

I turned, scanning the area. "You see anyone?"

Marion swiveled to look back. "You think someone's lyin' in wait?"

The road curved left and I followed the curve. No lights appeared in the distance, not a car, house or gas station. Anyone could be hiding in the dark. "Why would someone just ditch the car?"

Marion stared at me. "Turn around."

"Seriously, Marion. Why steal a car and then leave it in the middle of nowhere? What if this is a setup?"

"For what, for goddess' sake?"

"To get someone to stop? Rob them?" I imagined those three big hulking boys, their weapons, and us out here in all this darkness. "What if Pearl stopped running and that's why they left it? What if we can't drive it away?"

"Stop this damned car," Marion said and I stopped right there in the middle of the empty road. She took a deep breath. "Come on, Rev Lon. The universe has given us a very very big break here. Let's accept the gift with gratitude. Turn the key and drive away. Simple." She pulled the key from a pocket and dangled it in front of me. "I'll drive her if you're too chicken."

Chickenshit came my great-aunt's voice.

I pulled a U-turn. "Okay, but I want you to have a cell phone in hand so if anything goes funny, we call the cops."

Marion pulled her cell out of her purse. "Then ditch the drugs." She poked me. "Come on, Lon. This is like the movies. We're kick-ass heroines!"

"Kick-ass movie heroines know martial arts and have arsenals of automatic weapons strapped to themselves." I drove back around the curve, watching for any sign of life in the truck's headlights. "I don't."

Marion's eyes narrowed. "You have at least two weapons."

I snorted. "Yeah. Like what?"

"You can kick the hell out of anything. And that Taser. Tell me you've got the Taser."

I stopped the truck next to the Fairlane and touched my jeans pocket. The bulge was there. "I do." I'd shoved it in my pocket when we left town and forgotten all about it.

"Well, get that sucker out."

"I don't want to use it. What if I give someone a heart attack or something?"

"Well, first kick the crap out of 'em. But if that doesn't work, tase 'em."

The utter blackness of the night seemed to cup us as I pulled up next to Pearl.

No way would I do this for anyone but Linus.

"This will be a snap." My loud assurance sounded fake even to my own ears and my stomach twisted again. I took the keys from Marion and crawled out of the truck. She slid into the driver's seat.

"Hello?" I yelled. In the breeze, tree branches clicked.

Long weeds curled around the Fairlane's front bumper. The gravel shoulder crunched under my running shoes. *How stupid is this?* If I were watching this in a movie, I would be sitting in the audience screaming *Don't do it!*

I glanced back and Marion gave me a thumbs-up.

Linus. I peered into Pearl's black interior, wishing for a flashlight. It looked empty. "Hello?" My voice cracked. I didn't know what I'd do if someone answered. I pulled the cap off the taser, exposing the electronic ends.

Marion leaned out the truck window. "You're doing good, Rev."

The driver's door was locked, so I opened it with the key and the inside lights swelled on.

Pearl was not exactly empty. No person, but the front seat was littered with crap. An open bag of Nacho Doritos, three cans of soda, Marion's carefully made maps and notes, extra shoes and some sweats scattered across both seats. The troublesome leopard print bag sagged across the hump in the middle of the back seat floor, now empty. The whole car smelled like pot.

God, they'd been driving and smoking dope. It was a wonder they hadn't cracked up the car. I shoved the mess over and got in.

One turn of the key, though, and I knew we weren't taking Pearl anywhere. Because the engine turned over, sputtered, and died.

"Shit!" I searched the dash but Pearl had no warning lights. I wondered if I should open the hood and look at the engine. People always seemed to do that and quickly fix their problems. Thanks to Kyle, Gumbo and Brucey D., I did know how to get the hood off.

I slumped in the seat. Who was I kidding? I knew nothing about engines.

Marion backed the truck up next to me and hung out the window. "What's up?"

"It won't start." I tried again so Marion could hear. The car ground, caught, but died right away.

Marion squinted, concentrating. "Battery sounds okay. But don't keep trying it, or you'll wear it down."

"I don't suppose you'd like to look under the hood?"

"No!" Marion raised her hands to ward off my suggestion. "Messing with a car is like messing with a computer's innards. No way."

I touched the steering wheel, the gearshift and the dash as if I could divine the car's problem through healing touch. "Guess we know why the thief just dumped Pearl here."

Marion bent further down and looked inside Pearl. "Hey. That's my stuff. That bastard got into my stuff."

"Smoked your pot, too. The whole car reeks."

"Had his crappy little hands on my clothes. Yick!" Marion looked as if she'd seen something very slimy on her arm. "I'll have to wash it all before I can wear it."

"Good idea." Though more for the smell than any handprints, I thought. "I guess calling a mechanic in the morning is our only option. But I'm not leaving her here alone."

"You mean sit here all night?" Marion still studied her scattered things.

"It's just a couple of hours." I started to pick up the garbage.

"Call Red," Marion said. "Maybe she can talk you through some quick fix. Like a computer help line."

"I'm not bugging her at this hour."

"Lonnie!" Marion slapped the side of the truck. "Call the woman! Please!" She held out the phone. "Or I will. And then it will look weird that you wouldn't."

"God forbid I look weird to Red." I wasn't laughing. But I took the phone.

Red was up, of course. "Warming my hands around a hot cup of coffee," she said when I asked. "How are you? Or more to the point, what's wrong with the car?"

That didn't surprise me. It was just after five a.m. Why else would I call?

I decided not to tell her it had been stolen. After all, her family had taken care of it for thirty-some years and I'd lost it after just one day. "Well, we're trying to start it and it won't catch. The battery seems okay."

"Hold the phone out and turn the key, so I can hear it."

I held it out the window and turned the key. Cough, sputter.

"Was it running okay when you parked it last night?" Red paused. "It's kind of strange because it sounds like you're just out of gas, but if you'd run out of gas, you'd know it."

Gas! I hunted the dashboard for a gas gauge.

"I mean, you couldn't just park it completely out of gas," Red continued. "The chances of that are—"

"The gas gauge says a quarter full."

"How many miles did you put on it on this tank?"

I looked at Marion. "How many miles since we last filled it up?"

Marion twisted her lips as she did mental math.

"It doesn't matter," Red said. "You wouldn't have parked it out of gas."

"Well," I said, squirming behind Pearl's steering wheel, "the fact is we didn't park it. We—" Oh, man, how was I going to put this? "Well—"

"Someone *stole* the Fairlane?" Red's voice barreled from the tiny phone.

"About a hundred and forty miles," said Marion.

"But we found it," I said to Red. "Only it won't go. And we've gone about a hundred and—"

"I heard her," Red said. "That's a long way on that tank, given the mileage that thing gets."

"But the gauge," I said.

"Yeah." Red sounded almost apologetic. "It sticks. It's an old car."

"You might have mentioned that," I said.

"Good thing you didn't know, or you'd have filled it last night and that car would be long gone by now," Red said.

"There was a gas station back near town," Marion said. "Maybe four miles?"

"Probably a kid hot-wired it," said Red, "and he trusted the gauge. Plus, he never figured it for getting only eight miles to the gallon. He ran out of gas and you get your car back. Put some fuel in it. If it doesn't start, call me again."

"But wait. Can I drive it if it was hot-wired?"

"Lon, this car was built long before antitheft systems. It was probably hot-wired with a piece of wire and a screwdriver. It should start right up with the key. You can pull the extra wire out later. It won't affect the key ignition."

I felt my whole body lighten. We'd be on the road in no time. I thanked Red and jumped back into the truck. This would be solved in no time, no problem. "Sweet," I said to Marion and we high-fived.

Marion drove so fast, the truck's hood rippled. I was just about to suggest she slow it down a little when she slammed on the brakes. I lurched forward. "Deer?"

"Didn't you see him?" We coasted forward as she looked out the back window. "Somebody walking along the road back there. Headed toward Pearl." She stared at me. "He had a gas can."

CHAPTER THIRTY-THREE

I scanned the dark road behind us, saw no one. "You sure?"

Marion slowed the truck further. "Of course I'm sure. Want me to turn around?"

"To do what? Tell the guy to put up his dukes and fight?" I looked in the truck, at the bare concrete in the headlights, at the dark sky and even darker woods. No answers.

That son of a bitch, whoever he was, put Linus' life in danger.

I spun backward. "You know what? Yeah. Turn around. I'll scare him off."

Instead of turning, Marion sped up. "I have a better idea!"

"Hey! My car! Turn around!"

"Lonnie, listen!" She hunched forward, eyes glued to the road. "He's got to walk two miles. He doesn't know we're here, so he's in no rush. We don't need to beat him face to face. We can beat him back to the car. Get out of there before he gets back."

"Too risky. I could just—" My body slammed against the seat as she floored the truck.

At 5:29 a.m. we pulled into a self-serve gas station and E-Z mart. I was out of the truck before it stopped. "I'll get a gas can."

Marion was already brandishing her credit card. "We will take back Pearl!"

In the bright store, a young woman sat on a stool behind the counter. Large black smudges under her sunken eyes made her look sick as well as exhausted.

"Hi." I tried not to act like the crazed, desperate soul that I was. "My car's out of gas on the road back there. I need a gas can."

The girl, whose nametag said "Anjy," smiled. "You're the second person in an hour needed a can." She looked out at Marion who was putting gas in the truck. "The guy came on foot." She didn't move from her stool.

"Can I buy a can too?" The clock above her head said 5:31.

Anjy smiled again. "Oh, we'll loan it to ya."

I grinned. "Great! Thanks!"

She didn't move.

I looked around. "Can I have the can?"

She shook her head and long black locks fell like streaks before her face. "We only got one gas can. He took it."

I looked around. "You only have one?"

"Don't ever use it but once in a year, way out here." She tossed her head again. "Wait'll I tell my manager we had call for it twice in one night and at the same time too."

My eyes swept the aisles. Discount wine in paper boxes, a condom dispenser, magazines, beef jerky, caffeinated drinks stacked in a double pyramid. "There must be something else I can use."

She didn't move from her stool. "No, 'cause it's a federal offense to dispense gasoline into an unapproved container."

"But this is an emergency." I headed toward the car aisle. Pine-scented air fresheners shaped like buck heads. Travel mugs stamped with the words Everything's Better in Bliss!. 10W-30 motor oil. Blue rags.

I headed past canned soup and instant pasta dishes toward the coolers and then I saw them—plastic gallon jugs of distilled water. Two ought to be enough to get Pearl back here for a fill-up.

I brought them to the register and Anjy looked at me through narrowed eyes. "If I sell you that knowing you're gonna fill 'em with gas, I could get into a lot of trouble." She glanced up toward a security camera blinking from a ceiling corner. "This could even be some sort of a test. I mean what are the odds that two people would run out of gas out here at the same time?"

Marion stuck her head in the door. "The truck's ready, Reverend."

I raised a finger. "Just a sec."

Anjy's mouth dropped open. "Are you a minister?"

Normally, I hated playing the pastor card, but this was not normal. I smiled my best reassuring pastoral smile. "I'm a priest."

"No way." The girl pulled her hair from her face. "No way! What church has women pastors?"

"Episcopal," I said.

Anjy studied me. "I guess I should help out a priest, huh? Or I might wind up in hell? Like, could you damn me?"

"I can't damn you," I said. "No one can damn you."

Anjy shook her head. "Pastor Timmons says the devil is everywhere and he can damn you with sneaky tricks." Her gaze bounced between me and Marion. "Maybe this is a sneaky trick to get me to sell you gas in an unapproved container. Maybe letting you commit a federal offense is something that will get me damned to hell." She looked at Marion. "The devil can be anywhere."

"It's not a trick." I waved my cash in front of her. "I need the water. Please."

Anjy studied me, her eyes uncertain.

"Please," I said.

"You give me a blessing?" Her finger hovered over the final sale button on the cash register.

"Heavens, yes." I raised my right hand and made a sign of

the cross. "May the Lord bless and keep you. In the name of the Father, and the Son, and the Holy Spirit. Amen."

She pushed the button and the register dinged. "You know," Anjy said quietly, "there's a security camera on the pumps too. I can see whatever you pump into." She dropped the change into my hand and leaned in close. "But it's about time for me to sweep. Takes me about two or three minutes. And I can't see the monitor when I sweep." She grabbed a broom from where it leaned in a corner and tossed her head. "Have a nice morning, Reverend."

We filled the water jugs with gas, spilling only a little and dancing enough to keep it off our shoes. I held them between my feet as we raced back toward Pearl.

I scanned the road but saw no sign of the walker. "It's five forty exactly." Thirteen minutes since we'd seen him. "If he's there when we get there, just drive on by. I'll call the cops."

Marion leaned closer to the steering wheel as if urging the truck to run faster. "He's the thief, Rev. He ought to be afraid of us. Maybe he'll hightail it into the woods if we show up. Car thieves don't usually carry guns or anything."

"And you know this how?"

She pointed up ahead. "There!" The truck slowed as we neared the walker.

"Don't slow down!" I slapped Marion's arm down. "And don't point. Just drive!"

I struggled to make the guy out as we sped by. Dark hair, medium height with broad shoulders. Baggy dark pants and a bulky sweatshirt or jacket. Maybe facial hair. "How much farther?"

"Half mile."

In seconds Marion pulled behind Pearl, the truck sliding on the gravel shoulder. She grabbed her cell. "In case something happens."

I hopped out of the truck then grabbed the two jugs. "Turn around, so we can see him in your headlights."

The light from the truck twisted through the thick trees as Marion pulled a U-turn. I opened Pearl's driver's door to get light in the car. The stench of pot rolled out again. Then I pulled the gas door open and unscrewed the cap.

"You got the Taser out?" asked Marion.

I pulled the lid from one jug. "I've got gasoline here! I don't want three hundred and fifty thousand volts anywhere near me! Do you see anything?" I asked without looking up. *Focus, Lon,* said my smarter voice. *This is just like running toward goal with a defender on your ass.*

Yeah, except last time I did that, I wound up face down in the dirt.

Don't think about that now. You can win this one.

"All clear," said Marion.

I hesitated for one second wondering what any leftover drops of water might do to the car's engine. *Help, help, help,* I thought, and poured the liquid in.

Gasoline dribbled out the edge of the jug and down the side of the car. I stood as far back as I could to avoid getting it on my shoes, but drops still rolled across my fingers.

"Hurry, Reverend."

Like I wasn't hurrying. The liquid glugged out. "It only pours so fast, Marion." Which wasn't very fast at all.

The jug had nearly emptied when Marion said, "Forget the other one! Let's go."

"I haven't even got a whole one in yet." A gallon wouldn't get Pearl very far. I adjusted the angle of the jug, trying to get the liquid to move faster.

"You've got enough gas to drive away, and right now you need to drive away!"

I poured. *Just another few seconds—*

"Now, Lonnie!"

I looked up and saw the vague form of a man at the edge of the truck's headlights' range, arms unencumbered and pumping as he ran—not into the woods, but toward us.

Terror charged up my chest and throat. I dropped the nearly empty jug, scooped up the other and the gas cap, and leapt feet-first into the driver's seat.

"Go, go, go!" yelled Marion, revving the truck.

I turned the Fairlane's key. The engine revved, sputtered, died.

The truck's horn blared. "We're armed," Marion yelled. "And I'm dialing nine-one-one!"

Come on. Come on. I turned the key again and pressed the gas pedal lightly. "Help!" I screamed, demanded of some power beyond myself.

Suddenly everything slowed down. Grew silent, like a dream world. I could see myself, years ago, in the '72 Beetle my dad had taught me to drive. "It's a dance of clutch and gas," he'd told me. "Different in each car." I touched the pedals like I was juggling a soccer ball, and turned the key. The engine caught.

The silent memory ended as Pearl roared to life. I shifted into gear and floored the gas. The back wheels spun on the gravel and we leapt forward. In the rearview mirror I saw the open trunk snap shut, then the man flailing his arms just a few yards away. Marion roared away in the opposite direction.

Pearl's engine hollered and I shifted, then shifted again, still pushing on the gas. The speedometer needle swept across the dash-wide gauge and when I finally looked down, it read 127 miles per hour.

So this was what it was like to drag race a muscle car.

I had to remember to tell Red.

CHAPTER THIRTY-FOUR

I sped across dark wooded roads, turning left a few times to circle back. Once I knew I was headed back toward Bliss, I stopped to pour in the second gallon of gas. Then, because the roads were empty and my blood was full of adrenaline, I let myself floor it the whole way back to the gas station.

Marion paced next to the truck. When she saw me, she clasped her hands over her head and waved them like a victorious boxer. Then she bent through the window and hugged my neck hard.

"You, Reverend! You! Are a totally kick-ass heroine!"

I have to admit, I felt like one. I was so pumped up I felt like I could kick down walls. We went back to the hotel and I cleaned out the car while Marion showered, just daring that goon on the road to show back up here to retake the car. Let him try. Then

I made Marion sit in the car while I showered. I didn't feel like I'd missed a night's sleep. I felt ready to tackle my great-aunt's craziness and Star Hannes and the car thief all over again.

I was going to get my dog back. Nothing could stop me now.

At 7:04 we drove the two vehicles back to the Purple Slipper. I stuck a twenty in the truck's glove box while Marion returned the keys. When she reappeared, she had a bag between her teeth and two large coffees in her hands.

I took the bag. "My God, how many doughnuts are in here?"

"They were all fresh, and I couldn't decide on what kind, so I got a dozen. They're better for you than potato chips anyhow. Homemade. Better karma."

I waved to Shirley who had come to the door to watch our departure. "Better karma it is."

"First stop," Marion said, hunkering for comfort on Pearl's stiff seat, "the Mackinac Bridge."

I'd seen pictures. That was one big bridge. Normally I couldn't drive across one that big. But today I could. What was a bridge after what we'd been through last night?

Marion flipped through the pages on her clipboard. "That punk messed up my notes." She swatted paper noisily. "And it stinks in here." She opened a window and a freezing wind whipped through the car. Then she spread a napkin on my thigh then placed a plain doughnut glazed with chocolate on top of that. "Voilà!"

I took a big bite. The chocolate melted against the heat of my tongue. At moments like this, I wondered why chocolate wasn't one of the holy foods.

The rising sun shone white-yellow in a bright blue, cloudless sky, the kind of blue that only showed up on a crisp fall day in a place free of smog. The frost that dotted the fields glowed in the sun's first light. Very peaceful. No hint of the dark fright of just hours ago.

Then ahead, a white mist thickened below the bright blue sky, billowing and towering upward. A cloud on the ground. The bridge ramp disappeared into it and further on, the bridge's first suspension tower floated five hundred feet above the fog. It looked like a giant totem pole with the faces missing. The bridge itself was lost in the mist.

I regripped the wheel.

"Wait! The picture! Here!" Marion pointed to the last exit before the bridge. I jerked Pearl across two lanes of traffic and pulled into a parking lot at the reconstructed trading village of Michilimackinac. The fog curled around us as I watched car headlights rise upward on the ramp, then disappear.

"You know," I said, "my aunt knew I hated bridges. Bridges, piers, docks, anything suspended out over water." I shivered. She knew I had her to thank for that too—her and her little escapade on the pier in the storm.

"But you can't drive around Lake Michigan without crossing this bridge. I mean, the Upper Peninsula isn't connected to the Lower Peninsula any other way."

I didn't bother to point out Kate could have sent me on a driving trip anywhere else in the Midwest.

"You know," Marion said as she studied me and the car through the camera, "Pearl looks pretty good, considering she got ditched last night." She grinned at her own joke. "I looked like hell last time I got ditched."

I drew the breath to say it. To make the joke about the last time I got ditched, when I'd been whacked on the head, bleeding, semiconscious, lying in the middle of my front yard in the middle of the night when my girlfriend just ditched me then and there because she was too afraid it would get out—us being gay—and it would ruin her medical practice. I wanted to say all of that and get sympathy and then share a laugh about it. I was a kick-ass heroine now and could surely do it.

But I didn't. I just couldn't.

My skin felt clammy—part chilly fog, part frustration at my self-silencing—as we reentered the car and followed a fifth wheel camper being towed by a bright yellow truck up the bridge's ramp. Even if I was too chicken to tell my best friend the truth about me, I was not chickening out on this bridge. Everything around us was white, but I could tell it was very high.

"Lake Michigan over there," Marion pointed left, "and Lake Huron over there." She pointed right.

A funny dryness itched at the back of my mouth. "How long is this thing?"

"Five miles long," Marion said. "And three hundred feet above the water."

I blew out a whole lot of air.

"But that's nothing compared to the one they just opened between France and Spain," she continued. "The clouds—real clouds, not just fog—are below that one."

Mental note: never drive between France and Spain.

"Plus, once we get off this ramp," Marion said, and at that moment, we bumped from the ramp onto a green grid, "there's no concrete in the middle. See, only that grid. And it's see-through."

My stomach lurched.

"If you don't like it, you can pull out of the center lane. It's concrete on the edge."

I didn't like it but I liked the idea of edge even less. The railing barely looked three feet high. A child could step over it.

Above us blinked a warning sign: *High Winds. Reduce speed. RVs and trailers 20 mph.*

"Do you think that's a problem?" The trailer ahead of us was easily doing fifty.

"Nah." Marion shook her head. "It always says that."

I didn't bother to ask her how she knew.

"Though I'm glad Pearl's a heavy girl. Like me. No chance of blowing over the edge."

That cinched it. We were staying in the center lane, even if I could see through the road into the apparently bottomless fog below. Just a few more minutes and we'd be on land again.

I swirled my tongue around in my mouth. I needed water or gum or something.

Marion looked up through the windshield. "You ever wonder how they get these things to stay up in the air? Just those little cables holding up us and all these trailers and eighteen-wheelers? Doesn't seem—"

"Okay! Marion!" I tried to swallow, but my tongue stuck to the roof of my mouth. "Enough about the height." *Help, help, help,* I prayed. *I need a diversion.*

My cell phone rang.

At that moment the dangers of driving while talking on the phone seemed much smaller than the dangers of my terrified focus on the bridge and the deadly waters below. So I answered it.

"I'm assuming," Red's voice sounded weary on the phone, "you got the car no problem or I'd have heard."

I debated telling her about the mad race with the man on the road. The thief. Me in the role of kick-ass heroine. That I was gay and thought she was hot.

"Everything's just fine," I said. Then a gust of wind caught Pearl, shoving us hard to the right. I had to yank the wheel to stay in my own lane.

"Whoa," said Marion.

"Yeah, well, not everything," said Red. "How in God's name you can be hundreds of miles away and still make trouble here, I do not know."

I glanced in all Pearl's mirrors, double-checking nearby traffic. Trailer ahead. A pickup in my blind spot. A bunch of SUVs all around. The lanes suddenly seemed very narrow.

"Actually," Red continued, "I do know. You're on the damn phone. I should have taken it away from you when you left town."

"But then I'd be sitting with some backwoods mechanic somewhere waiting for someone to fix Pearl, not on the road to Star's fortune," I said. "And getting my dog."

"Careful," Marion said as the trailer ahead of us swayed over the lane line.

I pulled back.

"Besides," I said, "what trouble have I caused?" I mean, hell, I'd been chasing bad guys all night. No connection to Middelburg.

"Ivor Koontz is threatening to get a restraining order against you. Says you've been hassling Isabella."

"What?" Heat prickled my face. "That's bullshit!"

"Did you call her?"

"She's my parishioner, for God's sake. And works on several important church commissions. Of course I called her." And she must have told her husband.

The wind forced the car further right, and I needed both hands on the wheel, so I pushed the phone between my ear and shoulder.

"You ask her about Ivor's business?"

"I checked on the family."

"Watch out!" Marion waved her hands at the trailer whose brake lights flashed.

"Well, for now, stop calling her. Wait until he cools down."

The trailer ahead of me swerved again and I resisted my urge to lay on the horn.

I felt a prickle of guilt. I hoped I hadn't made Isabella's life any harder than it was. "She's got to get away from that bastard."

"No argument from me there," said Red.

My arm ached from pulling the car to the left. "You talk to Jack Putnam? Or Dale Zeerip yet? About Ivor and the troubles at work? Some dispute with Koeman about pay?" He'd had enough cash to buy tickets to Vegas, but still owed everyone at the poker game money.

"Lonnie, we are not having this conversation." I heard the crackle of her squad car radio in the background.

"Ivor Koontz is up to his neck in Koeman's death," I said. "Why else would he freak out and try to get a restraining order on me just because I checked to see how his wife was doing?"

"Quit asking questions, Lon. Just keep that car safe and come home and get your dog," Red said.

Screw her, then. I'd done a bunch of things she didn't know about. Outfoxed a car thief. Found out about that Thursday night poker game. She didn't want to talk, I wasn't going to tell her.

I felt the push of the wind let go of the car and relaxed my hands on the steering wheel. We had crested the arc of the bridge but still remained in a swirling white cloud.

"Hey, look," Marion said, pointing up from the window. "You can see the sky. The clouds are like wispy hairs up here."

I tried to look, steer and manage my phone all at once. I slid Pearl slightly to the left so I could glance around the trailer. The end of the bridge was still lost in fog.

"One thing," I said, "from before this trip. Someone's messing with the security cameras at the rec center. The ones

Jack Putnam installed. I saw him and Star and Gil Hannes having a hell of a fight about it one evening after soccer. Jack thinks Ivor is sabotaging his systems. And you and I know how well Star and Ivor work together when it comes to sabotage."

I was referring to their little plan for last May's Family Values Day celebration. A plan I'd discovered and busted up. I felt a jolt of pride. Maybe I'd been a kick-ass heroine all along and never known it.

"Why would Ivor do that?"

"Maybe we should ask why Star would do it? Ivor's probably working for her again."

Red just groaned.

Pearl lurched in the wind and the phone slipped from my shoulder as I struggled with the wheel.

Marion shrieked as the trailer in front of us swung three feet to the right, well into the next lane. The sedan driving there swerved into the narrow shoulder of the bridge. "They're gonna hit the rail!"

I kicked the brakes. The lap seatbelt bit into my hips and something tumbled off the backseat onto the floor.

The trailer swung left, then right, back and forth, until it eventually centered itself.

"Holy Goddess." Marion pushed against the dash.

My heart thudded in my throat. I slid my hand on the seat until I found my phone. "Sorry about that."

"I'm hanging up," Red said. "So you don't kill yourself."

"You really do care."

"Or worse," she continued, "wreck that car."

Someday, over a few drinks, I'd have to tell her the truth about what happened on the side of the road last night. But in the meantime… "Ask Ivor some questions, Red. Seriously."

"Drive the car, Lonnie. And stay out of trouble. Seriously."

Then just ahead the white fog dissipated and the multilane tollbooth marked the entrance to Michigan's Upper Peninsula.

I'd crossed over the bridge.

CHAPTER THIRTY-FIVE

The next stop on Aunt Kate's itinerary was Totem Village, a quirky shop just a mile west of the toll plaza in St. Ignace. We drove west on M-2 through a strip of tourist traps that looked like it had been lifted from an old *National Geographic.* On the left grassy parks led down to the northern shore of Lake Michigan. On the right little gray buildings with colorful signs offered pasties, smoked whitefish and fudge. Then we pulled off at a long, low log cabin fronted by several totem poles, a teepee and a chunky wooden Indian. Golden bales of straw and caddywampus piles of pumpkins threatened to tumble, so I parked well away from the building. A huge sign crossed the roof, letters formed from fake birch branches proclaiming "Moccasins, Indian museum, baskets, jewelry, live foxes."

The parking lot was empty, though I saw a few lights on inside. "Looks closed."

"Nah." Marion pulled her camera from her bag. "We got money to spend, they'll be open."

I stood near the car while Marion tromped a few yards away to take the photo. Then she tossed the camera back in the car. "I love kitschy places like this."

I hesitated next to the car.

"What?" She held her hands out as if checking for rain. She wore an eggplant corduroy big shirt with flowers sketched across the bottom in bright yellow and orange embroidery. Boot cut jeans wrapped tightly around her hips and tapered to a point above her purple spike sandals. She looked hilarious next to those totem poles.

She thrust her hands onto her hips. "There something you want to tell me, now that you're a kick-ass heroine?"

I could not figure out why, all of a sudden, she'd decided to probe into the unspoken parts of my life. But I didn't want to talk about it. So I deflected.

"Let me take a picture of you." We killed a few minutes posing her in front of wooden Indians, enormous pumpkins and bales of straw.

"Where to next?" I asked as we finished.

She looked horrified. "No way! We can't pass this up! Look at this place! God knows what treasures lie within."

I shook my head. "I'm not leaving this car."

She bit her lip. "Lonnie, whoever stole Pearl is long gone. Come on."

"Nope." I leaned against the door.

"Lonnie. You can't spend every minute between now and the end of this trip in that car. Whoever took it is probably still walking back into town after last night."

"Maybe he's really really angry at us," I said.

"You're paranoid."

"Maybe someone else will see this car and decide to steal it. There's a reason Red kept it locked up all those years. It's worth a lot."

"Paranoid," Marion said.

"Go ahead," I said, waving toward the shop.

Half an hour later Marion returned, arms full of bags. "You've never seen anything like it. Shelves so packed you couldn't see it all! Plastic squaw dolls with kewpie heads like when we were kids. They even have decoupaged slices of wood with pictures of howling wolves and stuff. And look!" She held up a rubber-headed tom-tom. "I haven't seen one of these in thirty years."

Our next stop was the Garlyn Zoological Park in Naubinway, just another five miles west. Though Marion begged, claiming a lifelong desire to see wallabies, and though it looked beautiful all nestled in a northern pine forest, I refused to go in.

"We are not leaving this car."

Marion grumbled and agreed only on the condition that I let her drive. "Michihistrigan is another twenty miles," she said.

"Fine." I grabbed my cell phone.

"You wouldn't be doing anything to piss off Red, would you?" asked Marion, eyeing my cell instead of the road.

"Just calling my mother." She answered on the second ring. Miraculously, I heard no appliances in the background.

"I wake you up?" I asked.

"Squeezing oranges for your father's juice," she said. I heard a thunk—probably a knife slicing a fruit in half. "He promised me one of those electronic juicers for Christmas this year."

"Good. Mom, I need to finish talking to you about Aunt Kate."

"Do you?" Thunk.

"You said she had something planned for my thirty-fifth birthday?" I tried to sound happy and light. I had to go carefully here. If my mom thought a conversation would be unpleasant, she simply wouldn't have it.

"She told me she had the most tremendous surprise for you!" Thunk. "She said she'd send you on a wonderful trip. In a new car. With a slew of cash." Thunk. Mom laughed. "Can you imagine? She always was a little off-kilter as your father would say."

"Is that Lonnie?" my dad hollered from somewhere in the house. "Tell her I said happy birthday a day late."

"Your father says—"

"Tell him I love him," I said.

"Lonnie loves you." Thunk.

"Mom, why did you send me to stay with her all those

summers if you thought she was off-kilter?" I'd hated my time with my great-aunt. I'd hated being ostracized from the family.

"Oh, Lonnie, you were so angry at your father and me for splitting up." Thunk. "Your sisters were just collapsing, but not you. You were angry and fighting and getting into trouble all the time."

"Well, hell, yes, I was angry."

"Lonnie." Marion's voice reminded me to stay calm. I nodded at her.

"We just knew it would be better for you—for all of us—to send you away. Where you could start fresh, be with new people. And Kate just adored you. Said you reminded her of herself, younger. Plus, she was so devoted to that church. We knew she'd be a good influence."

"Adored me? Good influence? She treated me like crap!" I remembered how she'd made me scrub her old floors before I could eat dinner. How she made me serve her friends tea in silence. How she always threatened to send my dog away any time I didn't agree or obey. How she'd forbidden me to go to church because "it warped young minds." Of course, I'd snuck in the next week and the rest was history. But still.

"And look how wonderfully you turned out!" my mom sang. "A priest. Helping the police. A great soccer player. So many wonderful friends." Thunk. "Lonnie, honey, I couldn't give you what you needed then. I just couldn't."

"She didn't either."

"She thought she did!" said my mother, ever chipper. "She said she wanted to be sure you didn't grow up to be stiff and wimpy. Too serious. Too chicken to take risks. So she had this birthday present all worked out."

Chickenshit.

Rage swamped me. Aunt Kate. Always always manipulating.

"Imagine," my mom said. "A car, vacation and cash. Sounds like the big prize on *The Price Is Right.*"

"Yeah." I didn't say much else. I was too mad.

"I need to finish this juice, Lonnie," my mom said. "I need two hands to squeeze it. You call me back when you can."

I clicked off and tossed the phone in the glove box.

"My great-aunt thought I was a chicken," I said to Marion. "Stiff. Wimpy. Too serious. That's why she arranged this trip."

Energy bubbled beneath my skin. I swallowed, tried to press it down.

"Maybe," Marion continued, "she wanted you to get more from life. Be with friends. Kick back. Be yourself. That's why here and not New York. Or Paris or something."

The energy—my spirit?—frizzled and stretched. "I'm not some angry wimp hiding from life. I'm always pushing for more. For better. That's why I can't let crap like Star's seven laws just happen. That's how I got into this mess."

"You're always fighting to free everyone else," Marion said. "But what about yourself? I mean, we all have our cages but maybe, if we always help others, we never get free. Just talking can set you free." She sighed. "I'm glad you know about the dope. Knowing you know, well, it makes me think about it in a different way."

"I'm gay," I said. It was out before I'd really thought about it, before I'd felt my mouth form the words.

Every part of me clenched, waiting.

Marion turned to look at me. She grinned. "Well, duh, honey. I've known that since we were teenagers."

Surprise roiled through me like a wave. "What? You knew? How? I didn't even know until I was in seminary!"

She laughed. "It was pretty obvious."

I flopped forward, leaning against Pearl's expansive dash. "Well, I wish you'd told me." God, the years of anguish that would have spared me.

"Wasn't mine to tell. And Lon?" She waited for me to look at her. "Being gay is not like stashing dope in your friend's car. Not even comparable."

Blah blah. Her words washed over me. She said it was obvious. I had to refigure my whole life. I mean, did everyone know? "Do the Flashes know?"

"What? That I smoke?"

"No!" I sat up. "That I'm gay!"

Marion shrugged. "Probably. I don't know. We don't talk about it. Occasionally we'll chat about fixing you up with someone and we sort of stop at agreeing that we don't know anyone right for you. No one ever says if it's because we can't think of any other lesbians. But I suspect that's the case."

I chewed on that. If everyone knew—or at least if all the people I loved and trusted knew—my life would be totally different. I wasn't sure how, but I just knew it would be.

"We don't talk about it because we love you, Lon. And you haven't talked about it with us yet. It's kind of like permission. You tell us you're gay and you can bet we'll be gossiping about how to find you a hot chick!" She waggled her eyebrows at me.

I heaved a breath from the depths of my toes. "I've been wanting to tell you for—well, forever."

"Wait a minute." Pearl bumped over a pothole and kept on. "Is there something else you want to tell me?"

"Wasn't that enough?" I grinned. But she was serious. "No. Nothing. Why?"

She checked the road, then reached across to open the glove box. She rattled her hand around its cavernous expanse then dropped something small and orange in my lap. "Then what's this?"

It was L-shaped. Had a cap on one end. "An inhaler?"

She sat back up straight. "Of course it's an inhaler. Albuterol is an asthma medication." I saw the drug name stamped into the plastic case. "And if you've developed asthma, it's okay. You'll be fine. You'll still be a great soccer player. No one will care."

Things started to click together in my head. "The last few days. All the questions trying to get me to tell you something. You've been trying to get me to tell you I'm asthmatic?"

"We'll still love you, Lon."

"You thought *this* was the secret I've been tiptoeing around?"

"Well, I wasn't sure until yesterday morning when I found it on the floor of the car. After we jumped the curb in Grand Haven and dumped my stuff everywhere? But I know how much anything that would compromise your soccer would crush you—"

I laughed until tears ran down my cheeks. Marion watched me carefully. "Seriously, Lonnie, no one cares. Medicine controls these things."

"It's not mine. God." I wiped my eyes. "I thought you were pumping me to tell you I was gay."

She smacked my arm. "Why would I care that you're gay?" She smacked me again. "You think I'm a bigot!"

"No, no." I fell all over myself apologizing and laughing. "You're not a bigot. And I don't have asthma. And if I did, I'd tell you. I promise. I'll tell you anything."

Eventually she laughed too. "Let's split a doughnut."

As I pulled the doughnut bag into my lap, I tossed the inhaler back into the glove box. "Wait a minute." I pulled the inhaler back out and studied it. No label. "If this isn't mine and it isn't yours, whose is it?"

CHAPTER THIRTY-SIX

We decided the inhaler had to belong to Red, since it didn't belong to either of us and Marion had found it before the car got stolen.

"Though it would be sort of funny," Marion said, "to think about a car thief losing his asthma medicine in the stolen vehicle."

I agreed it would serve him right. Plus, it would be a cool way to catch a criminal. Imagine the lineup. *Him, Officer,* I'd say, *the one with the wheeze.*

"So call her." Marion tossed me her cell. "Tell her we found her inhaler. She must be wondering about it."

Suddenly, the idea of calling Red Carson filled me with terror. "She probably has a backup." I slid the phone back across the front seat.

Marion narrowed her eyes at me and scrunched her lips.

"Don't want her to have to pay for a new prescription if she doesn't need it." She slid the phone back to me. "Call her."

I flipped the phone back onto her lap and hunkered against the door. "You call her. I'm taking a nap."

Marion picked the phone up and tossed it into my chest. "I'm driving. Unsafe to phone and drive. You call her."

I snapped the glove box open and threw the phone in. "No need to call her."

We rode in silence for a few minutes. Woods towered on either side of the highway, the pine trees so dark green they seemed almost black amidst the flashy oranges and yellows of the turning oak and maple. The ground disappeared into dark shadow and tangled masses of undergrowth and fallen limbs. I knew bear lived there, and cougars and moose. It seemed primeval, mysterious wilderness on either side of us. It felt both terrifying and inviting. I wanted to walk there, in the shadows and tangle. Face that mystery.

"So, do you know if Ivor Koontz even owns a gun?" Marion asked out of the blue. "Or did he borrow one from someone recently? Did he lose big at poker? Or, if he gambles at poker, might he gamble somewhere else? Maybe that's why he didn't pay Koeman the overtime he owed him, because he didn't have the cash?"

I pulled myself back from my fantasy. "Don't know. I'm not investigating, remember?"

Marion rolled her eyes dramatically. "Will you just call the woman?"

I closed my eyes and leaned back against the door. "Napping."

"So, you think she's cute, huh?"

I snored. Loudly.

"Call her."

I opened one eye. "Is Red Carson gay?"

Marion shrugged. "Only one way to find out."

Yeah, but that meant having to tell her I was gay first. Marion may have known. Marion may not have cared. And maybe most of the Hot Flashes suspected. But they were my team. My family. Red Carson was none of those things.

"Call her."

I closed my eyes and snored again. Joy bounced around my body. The hilarity of my outing scene with Marion which someday would make a great story. The news that the Flashes didn't care. Plus, Marion didn't say Red Carson was straight. Which meant she might be gay. I let my mind linger on that possibility for a nice long time.

"I know you're awake," Marion said. "You're grinning. So open your eyes. We're here." We bumped off the road onto a gravel parking lot in the middle of a great field, browning and brittle. At one end stood a lush course of greens, waterways and obstacles.

"Michihistrigan Mini Golf," Marion said.

The two-story building next to the course housed a tavern and family restaurant, at least according to its signs. A neon orange banner flapped from the balcony welcoming hunters and promising an all-day breakfast.

"I like the looks of that," Marion said. "Bacon, eggs, toast, coffee. I want it all."

I grabbed my wallet, stomach grumbling. "Me too."

"Ah." Marion grinned as we stepped from the car. "Hunger tops paranoia every time."

I froze. "You're right. We can't leave the car."

Marion flapped in exasperation. "I didn't mean that!"

"We can't leave the car."

Marion shook her head. "No way. We are not just driving away like at the zoo. Unh-uh. Because even if my stomach can be ignored—and by the way, you do that at your peril—my bladder knows we stopped and it insists on using a potty."

I sat on Pearl's hood. "Get takeout. Then come babysit so I can go too."

"Fine. But you're wrong if you think I'm sitting up half the night tonight guarding that car." She strode into the restaurant, bag swinging, ankles never wobbling over the gravel in those astonishing high-heeled shoes.

I missed Linus. If he were here, we'd have passed the time playing fetch with Toad. I could have watched him sniff around the edges of the lot. I loved him more than I'd loved just about anything or anyone in my whole life.

For some reason, I thought again of the scene at the crucifix yesterday. Of the church's continual emphasis on victimization and suffering and guilt and unworthiness. About how much more I loved my dog than the institution I worked for.

Was that okay for a priest? Or should I love the church more than anything else?

I loved what I thought the church could be. Social justice. Everyone welcome at the table. A message of victory and fulfillment and love for everyone. If I weren't a priest, I didn't know what I'd be in the world.

My bladder had reached panic-inducing fullness when Marion finally returned carrying breakfast in Styrofoam containers. "Pick up the coffee on your way out."

A quick visit to the bathroom decorated with decoupaged plaques of German shorthaired pointers and wild turkeys, then I picked up the coffee and returned to Marion, who sat on the hood reading a brochure and downing her food.

"Says here this course is shaped like the state of Michigan with major cities as holes. We're way ahead of schedule..." She sipped her coffee. "I'd whoop your butt."

I knew what she was up to and wasn't going to be suckered. At least, not while I ate. But still, it gave me an idea. "What if Red Carson could tell us how to disable the car? So it couldn't get stolen? Then we wouldn't have to worry about it now or all night tonight."

"If it means you're going to call her," Marion said grinning, "then I vote yes."

We ate quickly and dialed.

Red picked up after one ring. "You lose the car again?"

"No." It irked me she thought I was that careless. "And I'm not going to either, if you can teach me how to disable it." I slid my hand along the cool edge of Pearl's hood.

"I was joking!" Red said.

"I'm not."

"Statistically—"

"Please don't make us sleep in the car!" Marion yelled.

Red sighed. "Let me get my coffee."

"Be nice to her!" Marion whispered.

"I am!" I whispered back. Then I hopped off the hood and walked away.

"So, you got the car back no trouble, huh?" Red asked.

"No trouble." I dug my toe into the gravel. Was lying good for a relationship?

"Well, do you think you can open the hood of the car?"

I gave Marion the thumbs-up and we started pulling hood pins. "Oh, we can take the hood off. No problem."

"Well, it's gonna get more complicated than that. Remember that little tool kit I let you in the trunk?"

"Wait," Marion said as I grabbed the toolbox. "Does this involve tools? Maybe it's not such a good idea."

"She said she'd talk us through it." I set the tools down near a front tire and picked the cell phone off the fender. "How hard can it be?"

"Damned hard if you don't know what you're doing," said Red on the phone. "You don't really want something just anybody can figure out, right?"

She told me to find a ratchet and a spark plug socket.

I stared at the tools. "I can find the duct tape."

Marion's orange toes appeared next to the toolbox. "I know I suggested this, but I withdraw my suggestion."

"Piece of cake." I had Red coaching me. No way was I backing out now.

"I'm guessing you're in some sort of sleep-deprived bacon-induced manic state," Marion said. "Don't do this, Rev." Then she yanked the car door open so hard and flopped inside so firmly the big car rocked.

I ran my hand through the tools. "Okay, Red. You'd better tell me what those things look like. I'm not getting any support on this end."

"I do not do car engines." Marion clucked her tongue.

Red, all business, described the ratchet and the spark plug socket until I found them. "Set them aside. First step, disable the car. Second, get it going. Whole thing will take about twenty minutes. Practice a few times and you'll get faster."

I bounced on my toes and studied the engine like it was a defender near the goal. "Ready for step one."

"Pull all the wires off the distributor cap."

"Pull the wires off the distributor cap?" I repeated.

"Jesus, Mary, Joseph and the great goddess Gaia!" Marion threw her hands up.

Red told me where to find it. "There's a bunch of wires running from a plastic thing to the spark plugs."

The first wire I saw sticking out of anything was one about eight inches long, wrapped around the red pole on the battery on one end and around another red wire on the other. I described it to Red.

She laughed. "Thank your car thief for that. It's how he jumped the car. He linked the battery to the ignition coil. Probably crossed the terminals of the starter solenoid with something metal, like a knife or screwdriver. It fell off when he drove. Just pull it off."

I did, then found the distributor cap. I hesitated. Did I trust her or not? Was I a kick-ass heroine or not? I yanked and they came free.

"That was the ten-second part," Red said.

"And now I just put 'em back on?"

"Yes, but." Red paused. "They have to match spark plug to cap in an exact order. I'd tell you the number of possible combinations, but I don't do math, especially at this hour." She bit into something crunchy and chewed for a second. "You want to know how a distributor and distributor cap work and what we've got to do to it? Or you just want to know what to do?"

I glanced again at the wires. "Just get me back on the road."

"You need a second person behind the wheel to do this."

"Marion's there."

"Okay," said Red. "First, you're going to remove the number one spark plug from the distributor. It's the first one to the right of six o'clock." Red explained how to use the tools to pull the plug out.

I juggled the tools, wires, one spark plug and the phone. I waved with triumph at Marion. She scowled at me through the windshield.

"Now put a thumb over the hole where the spark plug was."

"Is it wise to stick my hand in a car engine?" I asked as I lowered my hand.

"Not generally, no," said Red. "Which is why when your friend Marion turns the key in a minute, she needs to be careful not to actually start the car."

I yanked my hand back out. "What happens if she does?"

Red chuckled again. "Relax, Reverend Squires. That was a joke. She can't. That's the point, remember?"

"Right." *Duh.*

"Still, just bump it. Turn the key quick on and quick off. Don't drain the battery."

Marion listened to the instructions with a grimace. "I do not like this at all."

I put my thumb over the hole in the cap. "Ready."

"When she bumps it, you feel for pressure. It should push your thumb right off the hole. That means the piston is rising in the cylinder and it will fire next. But it could take eight tries. There are eight cylinders in that car and it might have to work its way around."

I bent back into the engine. "Too much info." I covered the hole with my thumb, then looked at Marion through the windshield. "Bump it."

Marion winced, her eyes closed, and switched the key on and off. I felt the engine turn, but nothing under my thumb.

"Again," I said.

Marion still hadn't opened her eyes, but she did it again.

Nothing.

"Again."

A pop of air pushed my thumb from the hole. "That's it!"

Marion opened her eyes. "You still got all your fingers?"

"The number one plug," Red said, "will be the next one to fire. Here's what to do."

When I pulled the distributor cap off, I thought Marion would have a conniption.

"Just check the position of the rotor," Red said. "Where the metal tab is about to touch, that's where you want to connect the number one spark plug wire. And then, back to the spark plug, of course."

It was actually pretty easy when I knew what to look for. "Okay!" I felt good. "Do the rest go around clockwise, or counter-clockwise?"

"You wish," Red said. "Firing order varies on cars."

I sagged. "Do I have to do this for every plug?"

"I have the firing order memorized, Reverend. So listen up." She told me exactly how to reconnect the wires in reference to the number one.

"Okay. You should be ready to go," said Red.

I held up crossed fingers. "Give her a crank."

Marion turned the key and Pearl started up with a roar. "Woohoo!" Marion hollered.

"That's a sound I like to hear," said Red. "In good time too, because I have to get into the shower. You all set?"

"Perfect." My hands were covered in grease and I had nowhere to wipe them. "You've been a big help, really."

"Yeah, well." I imagined her big grin.

"You've given me an interesting morning," said Red. "Bring that car home, Rev. Your life around here will get a whole lot better."

I hoped she meant that she'd be part of it.

"Wait!" Marion sprang shouting from the car. "Tell her we have her inhaler!" She handed me a napkin to wipe my hands.

"We have—"

"I heard her," Red said. "What are you talking about?"

I explained about the inhaler Marion had found and when. How she'd thought it was mine. But it wasn't. "It's no big deal, you know, if you have asthma," I said. "If you want it kept quiet." Maybe it was a problem with the force or something. "We won't tell."

"I don't use an inhaler."

"Not hers," I told Marion.

"Then whose?" Marion said.

"Someone must've been in the car," I said.

"While it was in my garage," Red finished.

None of us liked that thought at all.

"You're sure there's no marks of any kind? Pharmacy? Date?" Red asked after we walked her through the details again.

I turned the inhaler over. "Just the medicine name molded into the plastic. And a counter. It says forty-six. Nothing else at all."

"Lonnie, I can't tell you how sorry I am," Red said.

I watched a family with four kids tumble out of an RV and dash for the mini-golf hut. "You didn't do anything."

"I was supposed to keep that car secure. And clearly someone was in it."

That hardly compared to letting it get stolen, but I said nothing.

"I'm going to look into it," Red said and then hung up.

"You know," Marion said. "I'm feeling a little crazy. And we're way ahead of schedule. What do you say to a little mini-golf?"

So, fingers crossed, we disabled Pearl and went to play mini-golf. The sun cracked through the white sky at about the point we both hit par on the hole around Lansing, so by the time we finished our cheeks glowed with wind and sun and our blood pumped with fresh air, hot dogs, and way too much full-sugar, full-caffeine soda.

We felt great.

And we felt even greater when, after only twenty-five minutes of trying and a minimum of swearing, we got Pearl running again. We were just about to leave when Marion shrieked. "The photo! I almost forgot." She dug the camera out of her bag. "Dammit!" She hunched over the camera.

"What?"

"Memory card's full. Don't know how that can be." She held the camera out. "This is a two-gig memory card. It should hold like seven hundred pictures." She looked at me. "I've taken like thirty."

"I took some at Totem Village," I offered. "Maybe I hit a switch or something."

She pushed another button or two. "Yeah. Maybe you switched it to video and left it on, filled the card. If we just look at what's on here..."

Muffled sounds started coming from the camera's tiny speakers. A man's voice, laughing hard.

"Great goddess of the moon and mountains." Marion's eyes popped and she thrust the camera toward me. "What is this?"

We stared at the tiny screen. The picture sprang around, as if the man handling the camera didn't know it was on.

Then came a man's voice in the distance. "Yeah. Friggin' HD's the way to go."

Tan and brown swooshes of color smeared across the screen.

The figure of a man appeared and spun like crazy clock hands as the camera turned.

"Who's that?" Marion asked. "Where is he?"

The camera swung to a ceiling, struggling to focus on a band of fluorescent lights.

"Make sure that thing's wide angle is on," said the man. "Don't want to miss a thing."

"No." A second voice, closer, lower.

"You know those voices?" I asked Marion.

She shook her head.

Grunts and heavy breath punctuated the camera's jerks until it finally settled. Wooden benches, two rows of floor to ceiling brown lockers, shiny tile floor.

"It's a locker room," I said.

"It's our locker room!" Marion said.

Offscreen, the first voice. "Make sure the motion detector works."

And the video ended.

"Great goddess. Was that our locker room?"

What and who and how? We stared at each other.

"What motion detector?" Marion asked. "What for?"

My brain swirled with ideas and images, like a spinning painted plate. None of it made sense.

"Is there another video?" I tapped the camera.

Marion clicked through the controls and sure enough, another video started. The picture was filled with a man's hand, slender, long-fingered and out of focus, waving in front of it. Then the hand moved away.

"It is our locker room!" Marion shrieked. "I'm freaking out!!"

"It's on," came the voice nearest the camera.

Steps on tile. "Good," came the other voice. "We'll get the fuckers this time. Let's get out of here." The big man stepped on screen and the video blipped to black.

My scalp prickled. I'd seen that man before. And he'd been dead.

CHAPTER THIRTY-SEVEN

Marion and I sat on opposite sides of Pearl's hood. The camera lay on the metal between us, right behind the hood ornament. We both stared at it as if it were a raging scorpion.

"Our locker room?" Marion murmured over and over. Each time she said it, she shook.

I tried not to think about that. Randy Koeman and someone else. Setting up a camera in the women's locker room of the new rec center. Somewhere up in the ceiling. On a motion detector.

Randy had wound up dead. He'd boasted of money coming in. Someone had been messing with the security cameras at the rec center. Ivor Koontz had to be involved. My head swirled. *Yuck.*

Marion wiped her mouth with the back of her hand. "I might be sick."

"We have to see if there's more," I said. "What they filmed."

Marion shook her head slowly. "No way. I've seen enough. If I see a clip of us undressing in there, I'm going to vomit."

I gingerly reached toward the camera. "We have to know."

She shook her head harder. "I don't. I know my memory card is full because it's someone else's. I don't know how I got it, how it got in the camera, or what's gonna happen next. But I don't want to know." When she looked at me, I saw tears in her eyes. "I want to go home to my family."

I tried to smile. "I know it's creepy, Mare, but it happened days ago. We're safe."

She barked a fake laugh. "Yeah, Miss I-Have-To-Disable-My-Car-To-Leave-It. That's us, safe and sound."

I picked up the camera. "Fair warning." And I clicked play.

The next video fired up with a parade of sodden, muddy women clicking and dripping through the locker room. My Hot Flashes.

"Oh, shit!" Marion shoved herself off and began circling me and the car with quick stomps.

I scanned the group—I wasn't there. That clinched it. This was taken that night we played in the pouring rain. The night I went facedown in the mud. I'd stayed behind to talk to Red. I hit the fast-forward button, watched my teammates towel down, undress, put on civvies at a sped-up mechanical pace. And sure enough, in a few seconds, I speed-walked past the camera, straight into the shower room, which, mercifully, was not on the camera.

I stopped the video.

"They're pornographers!" Marion's voice came from behind me as she kept up her worried circling. "And they used us."

"It was Randy Koeman. And I'll bet you anything he was working with Ivor Koontz."

"You have to call Red," Marion said as she passed me. "Tell her what we found."

"No."

"No? Are you nuts?"

"I'm going to call her," I said, jumping down from the hood. "But not yet. Not until I've watched the rest of these. There's more."

Marion emerged from the car butt first, waving a smoking stick of sage and muttering I couldn't tell what.

"Come on," I said. "We need a walk." She didn't argue.

We tramped across the Pine Ridge Loop, a 1.4-mile walk through cool maple and beech forests lit up with late golden sunshine. The last of the fall butterflies tiptoed across the yellowing weeds. Maple leaves mottled with red, orange and yellow carpeted the path. The beech trees towered on trunks as smooth and gray as elephant skin, many leaves still green, others tinged with yellow. On one side—I presumed the north—the trees' trunks were black with moisture, so that the moss and shelves of white fungus that grew there glowed. Everything smelled like moisture and woods and autumn.

We'd walked about ten minutes in silence when Marion finally relaxed with a whoosh. Shortly after that we emerged from the woods into an open marsh with a smooth blue pool in the center. The weeds that framed it had turned that aged green of dying summer. Silken stars of milkweed seeds bursting from their stiff brown pods shaped like elf shoes. Each seed lofted into the air on white wings, some traveling high and out of sight, like a released helium balloon. Then we heard it: a mournful, sonorous call from somewhere on the water.

If I heard that in the middle of the night, it would scare me to death. As it was, it was heart-breakingly lovely.

"Swans," I said. And sure enough, within a few seconds, two of the massive white birds drifted from their spot behind a twist of weeds.

"Picture," Marion whispered, pulling the camera from its case.

"I thought—"

"I switched the memory card," she said. "The new one I brought was in here. So we're good." She took several shots of me, the birds in the background. Eventually they glided out of sight.

We returned through the woods, enjoying the peace and quiet. Nothing looked amiss as we crossed the parking lot. Pearl stood alone in the corner of the lot. But about halfway across the macadam, Marion stopped and clutched my arm. "Something's not right."

Marion stopped in front of me. "Please, Lonnie, I beg y
Don't watch them around me. Not in the car. I—I can't bear
The bad energy has me completely unwound."

She looked completely unwound, a wild fright in her ey
I'd never seen. "Okay. I won't do it now. But until I know it al,
I'm not calling Red. I don't want to bug her with half the facts,
Okay?"

Marion bit her lip.

"We'll just keep driving, finish the day, then later, when you're
in the motel, I'll go for a walk, finish watching, then call her."

"Then lock it in the car. I'm not sleeping with that horrible
karma floating around the room." She pointed at the camera, but
wouldn't touch it.

"Promise."

She nodded. "Okay. But keep it away from me."

I looked at my watch. 1:56. "Where to next, oh navigator?" I
wanted to get her back into Marion-mode.

"Seney National Wildlife Refuge." She spoke without taking
her eyes from the camera. "About forty-five minutes north. Then
Escanaba to Sand Point Lighthouse and to spend the night.
Another two hours or so."

"Let's go!" I tossed her the keys, which she dropped.

I chattered manically the whole way, reading to her from the
clipboard of travel notes. But my brain chewed on something
completely different: how did that memory card get into Marion's
camera? Nearly an hour later, we passed through a little burg
called Germfask, then turned off to the Seney Refuge. "Thanks
for trying, Lon," Marion said as I parked. "But that thing in the
car is bad bad energy. I brought sage. I'm taking our photo, then
smudging the car before we do anything else."

I expected the refuge to be crowded on a sunny October
Saturday, but it wasn't. Still I pulled us to the farthest corner of
the lot and studied the park map while Marion got the shot, then
smoked the bad spirits out of the car.

Maybe what we both needed was a walk. We'd been rattled
and badly. Maybe a little time in a refuge would suit us both.
A half hour here wouldn't matter that much when it came to
getting to Escanaba.

The car looked fine to me. We stood facing the passenger's side.

"See that red, beneath the car?" She pointed an orange-tipped finger. "That's my makeup case. It was in the glove box. And I did not drop it there."

I brushed her grip off. "Now who's paranoid? That's probably an old Coke can or something."

Still we approached slowly, silently, and in a few more steps, my gut sunk. Not only was it her makeup case, but the car door was ajar.

We ran to the car.

Someone had thoroughly, messily searched Pearl.

CHAPTER THIRTY-EIGHT

I bent, one hand in the guts of the engine, the other gripping a tangle of spark plug wires. "Again!"

Marion bumped the car and I felt the whoosh of air. Finally!

I recited the order of the distributor cap firing as I replaced the wires. *Please let this work*, I prayed. "Go!"

The car rumbled and Marion hopped to help me replace the hood.

"Faster we're out of here," she said, "better I'll feel."

"Admit you're glad I made Red teach us how to disable the car." I twisted the hood knob tightly.

"Wrong, Squires. If you hadn't done that, we'd have been out of here ten minutes ago. Instead we're sitting ducks for whoever to come back and get us."

"Wrong, Freeley. If I hadn't done this, we'd have no car to

get out of here with." We crossed in front of Pearl as I took the driver's seat.

"Wrong." She slammed her door. "This wasn't a car thief. Car thieves try to steal cars. They take hoods off and hot-wire them. This was someone searching the car for something else." She shuddered.

I backed us out and got us on the road, watching every mirror for signs of someone following us.

"You left the windows partly down," I said. "Any petty thief could have hoped for a wallet or a camera."

"That was to let the bad energy out!" She struggled to get her seat belt latched. "Besides, look at this mess. This was no petty thief."

Everything inside the car had been turned upside down and emptied with a force that suggested it might have been done by an agitated bear. A can of Pringles that had been in the front seat showed up under the backseat. Tweezers from Marion's makeup case had glittered from the concrete ten feet from the car. Maps, notes, sunglasses, papers, food, drink, everything was accounted for, just tossed about. It was a mess.

"What were they looking for?" I hoped she wouldn't say what I was thinking.

"This." She held out a fist and opened it. The memory card in a tiny plastic case. "I changed it out of the camera, but I kept it in my bag. So the energy could clear the car. Those pornographers were here." She made a face like she'd bit into something severly undercooked. "They're following us. We have to get rid of this thing."

"We can't just ditch it, Marion. It's evidence."

She dropped the card back into her bag. "I know."

"Besides, that card isn't all bad energy. It has our pictures on it too. This whole trip so far."

"I know." She sounded heartbroken. "I think it's dangerous to have around, that's all."

"But don't the good pictures sort of even the card's energy out?"

"I don't know," said Marion staring at her bag as if it contained a poisonous cottonmouth snake. "I just don't know."

I drove us south and west again the two hours to Escanaba and as I drove, I thought. I needed to see the rest of the videos on the card, that was first. I wanted to see if the second man, the man fiddling with the camera ever showed his face, or got called by name. I'd hand it all over to Red when we got home tomorrow evening. But in the meantime, well, depending on what I found out, I just might tip Artesia Collins off first. I trusted her more than I did the police to dig into the matter and find out if Star Hannes was involved.

I couldn't quite fit it together. Randy Koeman was involved with someone shooting videos of us undressing in the locker room. Us and presumably anyone else who used it, though so far we were the only team. The basketball floors wouldn't be done until next month. And Randy Koeman owed everybody money. So maybe he'd done this for some extra cash?

Why hadn't Ivor paid Randy the extra overtime he owed him? Was Ivor strapped for cash? Was he doing this for someone else—a third party—to get money?

Jack's security system didn't work right. But this didn't seem to be a part of that. In fact, I remembered Jack told me about his plan to set up a second system of cameras on motion detectors to catch anyone messing with his system. Looks like that's what Randy and partner had done. So I couldn't figure out why they would have messed with Jack's system.

Did any of this tie in with the person or persons who had just searched our car, taking nothing? Or was that the car thief of last night, following us to try to steal Pearl again? Or might Marion have been wrong about when she found the inhaler? Might the car thief have lost it in the car and come back for it?

Who would want footage of the Hot Flashes undressing?

Who had shot Randy Koeman in the back? In the dark?

How did Star Hannes fit in? Because I remained sure she did.

This last was the question I kept circling around, because it was the most important. At least to me.

At 5:46 we rolled through Ludington Park on the north shore of Lake Michigan, just outside of Escanaba, and up to Sand Point Lighthouse. Not many people had come to the park in the gray chill, but a few cars dotted the lot. At the end, the brightly whitewashed house-sized building with the bright red roof stood pleasantly beneath the gray-white sky.

"Heck of a day," I said.

"Let's get the picture and go," Marion said.

The car wouldn't leave our sight, so we didn't disable it. As we walked to the lighthouse, the lake breeze wound around us, chilling our flesh. The water twisted, peaking here and there into tiny whitecaps as the wind curled around it. In the west the white sky grew pink but also held dense dark shapes, thicker clouds approaching on the prevailing winds.

"I'm starving," Marion said.

"Picture. Then food."

She took one of me with the lighthouse, then another of me sitting on the car with the light in the background.

"That'll be a nice one to give Red," Marion said.

Heat sprouted through me. "No way. No."

Marion laughed. "God, Rev, you're worse than a teenager. I can't wait to get home and watch this develop."

I was about to lambaste her in return when I spotted a young guy, baggy jeans, hooded sweat jacket, dark hair and eyes, walking toward us from a picnic table in the center of the park. His hands swung empty by his sides. "Hey, can I talk to you a minute?" he shouted.

Marion sidled up next to me. "Phone in hand. Taser?"

What a change this was from her hail-fellow-well-met attitude of the other day—my God, was it just yesterday?—when we met the car guys in the gas station. Still, I touched my pocket. The Taser wasn't there. I'd tossed it in the car earlier in the day. Before someone had searched everything. No telling where it was now.

"We're kind of in a rush." I unlocked Marion's door and walked around the back of the car.

The guy kept coming toward us. Twenty feet. A glance back over his shoulder. Fifteen feet. He looked younger than I'd thought, maybe sixteen, with a sparse mustache and soul patch and acne. He was considerably shorter than me, maybe five seven, and tubby around the middle.

"Wait!" He held up his hands. Empty. "Just listen to me."

I wished for Linus, big and black, with his glimmering white teeth and hefty bark.

"You have to let me have the car back," he said.

Marion sucked a lungful of air. This was our thief!

"I have to get—there's this guy." He blinked rapidly and looked behind him again. I followed his gaze and saw no one.

"Is someone putting you up to this?" I asked.

"You caused this mess," he said. "If you'd left me alone you'd have your damn car and I wouldn't have this guy after me. With a gun." Then, angrily, he dashed the back of his hand against his eyes. He had begun to cry.

Twenty minutes later we sat in a Big Boy restaurant, Marion and I in one half of the red pleather booth, the guy—a boy, really—sitting in the other. We'd wound up here after Marion, seeing his tears, had decided to mother him. I'd told him I wasn't giving him the car or anything else until I knew what the hell was going on, and he'd said it wasn't safe to talk there and gosh was he hungry.

Now that he wasn't so frightened he sat giving us the "f-you" stare across the table laden with burgers, fries and malts.

Marion had grilled him while we ate. Peter Sutter hailed from Holland, Michigan, just south of Middelburg. He was sixteen. He had an older sister, nineteen. His dad had split two years ago leaving them nothing and his mom had left the kids and gone south, to the Carolinas—he wasn't sure which one—to find work. For fun, he played video games.

"You trying to get into a gang? That why you're after my car?" I asked. Marion kicked me.

Peter swallowed burger and wiped his mouth on his sleeve. He stared at me and I couldn't get a sense of what was going on behind those eyes. "No. I just wanted a ride's all."

"You're a bad liar," I said. His eyes lurched away. "You said you had to get something. And you mentioned a guy with a gun." I got the "f-you" look again, so I shrugged and wiped some fries through ketchup. "Your call, man. We have the car. And we're calling the cops. You want that situation to change, you change it."

Next to me, Marion bit her lip. I could tell it was killing her not to mother this kid to death.

His face clouded. "If you'd left me alone, I'd have brought it back. I'd be on my way home. You ruined it by taking the car."

"You took it first!" Marion said.

"Why?" I asked.

"I can't tell you, okay?" He pushed his plate away. "Just give me some time to—just give me some time with it."

"What are you looking for?"

Marion leaned forward and whispered, "Did you smoke all my dope?"

He grinned at her. "Thanks for that. Let me know I could take my time, 'cause you wouldn't call the cops. Didn't want rumors about a pothead priest getting out."

She leaned back, picked up her malt, and sucked the straw.

"Your gas gauge's for shit, though," he added.

"What do you know about video cameras?" I asked.

This caught him off guard. "Enough. I put stuff on YouTube. Everyone does."

The thought of my soccer team undressing on the Internet made me queasy.

Marion set the malt down slowly. "Are you after the memory card?"

Peter scrunched his face in overblown adolescent impatience. "What? No. I don't even know what you're talking about." He pulled his plate back and pushed the last chunk of burger into his mouth.

"Marion," I said. "Remember our story about how the dope in the car wasn't ours, but belonged to the thief? When we turn this brat in, if he brings it up, we stick with that. Then he goes down for stealing a car and drug possession. No one will believe him over us." I turned what I hoped was a wicked Star-Hannes-style smile on him. "Now tell me why you drove hundreds of miles to get that memory card. Who put you up to it?"

"Add pornographer," Marion said. "Car thief. Pothead. Pornographer."

"What?" Chewed bun spit across his plate and he wiped his mouth on his sleeve again.

"Use a napkin." Marion's voice held more disgust than I'd ever heard.

"I'm no pornographer." He looked young again, teary. The cocky façade vanished. "I just need—" He sighed. "Look, you can't tell anyone, okay?"

"No deals." I crossed my arms.

"Just—I swore." He took a big breath. "I need to get my sister's asthma inhaler, okay? But you can't tell!" The words came in a gush. "She told me if anyone found out it was hers she'd have to leave town. Go with mom. And I can't stay alone 'cause I'm a minor and she said I'd have to go with Dad and I just can't do that." He blinked back a tear. "I just can't."

Marion softened instantly. "Oh, honey, we would have given you the inhaler if you'd just asked."

"I couldn't!" He was mad again now. I wondered if he was even sixteen, given the mood swings. "No ties to my sister." A tear plopped onto his cheek. "I couldn't even do that right."

"Well, you certainly tried very hard." Marion began digging in her bag. "It's right here."

I put a hand on her arm. "You can have it, Peter, but you have to tell us how it got in the car." I owed it to Red to explain how the car got accessed, even if I did keep the kids' identities secret.

He shrugged, but without attitude. "I'm not sure. She said she and some friends knew how to get into the back part of Carson's. Hung out in the car. Someplace different, you know? She lost the inhaler about two weeks ago, but didn't know where. Knew she had it at the soccer field, but not since."

"The soccer field?" Marion and I said in unison.

"She's that girl—" Marion began.

"—who ran me down," I finished.

"She had an asthma attack right after," Marion said.

"And I saw her going back there a few days later." I remembered the car that almost hit me, the driver coughing.

"Allergies have been bad," Marion said to Peter. "Has she been all right without it?"

He shook his head.

Marion yanked the inhaler from her purse and slapped it on the table before I could stop her. "Take it."

"Wait." I reached but he snatched it. "You've been following us? I never saw you."

He grinned, tough guy again. "Duh. I read your itinerary in the paper. Sometimes I was behind you. Sometimes just ahead." He wiped his mouth with the napkin. "Thanks for dinner."

"About the guy with the gun," I said.

"Yeah, threatened me. I was looking for the inhaler this afternoon, in that parking lot out in the middle of nowhere."

The Seney Wildlife Refuge.

"He just snuck up and yanked me out of the car and said if I didn't get out of there he was going to either beat me or shoot me. So I ran. But I had to get it. So I followed you here."

"A park ranger?" Marion asked.

"Some skinny guy in hunting camo, with leaves all over it. He had crazy eyes and I believed him. But I had to get Tina's inhaler. I can't—we have to stay in our house."

"Kyle," Marion said to me.

"Or one of them," I said. "They did like helping us last night."

"Our guardian angels," Marion said. "Think they caught up to us after hunting?"

"Some angel." Peter glanced around the restaurant. "I just hope he isn't around here now. I want to go home."

"We'll call him off," I said.

Peter rose. "You won't tell, will you? That it was Tina's inhaler?"

"Just go home," I said. "Stay out of trouble. When I get home, I'll be checking on you." Two kids alone. Someone had to check.

He hesitated only a second before bolting out of the restaurant. We watched him get into his car and drive away without a hitch.

I handed Marion the bill. "You pay. I'm calling Kyle and gang."

Funny thing was, when I got Kyle on the phone, thanked him but asked him to back off, he had no idea what I was talking about.

CHAPTER THIRTY-NINE

That evening, Marion begged me to go to a movie in Escanaba because she needed to free her mind from its bad karmic tsunami. She claimed my detective mind would put things together better if I stopped thinking for a while. The car was safe since we'd sent Peter home, she reasoned. Mostly, she didn't want to spend the whole evening and night in the same space with the pornographic video chip.

We found a theatre that showed Jeff Daniels' film *Escanaba in Da Moonlight* every night at seven. We laughed for two hours. It really did cleanse our auras, as Marion put it.

Shortly after nine o'clock we returned to our motel room armed with fresh munchies and pop for the long drive the next day. We walked down the dark outside corridor to our room, chill whipping around us. It hadn't rained, but a light mist filled the air, dampening everything. Even my bones felt wet and cold.

"I feel better," Marion said, clacking down the concrete walk ahead of me. The motel felt shadowy and dark, not only because night had fallen and the mist bounced reflections off everything, but because about half of the lights outside the room doors were not on. "Like now, everything is going to change." Stopping in front of door forty-seven, our home sweet home for the night, she hitched the two paper bags she carried onto her hip like toddlers and shoved a hand into her pocket.

"I got it." I gripped soda in one hand and pulled the key— an old-fashioned metal one, no fancy key cards here—from my pocket.

"You're gonna call Red tonight, right?"

I tried to fit the key in the lock, but our door light was one of the ones not burning and in the shadows I couldn't see. "No." I jerked the key back and forth where I could see the lock, but I couldn't fit it into the slot.

"But you have to tell her what we found out. The inhaler. The video."

I bent, squinting, still sliding the key. "I haven't watched all the videos yet."

"You're not going to—"

"Argh!" I shook my head in frustration. "I can't see a thing here. You got a flashlight?"

Marion gave a short laugh. "No. You need to borrow those night vision goggles Lucy was talking about. Her husband ordered 'em, remember?"

"Could've used 'em last night on the road with Pearl!" I slid my finger against cool wood then cold metal, until I felt the lock and the slot. The deadbolt squeaked and the door opened.

Marion flipped on the light switch next to the door. "Maybe you could wait until morning to give that video any energy. Things are good right now."

I locked the door behind me. "I won't watch it near you, promise."

We set our bags next to the luggage we'd brought up earlier. The array of junk food looked fabulous. Just the sight of a bag of

Nacho Doritos made my mouth water. "At least we'll survive the trip tomorrow."

It was going to be a long drive. We had to get from Escanaba to Pembine, Wisconsin to visit Long Slide Falls. That should take only a bit more than an hour, but then we had to drive to the south side of Chicago for a photo in front of one of the gargoyles at the University of Chicago in Hyde Park. That was a six-hour drive. And from there we had to find the Hesston Steam Museum in northern Indiana, an hour east of the city along the southern shore of the lake. Then we cut north to Holland for a photo near their famous windmill, and then home. It would be a long day of driving, but by tomorrow night, we'd be home in our own beds. Monday morning, I'd have my dog back.

I flopped on the bed. "I hate to admit it, but I'm hungry."

Marion kicked off her spike heels and tossed me the phone book. "So, order pizza."

Good thing we ordered when we did, because Papi Barcelona's Pizza said they needed ninety minutes to cook and deliver a thick-crust pepperoni. "See," said Marion, snuggling back against her pillows and flipping channels like a man, "it'll be a midnight snack."

We watched some reality nonsense for a few minutes, then Marion tossed my cell phone into my lap. "Call Red. Tell her whatever you want. Even the video. I'm a big girl."

"It's too late," I said.

"Then I'm calling her." She grabbed her cell. "You won't do it because you've got issues, but you know, kids broke into her garage. More than once. She should know."

I stared at her. Her copper hair flamed against the browns and yellows of the sunflower patterned wallpaper. "What do you mean I've got issues?"

Marion lifted her eyebrows and blinked innocently. "Nothing."

Heat prickled my face and neck and I wanted to bury my head beneath a pillow. "I do not have issues."

Marion grinned. "It is going to be so much fun watching this." She pointed to my phone. "Call. Or I will."

So I did. "Hey. You sitting down?" I asked Red. Then I told her all about the car and Peter.

At 10:42 we sat in our pajamas watching adult cartoons when my cell rang.

"Pizza!" Marion said.

"Red," I said.

"I did some follow-up." Red sounded giddy, like I did when I scored from way out. "You are not going to believe what I'm about to tell you."

"What?"

Marion heard my tone and muted the TV.

"I went down to Holland, to the Sutter house," Red said. "Unofficially, you know. Like you suggested. I didn't want to freak the kid out, but just find out what's been going on. Tina answered. She's definitely your soccer nemesis. Not too happy to see me there, I can tell you."

"Yeah, the brother practices some 'tude too."

"It only took a few questions for this kid to spill her guts. Like you said, mom gone and dad an abuser they'd rather not see again. She doesn't want social services involved. She's supporting them just fine she says."

"How?"

"That's what I asked. That and how did her inhaler get into your car. She stalled until I mentioned that I could charge her and her brother with all kinds of crimes, but I might not if I knew the truth and out it came." She laughed but I could tell it wasn't funny, whatever it was. "She's been having sex. For money."

I grimaced. "Prostituting to support her brother."

Marion made a face too. "Poor kids."

"It's worse," said Red. "She was having sex with Gil Hannes."

I think I stopped breathing. In fact I'm sure of it. I could not believe my ears.

"What?" Marion whirled her legs off the bed. "What?"

I honestly thought I might cry, because Gil was so icky and because it served Star right. Except it didn't, of course, because no one, not even Star, really deserved this.

"What?" Marion demanded.

"She was seeing Gil Hannes."

Marion's face twisted as if she'd bit into dog poo. "Inside Pearl? Where we've been sitting for two days? Gross!"

We all sat in silence for a few seconds, tortured by our own visions.

"Gross," I repeated quietly.

"It had been going on for some time," Red said. "The girl says it was true love, even though she was taking his money. But then he broke it off."

"Of course he did." I pulled my fingers through my hair.

"Dumped her, didn't he?" Marion asked.

"On Friday last week." Red paused. "Right before Randy Koeman turned up dead in a ditch."

That made me sit up straight. "You think Gil killed him?"

"Oh great goddess." Marion stood and started to pace. "There was a murderer in our car too. Pornographers. Fornicators. Murderers." She headed for her tote. "Where's my sage? I've got to smudge everything again."

"Gil dropped Tina because he claimed someone was blackmailing him. He showed her the copy of the film that someone had sent him."

"A video of them having sex in Pearl?"

This made Marion dig through her bag even faster.

"No." Red sighed. "In the rec center. Women's locker room."

Things started to click together in my head fast. I glanced at the table by the television where our suspect memory card lay in its plastic case. "They had sex in the rec center too?"

"I so do not want to hear this," Marion muttered, arms flying.

"Heard a noise outside my garage. Thought it was me. Got scared. When Gil got his keys to the center, they moved."

"And the blackmailer?"

"Haven't found him yet."

I wondered if the memory card we had held the original video. Randy Koeman and someone else shooting us undressing and got Gil and Tina by mistake? Or was it the other way around?

"Found it!" Marion raised the smudge stick high above her head. "Now, my lighter."

"Tina then tells me—because once she started talking, she didn't stop—that she thinks Gil killed Randy Koeman."

"No way!" I said.

"The timing makes sense. If Randy was the blackmailer, Gil would do anything to shut him up. After all, he dumped her, didn't he, and he loved her. Or so went her reasoning."

"Lighter!" Marion held it up in triumph.

"Just don't set off the smoke detector," I said to her as the dry herb caught and a flame leapt up.

Marion stared at me, horrified, then blew the sage flame out with a whoosh. Instantly a plume of blue-white smoke flowed upward.

"Gil doesn't seem the type to shoot someone in the back," I said.

Marion waved the smoke wildly.

"Maybe not. He confessed to everything else, though," Red said.

"You arrested Gil Hannes?" I couldn't believe it. Couldn't imagine Star's devastation. And, I admit, couldn't imagine what Artesia Collins would make of it.

"No, of course not. My God, Lonnie, it's only been an hour and a half. I couldn't get a warrant that fast. I just wandered over to Hannes' place for a little chat. Star wasn't home and Gil spilled. Literally, in fact. Cried like a baby. Told me a man called him, mailed him a copy of the tape from inside the rec center."

"Great Goddess Gaia," Marion intoned, slowly walking in front of the silent television. Sponge Bob jerked and shrank, evidently in trouble with Mr. Crabby.

"Hold on!" I suddenly understood something. "Gil's the one messing with the security cameras! He turns them off to sneak Tina in. They do their thing. He turns them back on. Then he covers by making a big fuss about how the cameras aren't working."

"Send white light down to surround us and protect us," Marion said.

"You got it, detective," Red said. "And everyone fell for

it. Koontz was only too glad to spread the idea that Jack is incompetent since, as you've said, there's bad blood there."

"Koontz could be involved. Even working for Star, if she suspected!"

"Heal the space between and among us." Marion reached the door, turned on her heel, and paced toward the bathroom.

"Could be." Red paused again, but didn't ask me any more questions. "Gil says no one else has called since Koeman's death. I'm inclined to think the two are connected, but I have no evidence."

I knew there was a second man! But I wasn't saying anything until I saw those tapes.

"So how did Gil and Tina get into your garage in the first place? I mean, you kept it locked, right?"

Marion paused in front of the television, circling the screen slowly in front of an ad for Old Spice. "Archangels Michael and Gabriel, protect us."

"Regular deadbolts on the front and office doors. But just a padlock on the old service door in the back. Gil says he looked up on the Internet how to break into old padlocks and he did it in about a minute one night. And yes," Red said. "This is going to make my life absolute hell when it comes out in the reports."

"Do you think the blackmailers had tried to catch them on camera in the garage? Like maybe they made the noise that spooked Gil?"

"Maybe. Maybe they drove them out on purpose, because it would be impossible to get a decent video image in that dark garage, but a lot easier in the rec center. I mean, if they'd turned lights on in my garage in the middle of the night, someone would have noticed. But security lights are on throughout the rec center twenty-four seven."

"Yeah. Shooting in the dark probably requires some pretty sophisticated equipment."

"Bad energy, begone!" Marion spread her hands above her head. "I cast you out!" She twirled, her smiley face fleece pj's spinning around her.

"So?" I asked.

"Gil certainly had a lot to lose if Koeman were the blackmailer and stayed alive and this got out."

"Yeah, like his man-parts." I could only imagine Star's reaction to all of this. And while I wouldn't mind seeing her high and mighty self taken down a few pegs—a lot of pegs, really—I didn't envy her the discovery she'd been betrayed by her partner. I wouldn't wish that on anyone, even my worst enemy. And this would be so very public. I shuddered on her behalf. "Where is Star anyway?"

"Not at home," Red said. "Gil said she had dinner with some big potential donors. He expects her around one."

"Where are you?" I'd been thinking she was at home, but would she have left Gil alone with all these questions unanswered? Especially if she thought he'd done it?

"In my car. My private car. Just a house down from Hannes'. When Star comes home, we're all gonna have a little talk together. I can't really do anything anyhow until I find that video. 'Cause knowing it actually existed would change things."

"You didn't get it from Gil?"

"He destroyed it. Of course."

If the card we had did have that footage on it—I could break this case for Red. But no false hopes. I'd let her down enough. I wasn't saying anything until I watched it all myself.

"Lonnie!" Smudge stick held out like a conductor's baton, Marion stood in front of me. "You need to pray. Now."

I waved at her to give me a minute but she would not be denied.

"Seriously, Lon, the spirits are at war here. You're consecrated or whatever. You need to pray." She looked about to cry.

"Call me later," I said to Red. "Any time. We've got more to talk about."

CHAPTER FORTY

"You must know some sort of cleansing prayer," Marion said. "Some sort of exorcism to really punch the bad energy right out of here!"

I grabbed the camera off the TV stand and switched out the SD cards.

"No!" Marion grabbed the camera from me. "Don't play that again! That's what's bringing the bad karma back. We never should have kept it. We should throw it away."

I stretched for the camera, but she held it high. "Give that to me," I said. "Go smudge the john if you don't want to see it. I have to check something for Red."

"You aren't supposed to be sleuthing." Marion stood, one hand overhead gripping the camera, the other scolding me with a stick of smoking sage. "Why didn't you just tell her about it?"

"What if it's not the one? You want the video of the Hot Flashes made public? Or worse, what if it is the one? How do we get it to her and not mess up the whole trip?"

She studied me.

"I have to get Linus back! I don't want something I don't know screwing that up."

She shook her head. "It's asking for trouble."

"I didn't seek this out," I said. "It got dumped on me—and you—literally. By fate, or karma or the goddess or the universe or whatever. Aren't we supposed to deal with what the universe gives us? Isn't that what you always say?"

Marion squinted at me for a second, heaved a round sigh, and tossed me the camera. "I hate it, but true."

I clicked through the video clips quickly, past the camera getting set, the locker room scene with the Hot Flashes, a buzz-cut young janitor cleaning up, Ivor Koontz and one of his workers popping a ceiling tile to check the wiring on a light, and then, finally, in the dull yellowed light of the security system, Gil Hannes and Tina Sutter twisting in. She giggled. He lapped at her like a dog. Belts unbuckled, pants came down. She squealed in appreciation while he thrust and moaned. It didn't last long. Then it started again when he said the only complete sentence either of them uttered—"I love you"—then slid his head between her legs.

The progress bar showed this video clip was less than half over, but I didn't need to see anymore. I had the evidence Red needed—there had been an affair, there had been a tape.

"What I don't get," said Marion, sitting on the bed opposite me, smudge stick sticking upright between two fingers like a forgotten pencil, "is how this got in my camera in the first place."

I carefully pulled the card from the camera and stuck it in its case. "I figure they hid it in the car. When everything spilled in Grand Haven, you just picked it up." I stuck the other card in and put it all back on the TV table.

"But why would they hide it there when they knew Gil had been there?"

I shrugged. "Because they'd already scared him off and knew

he wouldn't be back? And because it was safe because this car hadn't left town in forty years?"

Marion chewed on that. "So how did the blackmailer get the card into Pearl? I mean, how many people know Red's lock combination?"

"Gil figured it out from something he read on the Internet. I suppose the blackmailer could have too."

Marion bounced on her bed. "Maybe he just watched. I mean, he's a watcher, right? Mitchell got the combination to Cam's new bike last spring, just by watching. You know, Cam's the big brother, he ignores Mitch. So Mitch played dumb, watched him unlock it then had the bike whenever he wanted it." She smiled and shook her head.

"Yeah, but Gil always went there at night. How would someone see in the dark?" My eyes lit on the grocery bags full of munchies we'd brought in. The paper bags had an orange design printed on the side. A buck's head.

I thought about Kyle, Gumbo and Brucey D. The man in camo who had scared Peter. All the banner's and traffic and cars with dead deer on their hoods we'd seen. Red's long hours. The hunting widows—even among my soccer friends.

My heart hiccupped and began to run. "Someone would see the combo if they had a hunting scope or night vision goggles."

Marion nodded. "Sure. But they'd have to be—"

"Marion, don't you get it? Lucy told us. Her husband. Jake. He loaned his stuff—that exact stuff—to someone. That was before Koeman got shot."

Marion blinked. "I think you're right."

"Who? Who did she say he loaned them to?"

She shook her head.

"We have to call her. Right now."

Marion put a hand on my lap. "No. It's too late. She's got six kids. Four under the age of four!"

"It's about a murderer!"

"It's about your hunch. And four little kids sleeping. You've never been a mom, so trust me. Call in the morning. Unless you want to lose a teammate. Right now—" She thrust the sage at me—"pray."

I took the stiff chalky stick. "I don't have a prayer book. I have to make something up." She shrugged. I stood. Turned the TV off. Looked at the small room, with orange bedspreads, yellow sunflower wallpaper, brown and orange grocery bags. Marion sat on the other bed, her feet between the beds, waiting.

I raised the stick. "Help, help, help." I lowered the stick. "Do we need more?"

Three loud raps came from the door.

"Pizza!" Marion leapt up. "Your prayer worked. At least some."

I tossed the stick to her. "I'll get it." I grabbed my wallet from where I'd dropped it next to the grocery bags. "But then we're calling Lucy." I disconnected the slide bolt from the door. "I don't care what time it is." I gripped the cold faded doorknob and turned. "We need to find out—" I pulled the door open— "who borrowed those night vision goggles from the Vogels."

"That," said the thing at the door, "would be me."

CHAPTER FORTY-ONE

His fist slammed my chest and I fell back onto the bed as everything in the room went dark.

Space alien. Giant bug. Creature from the Black Lagoon. The images exploded through my mind as I forced myself to somersault backward, landing between the beds. Marion's bare feet poked me in the back. Had she not moved? I reached up with my other hand. Felt her knees, tried to find a wrist, her shirt, any way to get a grip and pull her down. Out of the line of fire.

I was pretty sure I'd seen a gun.

A gun. Autumn foliage camo. Big science fictiony goggles.

A man with a gun who could see in the dark.

"Oh!" Marion's voice. Surprised yet small. As if she'd stumbled upon a monarch butterfly in a quiet woods.

"I have a gun to your friend's head," said the man, his deep voice filling the dark. "And believe me, I can see you. So get up and sit beside her like a nice lady."

I moved, groping. Sat so my thigh pressed against Marion's. The mattress sagged backward and I had to fight to keep from tumbling back into the dark.

"Where is the fucking memory card?"

"Over there." I pointed toward the TV. The sudden loss of light felt infinite, loud. Thrumming with energy. My eyes stretched to see something, anything inside of it.

Then a shadow moved within it, darker than the black around it. Him. I heard plastic against wood as he picked up the card.

"Thanks. It's been a pain in the ass chasing this. And that kid, what a pain in the ass, huh? Still, he'll come in handy."

Light from the motel walkway, glowing from several doorways down, seeped around the closed curtains, throwing his dark shape into relief. Baggy, tall. Firm strides. Not afraid.

That, more than anything, made me very afraid.

"Here's what's gonna happen." His voice rumbled from near the television. "We're gonna walk to that car. Then, you're going to do whatever it is you have to do to make the damn thing run." He paused and we didn't say anything. "Yeah, I know you've fucked around with it. I watched you."

Suddenly I heard Marion's breathing, fast and hard, like she'd been charging down the line on a breakaway.

"Then," he continued. "We are gonna drive away. No fuss, no muss, and everything will turn out just fine. Got it?" Silence. He slammed a hand on the TV stand. "Got it?"

Beside me Marion jumped, her breathing jerking. "Got it, got it!" She jumped to her feet. "Got it."

"I need some light," I said. "To find the keys."

"You don't need light," he said. "You got me." The keys jangled—evidently he'd picked them up too.

We put on shoes and went outside, me first, then Marion, then the man who, he told us, had a handgun in his pocket pointed straight at her spine. "So no fuckin' around."

"We won't," Marion whispered. "You won't, right, Lonnie?"

"She won't," said the man.

The wind whipped the cold pre-snow mist into a frenzied dance of silver around the few lights shining. Barely a sound other than the wind and my blood, both rushing around my ears. The man wore autumn leaves hunting camo, high-laced military boots, a brown knit balaclava over his head, nose and mouth, and the night goggles. If anyone had seen us, they'd have known something was wrong. But the streets stood utterly empty.

He keyed open the door and stepped back. "You." He waved a sinister hand-in-pocket at Marion. "Driver's seat." He shoved Marion toward the car and she stumbled, right foot twisting off her sandal. She squeaked.

"Now," he said to me. "Make it run."

So Marion and I went through our ritual with the distributor cap. Sweat dripped along my triceps as I bent into the engine, hoping like hell I didn't miss the puff and piss this guy off. Pearl grumbled to life and he and I replaced the hood, screwing it down tight. I took a step back as he hauled Marion from the driver's seat.

"You've got the memory card and the car," I said. "We don't know who you are. So let us go."

Marion stared at me with large, lost eyes.

"Fuck, right." He coughed out a laugh. "I know you saw that card. I overheard you talking earlier, about calling the cops in the morning, telling 'em everything."

"We didn't," Marion said. "We won't. Will we, Lon?"

"That's right, you won't." He shoved a roll of duct tape that he'd pulled from one of his capacious pockets at Marion. "Strap up her hands behind her back."

"You don't need to—" I started.

"Do it. Or I'll shoot your friend, then you."

I turned and held my hands behind my back while my best friend taped my wrists together. Then, gun still on Marion, he pulled the driver's seat forward and shoved me in the back. He slammed the seat back, smacking me in the hip and knocking me face first into the seat.

While I struggled to right myself, he taped Marion the same way and shoved her in the front. Then he got in the driver's seat. "No worries, ladies. Just a little ride."

I managed to shove myself into a sitting position as he lurched backward out of the parking space. What did he have planned? My mind scrambled and none of the options were good. He wanted to stop us from telling what we knew, what was on that chip. He was going to take us somewhere and shoot us.

I wanted to cry. Marion's kids growing up with no mother. Linus stuck forever in a pound.

"You know." I pushed my hands hard into the seat behind me, trying to scrunch up to a more comfortable position. "We've already given a copy of the chip to the police. They know what's on it."

"Lonnie!" Marion shrieked. "Don't—"

I didn't want her to reveal the lie. "There's no point in whatever he has planned, Marion! He might as well just let us go."

"There's plenty of point," he said. We drove north out of Escanaba, back the way we'd come today, along Highway 2. On our left, the vast expanse of Lake Michigan loomed a solid blue-black nothing.

"That pain in the ass boy's prints are all over this car. I saw to it this afternoon when I warned him off. Let him touch everything before I kicked his sorry ass. Anything happens to you, it's him they'll come after." He held up a gloved hand and wiggled his fingers. "They got nothing on me."

It was true. Probably not even any hair, given the getup he had on.

"They'll have nothing on you if you just let us go," I said. "We don't know who you are either."

"We don't." Marion's voice squeezed from some desperate lost place within. "Please." She sounded drunk, bewildered, amazed, like someone suffering from dementia. Her face glittered with wetness.

I pulled against the tape which tore at my skin. In the movies, people with their hands tied behind their backs get free somehow. I felt around behind me, against the seat, along its connection to the wall of the car for anything sharp. Nothing.

It only took another minute or two before houses disappeared altogether and we barreled forward down a lonely road, following the cone of light thrown from Pearl's stacked headlamps, through a forest darker than the night itself. Out here, no one would hear us. No one would help us. He wouldn't have to drive us very much farther. He could walk back to wherever he'd parked his own car and be long gone by morning.

Sweat stuttered down my back. I twisted my wrists against the tape again. Could I pull hard enough to break bones, slip a crushed hand out? I shoved my hands around the seat again, into the crack between the seat back and seat bench. A bolt, a metal bracket, I needed something to nick this tape.

My knuckles hit something hard. A cylinder. I grabbed it, pulled it out of the seat. Short, with a ridge in the middle. I pulled and a cap came off. The lipstick stun gun.

I could flatten him. If I could get it to him.

Before I'd thought two seconds, I flew sideways as he whipped the car off the main road onto an unpaved two track. A small sign announced this seasonal road was not plowed in the winter. Probably meant nobody lived back here either. I licked my dry lips and teeth.

I had to figure out a way to fall into him when he pulled us from the car, to make sure the leads of the stun gun touched him. He'd go down and we'd have some time to run like hell, maybe get back to the road. Maybe flag down help.

If he didn't drive us too far into these woods.

If he didn't shoot us in the car after all.

With a jerk that knocked me forward, he began to slow the car. "End of the line, ladies."

"My kids," Marion murmured.

I yanked against my taped wrists, energy crackling across my skin. I'd gotten her into this. If it wasn't for me losing my dog, for my crazy great-aunt, she'd be home in bed with her husband, probably in matching smiley-face fleece pajamas. I tried not to imagine her kids without her. The Grind without her. Middelburg without her. Her lying dead in the woods.

Heat seared from my chest down my legs and arms. I saw the back of his head, then only swirls of black and red and purple. My body felt swollen, electric, sick, about to explode with poison and blackness. I yanked against my wrists and butted my head into the back of the seat. "You son of a bitch." The seat bounced forward an inch.

"Please," said Marion quietly, "my kids."

I felt as if an egg inside of me had cracked and something new, some different kind of energy moved through my body mixed in with the black rage. I wasn't thinking anymore. My body wanted to take over. It knew what to do.

I slumped down in my seat, feeling my muscles. Bracing my shoulders against the back of the seat, I lifted both my legs. My abdomen crunched and my knee popped, but I felt the power of my core settle there, preparing, as it did before I took a long shot from the field. I knew I could do this. *Thank you, thank you, thank you*, I prayed and kicked the back of the seat with all the power of my soul.

I drove the man's seatback practically to the steering wheel, with him in between. Unprotected by a shoulder harness, he snapped forward. I kicked a second time, harder, and his head met the steering wheel with a crack that set my teeth on edge.

The car banged off the dark road and jerked to a stop at a tilt in the shallow ditch. Still in gear, it coughed, then stalled.

I stayed rolled up, ready for another kick. Nobody moved.

"Is he out?" I hoped I hadn't knocked Marion out too. She'd had no belt on, no hands to brace herself with. I didn't hear anything, but I didn't want him tricking us.

Marion turned slowly. "Yes. Did you kill him?"

Did it matter? "Get out of the car."

I prayed a silent blessing on those ridiculous sandals as Marion slipped out of them and used her toes to open the door. As soon as she wriggled from the car, I scooted to her side and propelled myself out.

I had to get her out of here. "Get to the road. Get help."

"You can't stay up here with him."

"We need to split up, in case he comes to. He can't chase both of us."

She shook her head so hard her whole body twisted. "You have to come."

"No," I said. "Get help. If something happens to me, get Linus out of the pound. Promise me."

The man behind us groaned.

"You want to see your kids?" I asked. "Then go!"

She nodded and, as best she could in bare feet with hands taped behind her back, ran down the road.

I walked around the car and looked through the window. He was slumped over the steering wheel, night vision goggles askew over his left ear. Breathing. I had to get those goggles. If he did come to, he'd have a much harder time finding either of us if he couldn't see.

I tucked the stun gun in my underwear to free both hands and nearly dislocated a shoulder trying to pull Pearl's door open from behind my back. I pulled and twisted until tears stung my eyes and my nose watered, but I couldn't get my hands high enough to reach the goggles. Finally, I boosted myself backward on the lip of the car, arching my back against the roof, until my fingertips found the goggles, gripped the strap, pulled.

He fell against me and I jumped from the car, clinging to the goggles which slipped from his head, but not before he tumbled from the car onto the gravel below.

I looked at the pistol beside him on the seat. Could I—?

He grabbed for my leg. "You are so dead!"

I ran like hell up the road into the woods.

Damp ferns pricked my knees as I shoved through them. The goggles slapped my butt. A shot exploded behind me and I nearly fell into the ditch from horror. He was up. He had his gun. Thank God he couldn't see.

I had to keep away from him, but not so far that he'd quit looking for me. I didn't want him going after Marion. The cold wet air pressed around me as I ran. My shoulders ached and my fingers tingled.

I lurched forward at the crack of another shot which smacked into a tree to my left.

He wasn't tied up. He would outrun me.

CHAPTER FORTY-TWO

I hear him gaining on me and there's no place to hide.

My feet skitter across gravel, slipping in the uneven path. My knee shrieks with pain. Sweat slices across my face. No options. I need my arms to pump, to keep my feet flying, but they pull against the tape.

I don't have long. He'll catch me. But what else can I do?

I run harder. I hear him cursing behind me. His clunking boots.

Don't battle.

That inner voice. I remember the slide I took on the soccer field. I didn't listen then.

Hide. I hear Red's voice, telling me to stay out of Star's sight. I ignored her.

I need to listen now. Before he gets closer.

I spin my body and hurl the goggles as hard as I can across the road. They clatter into the trees. I force myself to slow, to control my breath. How am I going to do this? How can I hide?

I remember myself face down in the mud, sliding, and I get it. The only way I am going to get out of this. I kneel, then slither into the ditch, slipping between the ferns, hoping I'm not leaving an obvious trail.

His boots pause.

My chest burns to pull a deep breath, but I tighten my jaw as I roll on my side. I reach into my underwear and pull the Taser out, tug off its cap.

The ferns around me seem to jerk with each impact of his thick boots as he runs up to, then by my hiding place. My foot twitches. I long to run. To fight.

No, I tell myself. *Lie here. Do nothing.*

Minutes pass. Lots of them. Maybe a whole night's worth of minutes marches by. My arms begin to numb. Eventually, I hear him walking back down the road, talking.

Talking to me.

"You won't get away with this, bitch. Not on your life. Because I know who you are. Even if you get out of here tonight, it won't take me long, you hear? You or your friend. Maybe her family too. You'll never know when I'll find you next."

And he walks by me shivering in the ditch. Soon I can't hear him anymore.

My body relaxes, but my mind whirls. I can't let him come after me. Marion. The kids.

I have to stop him.

I wriggle to my feet, then walk slowly down the center of the two-track, where tall grass nicks my shins but deadens my footsteps. Feeling comes back into my arms with a burn that nearly makes me shriek.

I get the stun gun in my hands, pull the loop to fire it up. I just have to get my back up against him and nail him. Then keep stunning him for as long as it takes.

Pearl's headlights still glow in the dark and he's there, bent into the trunk of the car. He flings the tool kit into the middle of the road with a shout of disgust and circles the car, bending into the backseat. He cracks open one of Marion's sodas, leans forward over the roof of the car, and begins to drink.

I don't need to calculate how fast I can move or the distance between us. He'll go for his gun, but I can spin faster, connect with him and he'll be flat.

I hope the Taser won't flatten me at the same time.

Help, help, help. I bury my head, square my shoulders and run.

He hears me, turns, but I'm faster. I kick Pearl's open door against him and he falls sideways with an oomph. The gun goes off in the car and both of us shout. He pushes himself up, but I kick again and spin, slamming my back and the Taser into him. I hear a whoosh of air and his head cracks into the edge of Pearl's roof.

I step away and he slumps to the ground. He's out, I can tell from the slow deep breaths. So I toe the edge of his mask until it catches on the rough edges of my sole and I pull. Short blond hair. Scrubby dirty blond beard. Dale Zeerip.

His was the other voice on the tape. Koeman's blackmailing partner. Videotaping the locker rooms to catch Gil Hannes in the act. Had the two fought about the blackmailing and Dale killed Koeman? Or had Gil killed Koeman and set Dale on a mission to destroy the evidence of his involvement and save his own life?

I wanted answers. So I stepped over him, got my hands on his gun, and waited.

CHAPTER FORTY-THREE

On Monday morning at 9:23, I ran into The Grind. Star Hannes and Red Carson were due in my office at nine thirty. We had some things to discuss.

God love 'em, the late breakfast crowd applauded when I walked in. I waved a hand at 'em, my fingers wrapped in Band-Aids. I'd bitten the nails on my left hand down to the bleeding point since the police arrived in the woods, arrested Dale and impounded Pearl. I still didn't know if I'd get my dog back.

I had, of course, lost all claim to my Aunt Kate's money. Marion could hardly believe it. When Maurice Brand confirmed that there were no exceptions to Aunt Kate's rules, Marion had snatched the phone from my hand and screamed about how unfair it was. Of course, this got us nowhere. When we hung up I took tremendous satisfaction in saying I told you so. Aunt Kate was a bitch, even from the grave.

So I had nothing to donate to Star's campaign. Maybe the money I got from the sale of the car, which would be considerably less now that a bullet had sliced through the seat leaving foam cascading like entrails from a deer. Nothing like what I'd promised her in order to secure Linus's release from the pound. After all I'd been through, I didn't know what I'd do if she wouldn't drop the charges. And I had no idea how to change her mind.

Red had been so busy tying up the ends of the case that she hadn't clobbered me for getting involved. In fact, she'd kept me up on the case, every time I called her—basically on the hour—asking about my dog. Turns out Middelburg's Ecclesiastical Super Sleuth had pretty much figured it out. When Dale woke up at the hospital and saw the charges he faced, thanks largely to the video I turned over, he made a plea. He and Koeman had stumbled on Gil's affair with Tina one night when they were out carousing after a poker game. They'd tried to get pictures in Red's garage, but Dale had stumbled and the noise scared the lovers off. They followed them, though, to their new meet in the rec center. Set up the cameras. "And the rest was cake," Red told me he said.

The frosting being video of the Hot Flashes in the locker room, I gathered.

Marion met me at the counter with a box of oliebollen, which translated into fat balls. Imagine a sort of raisin bread doughnut, except in balls, fried in oil, covered in powdered sugar. Super fantastic.

"Too bad Star isn't here." Marion didn't smile. "That applause would infuriate her." The skin beneath her eyes sagged, dark.

"You should be home," I said, "with your family."

Marion tried to smile. "They're at work and school. I can't just sit around with terrifying visions of what could have happened running through my head." She wiped an eye. "Here is better."

"We caught a murderer," I said.

Dale had confessed to that too. Things had gone well, he said, until Koeman just cut him out of the deal saying Dale didn't deserve it because he was the one who scared them from the garage and could have screwed up the whole thing. Dale had, in fact, gone on and on about how everyone else screwed him—first Ivor Koontz who always passed him by for overtime assignments, then Koeman who took all the overtime even though he knew Dale needed the money, and then again when he cut him out of the payoff. Red told me Dale remained convinced he'd done the world a service by killing "that pain in the ass." He didn't say what kind of service he'd have done by killing a priest and a mother.

"Maybe we did catch a murderer," Marion said. "But it wasn't worth it. Not to me. Not worth more than possibly losing my family. I just want things normal again."

She waved away my cash when I tried to pay. "I don't charge family," she said. We hugged.

I drove quickly to the parish house. Thought about Marion. About Aunt Kate. About Linus. Family, desperation. These made us all do strange things.

Red had explained to me that Dale had purchased several houses in Holland with the bulk of his parents' retirement savings—without mentioning it to them. He thought he'd make a good profit by repairing, renting, then flipping the houses. But he'd bought them with adjustable rate loans. When the bottom had fallen out of the market and his payments ballooned he was stuck. He couldn't let his parents know what he'd done. That he'd stolen. That he'd failed. He needed the money or else life as he knew it would end.

But when Dale killed Koeman, he thought Koeman had the video original on him. "He always kept it on him," the police report said, Dale citing this as another way Koeman screwed him. He'd searched the body. The rec center. Even the room at Frontline where they played poker. It never occurred to him it would be in the car until the morning Marion and I left, when he overheard "some old geezer" say something about never dreaming that car would move after sitting in one place for decades. Then he knew Koeman would have hidden it there. Safe in the scene of Gil's crime. "It would have appealed to his fucked-up sense of humor," Dale said.

I sat in my office, nervous, chewing the Band-Aids on my hands, watching the clock click past 9:30. 9:31. 9:32. 9:33.

Then Red, in uniform, looking worn but lively, swung in, grabbed an oliebollen, and slumped in a chair. "Do you realize you had two different guys tail you the whole way from Middelburg to Bliss, Michigan and you never realized it?" Powder sugar lined her lips. "I've been thinking about that." She chewed. "Don't let this Super Sleuth crap go to your head."

She meant, of course, that Dale had followed us, figuring he'd search the car for the memory card during that first night in Bliss. Only—surprise—the car was gone by the time he got there. Peter had already stolen it, looking for the inhaler. Dale panicked, but waited and when we rolled in with it that morning, then went on our way, he followed more closely. The first chance he had to search it was in the Seney Refuge parking lot but Peter showed up first. Dale chased the kid off then searched the car, but couldn't find the card because Marion had it in her purse. Dale watched everything we did that day, taking Peter to eat, going to a movie, overhearing us on the walkway talking about calling Red. He misunderstood what we'd said, thought we'd seen the whole blackmail video—which, at that point, we hadn't. It took him a few hours to work out a plan to get the video from us that night and frame Peter. And that's when he busted into our room.

I tossed a napkin to Red. "At least Dale didn't hurt Peter." I closed my eyes against the thought of the tragedy that could have become.

Red wiped her mouth. "Artesia Collins isn't camped out on your doorstep. How'd you manage that?"

I'd given her an interview last night, of course. Talked to the bishop too. Everyone was happy with the good press I was bringing them. But I still didn't have Linus back.

"Are you trying to distract me from the fact that it's—" I checked my watch, "nine thirty-nine and Star isn't here? What's going to happen about Linus? I don't have the car. I don't have the money."

Red held up a hand. "When you go into a soccer game against an opponent who has all the strength, all the advantages, what do you do?"

I blinked. "I would never go into a game like that!" How

could people not get the basics about sports? "You want to win a game, you never think they have all the advantages! It's not even about them. It's about you."

"Really? How so?"

I sighed. I didn't want to talk soccer. I wanted my dog back.

"How, Lonnie?"

"You only focus on yourself, what you can do. Giving it your all. When you've bottomed out, looking again, finding out what more you can bring. There is always something more."

"So." Red leaned back in her chair. "Quit whining and play soccer with Star Hannes."

"That's stupid. She'll want—"

Red held up a hand. "Think about it."

I tried, I really did.

At 9:52, Star entered impeccable as always in a black suit, cream blouse and strand of pearls. Subdued. Mourning even.

She had had a very bad thirty-six hours. It had all come out, of course. Her husband's affair with a nineteen-year-old soccer player and its capture on video. The blackmail. She'd adopted the same stance I'd seen more than once in the media—that of stalwart wife crapped upon by philandering husband. It was a twist to the usual scenario that she was the candidate, not him, and it seemed the whole thing would stand her in good stead with sympathetic and morally righteous voters.

"Come in." I offered the oliebollen, trying to look unterrified.

Star stood like she had a signpost for a spine. "I prefer to stand, thank you."

I resisted the urge to leap the desk and drop at her feet to beg for my dog.

"So, ladies," Red said. "It seems our agreement has hit a few snags."

"There is no agreement anymore," Star snapped. "She has no money to donate."

Oh God, no. My heart raced as I tried to come up with something, anything more I could bring to this. *Maybe my silence.*

"I'll drop out of sight," I said. "Stay completely out of the media. I won't appear at any public gatherings outside of my church and I won't comment about you, the laws, the campaign, anything, until after the election." Surely this would appeal to her. After all, isn't this what Red—and others—had told me all along? That to survive I needed to stay out of her way? To quit battling her? It had worked with Dale Zeerip on a lonely country road. Maybe it would work here.

Star smiled that snakey wicked smile of hers and the bottom dropped out of my gut. "You think that's enough to move me to drop all the charges against you and your dog?"

I needed more. My presence. "I'll leave town if you want," I said.

Red's head shot around. "Lonnie!"

"I'd like that a great deal," said Star.

"Now wait a minute!" Red said.

"I need a few weeks," I said. "Until the church gets another interim rector. But if you get me my dog today, I'll write a resignation letter."

"Lonnie! That's—"

"I want my dog back!" I said to Red. I willed myself not to cry. I already looked desperate. I didn't want to look utterly destitute.

"I'd like that a great deal," Star repeated, "however that is not what best suits my needs at this time. Right now, I need something more from you."

We waited.

Star's lip curled. "For some reason, everyone around here loves you. Middelburg's Ecclesiastical Super Sleuth." She almost spit the words. "Why they can't see you for the fake opportunistic immoral conniver that you are, I'll never know."

"Let's keep this civil, ladies," Red said.

I said nothing, but a funny little idea sprouted in my head.

"My husband has made many mistakes, most of them now grotesquely public, thanks to you. Had Dale been identified by more traditional means, Gil's indiscretions might have been handled a bit more quietly."

She meant, of course, that she could have manipulated the local system into hiding all kinds of details, at least until after the election. Maybe that could work to my advantage.

"But it is what it is." She fingered her pearls carefully. "And here is how it is going to go." She dropped the pearls and stared at me. "You will do everything you can to place yourself in the media from now until election time. Television, newspapers, Web sites, radio stations. Everything. You will embrace and capitalize on your popularity as Middelburg's Ecclesiastical Super Sleuth."

Okay, I admit it. I did not see that coming.

"And in each and every interview you do, you will mention my unwavering support for you and your efforts. You will mention my campaign and my initiatives with utter devotion. You will assure that this golden image of Middelburg's Ecclesiastical Super Sleuth is inextricably woven up with Star Hannes' Campaign for Congress."

Interesting.

Red looked at me. "Lonnie, you don't have to do this. There are other ways."

"There are no other ways," Star snapped. "That's my deal. Agree to this, your dog is free." She pointed at me. "And don't even think about reneging. Because I'll keep those complaints and refile them so fast you won't have time to throw a punch before I have that dog put down. Do you understand?"

"I do." I stood. "But there's one other thing," I said. I felt Red's eyes on me. "It's about that poker game." So far, nothing about the Thursday night poker game had made it into the papers. I'd not mentioned it to anyone except Marion. Dale had mentioned it to the police, I knew because Red told me. "You've heard about it, surely."

Star looked blank. "My husband was not involved in any way. Nor am I."

"No. But several people close to you are. Brady Wesselynk, a strong supporter of yours. Lex Brenninkmeyer. As Provost at Five Points, I imagine he would be most grateful to learn you helped his secret stay secret. He probably has many influential friends in the area."

"You have friends involved as well," Star said. "Parishioners."

I grinned. "Do you think the Zaloumi brothers care if the town finds out they play poker on Thursday nights? They're

Episcopalian—almost everyone in town has consigned us to hell already. There's a certain freedom in that."

I saw Red scratch her cheek to hide a grin.

"Your point?" I saw fear flicker in Star's eyes.

"How about instead of all that stuff you just suggested, you just give me my dog and I never mention the poker game to anyone?" Heck, I didn't really care if they'd played cards now and again. No skin off my nose.

"Why would I do that? You can't control what the police will share with the media."

I shrugged. "If the police mention it as one of a hundred clues in this murder case, and if Middelburg's Ecclesiastical Super Sleuth says it's irrelevant, then do you think much will be made of it? But what if that same Super Sleuth claimed it was the single most important part of solving the case?" I paused. I could see Star's wheels turning. "You could tell the men that you are the one who kept me quiet. By giving me my dog. They'd admire your sacrifice for them."

Star held up a hand. "Enough." She stared hard at me. "What if the media agreement stands, but in exchange for your silence on the games I agree to let go of the Faithful Heritage Initiative? I'll even recommend that the laws be altered to fit our current social setting better. You get your dog and your so-called freedoms back. But I still get the media boost."

I sighed. "Did you finally read all the laws? Or is public reaction to the initiative not what you planned? People don't like living by traditional law alone, do they?"

"I heard polls this morning showed a strong uptick in Star's favor," Red said. "Ahead of the competition, in fact. Maybe she doesn't need the Initiative anymore, thanks to her husband and the sympathy vote."

"So you're dropping the initiative anyway?" I asked.

Star's eyes twitched between us.

"Here's my final offer," I said. "I'm silent about the poker game, about what I saw of your husband on that tape and about your campaign and you give me my dog back," I said. "Right now."

She sniffed as if rotten air had floated through the office.

"I admire you, you know," I said. "You're a master at capturing the hearts of the people. And you work hard for your vision."

She raised an eyebrow. "As do you." She sniffed again. "I agree to your proposal. But I'm keeping the records. Just in case." And she spun out.

As soon as I heard the front door of the parish house slam below, I collapsed into my chair and into tears.

"I'm glad we're on the same side," said Red. "At least most of the time."

I wiped my eyes. "Can you take me to get my dog?"

She grinned. "You bet."

Then I heard it—pounding up the steps. Galloping. I looked down the hall just in time to see Linus' black head appear.

I screamed his name and he barked and ran into the office, skidding around the desk as I came forward and leaping—all sixty-some pounds of him—straight into my arms. I staggered under the weight but I didn't drop him. I held him and let him lick my face. He smelled horrible.

"You need a bath."

"I thought the same thing." Maurice Brand stood in the doorway. "But the lady outside assured me it would be all right to bring him in."

I set the dog down and sat on my desk. Linus bounced back and forth between the three of us. "Don't suppose you've come to tell me Aunt Kate sent a telegram from the grave and I can have the inheritance after all?" I asked.

"No." He stepped forward, handing me a business-sized envelope. "That is the title to the Pearly Gates. Whatever she's worth now, she's yours for attempting the trip."

"And the nearly dying part? Solving a murder?" said Red. "That ought to be worth the rest of the estate."

Maurice shook his head. "The trip wasn't completed as specified."

I grinned. "I told you and Marion both. This is how Aunt Kate always played. Her way or the highway. No in between." I nodded to Brand. "Thanks. Tell the secondary beneficiary good luck with the money."

Brand held up a hand. "You are, Reverend Squires, the rector of this parish?"

That surprised me. "Yes. Interim rector. Two-year term."

"Head clergy?" he asked.

I looked at Red. She shrugged. "Yes," I said.

Brand smiled—something new for him and it made him look kind. "Well, then, Reverend, I have some good news." He handed me a manila envelope.

"What's this?"

"Woman at the Well Episcopal Church is the beneficiary of a rather strange bequest," he said, eyes twinkling. "I can't reveal all the details, but this envelope contains, among other things, a receipt for four hundred and ninety-two thousand dollars. And some change. Contributed by an anonymous donor."

He waited while his words soaked in.

"She left it to the church?"

"I'm not at liberty to say."

I looked at Red and threw my arms wide. "She left it to the church!" I hugged her. Then I hugged Brand. I couldn't believe it. Aunt Kate had left her money to Woman at the Well Episcopal. And here I was. She couldn't have known. Somehow, I felt like I'd pulled one over on her.

"The money is in an account that was put in the church's ownership this morning." Brand pointed to the envelope. "Everything you need should be in there."

I beamed at him. "Can I take you to lunch? Dinner? Anything?"

He shook his head and bowed slightly. "I'm returning to Chicago. It has been nice to meet you."

I watched him go, my heart thumping, still not quite believing it. I emptied the envelope and Red and I pored over the papers together.

"It's for real," Red said. "You got your dog, the car and the money, sort of."

I got it all, I thought. *Or almost all.* There was one last thing I needed to take care of.

My mouth instantly went dry and my stomach flapped, but I did it anyway. "Do you, uh, want to come over for dinner tonight?"

"Sure," she said. "Do you want me to—" She stopped as our

eyes met. Something shifted between us and we both felt it, I knew. "Oh." She looked at the floor. I think she blushed. "What do you want me to bring?"

"Just yourself," I said.

She nodded.

I just might get it all, I thought, then looked upward past the ceiling.

Thank you, thank you, thank you.

Publications from
Bella Books, Inc.
Women. Books. Even Better Together.
P.O. Box 10543
Tallahassee, FL 32302
Phone: 800-729-4992
www.bellabooks.com

CALM BEFORE THE STORM by Peggy J. Herring. Colonel Marcel Robideaux doesn't tell and so far no one official has asked, but the amorous pursuit by Jordan McGowan has her worried for both her career and her honor.
978-0-9677753-1-9

THE WILD ONE by Lyn Denison. Rachel Weston is busy keeping home and head together after the death of her husband. Her kids need her and what she doesn't need is the confusion that Quinn Farrelly creates in her body and heart.
978-0-9677753-4-0

LESSONS IN MURDER by Claire McNab. There's a corpse in the school with a neat hole in the head and a Black & Decker drill alongside. Which teacher should Inspector Carol Ashton suspect? Unfortunately, the alluring Sybil Quade is at the top of the list. First in this highly lauded series.
978-1-931513-65-4

WHEN AN ECHO RETURNS by Linda Kay Silva. The bayou where Echo Branson found her sanity has been swept clean by a hurricane — or at least they thought. Then an evil washed up by the storm comes looking for them all, one-by-one. Second in series.
978-1-59493-225-0

DEADLY INTERSECTIONS by Ann Roberts. Everyone is lying, including her own father and her girlfriend. Leaving matters to the professionals is supposed to be easier! Third in series with *PAID IN FULL* and *WHITE OFFERINGS*.
978-1-59493-224-3

SUBSTITUTE FOR LOVE by Karin Kallmaker. No substitutes, ever again! But then Holly's heart, body and soul are captured by Reyna... Reyna with no last name and a secret life that hides a terrible bargain, one written in family blood.
978-1-931513-62-3

MAKING UP FOR LOST TIME by Karin Kallmaker. Take one Next Home Network Star and add one Little White Lie to equal mayhem in little Mendocino and a recipe for sizzling romance. This lighthearted, steamy story is a feast for the senses in a kitchen that is way too hot.
978-1-931513-61-6

2ND FIDDLE by Kate Calloway. Cassidy James's first case left her with a broken heart. At least this new case is fighting the good fight, and she can throw all her passion and energy into it.
978-1-59493-200-7

HUNTING THE WITCH by Ellen Hart. The woman she loves — used to love — offers her help, and Jane Lawless finds it hard to say no. She needs TLC for recent injuries and who better than a doctor? But Julia's jittery demeanor awakens Jane's curiosity. And Jane has never been able to resist a mystery. #9 in series and Lammy-winner.
978-1-59493-206-9

FAÇADES by Alex Marcoux. Everything Anastasia ever wanted — she has it. Sidney is the woman who helped her get it. But keeping it will require a price — the unnamed passion that simmers between them.
978-1-59493-239-7

ELENA UNDONE by Nicole Conn. The risks. The passion. The devastating choices. The ultimate rewards. Nicole Conn rocked the lesbian cinema world with Claire of the Moon and has rocked it again with Elena Undone. This is the book that tells it all...
978-1-59493-254-0

WHISPERS IN THE WIND by Frankie J. Jones. It began as a camping trip, then a simple hike. Dixon Hayes and Elizabeth Colter uncover an intriguing cave on their hike, changing their world, perhaps irrevocably.
978-1-59493-037-9

WEDDING BELL BLUES by Julia Watts. She'll do anything to save what's left of her family. Anything. It didn't seem like a bad plan...at first. Hailed by readers as Lammy-winner Julia Watts' funniest novel.
978-1-59493-199-4

WILDFIRE by Lynn James. From the moment botanist Devon McKinney meets ranger Elaine Thomas the chemistry is undeniable. Sharing — and protecting — a mountain for the length of their short assignments leads to unexpected passion in this sizzling romance by newcomer Lynn James.
978-1-59493-191-8

LEAVING L.A. by Kate Christie. Eleanor Chapin is on the way to the rest of her life when Tessa Flanaghan offers her a lucrative summer job caring for Tessa's daughter Laya. It's only temporary and everyone expects Eleanor to be leaving L.A...
978-1-59493-221-2

SOMETHING TO BELIEVE by Robbi McCoy. When Lauren and Cassie meet on a once-in-a-lifetime river journey through China their feelings are innocent...at first. Ten years later, nothing — and everything — has changed. From Golden Crown winner Robbi McCoy.
978-1-59493-214-4

DEVIL'S ROCK: THE SEARCH FOR PATRICK DOE by Gerri Hill. Deputy Andrea Sullivan and Agent Cameron Ross vow to bring a killer to justice. The killer has other plans. Gerri Hill pens another intriguing blend of mystery and romance in this page-turning thriller.
978-1-59493-218-2

SHADOW POINT by Amy Briant. Madison Maguire has just been not-quite fired, told her brother is dead and discovered she has to pick up a five-year old niece she's never met. After she makes it to Shadow Point it seems like someone—or something—doesn't want her to leave. Romance sizzles in this ghost story from Amy Briant.
978-1-59493-216-8

JUKEBOX by Gina Daggett. Debutantes in love. With each other. Two young women chafe at the constraints of parents and society with a friendship that could be more, if they can break free. Gina Daggett is best known as "Lipstick" of the columnist duo Lipstick & Dipstick.
978-1-59493-212-0

BLIND BET by Tracey Richardson. The stakes are high when Ellen Turcotte and Courtney Langford meet at the blackjack tables. Lady Luck has been smiling on Courtney but Ellen is a wild card she may not be able to handle.
978-1-59493-211-3